It Started
with a *Kiss*

NEW YORK TIMES AND *USA TODAY* BESTSELLING AUTHOR
MELANIE MORELAND

It Started
with a *Kiss*

Friendship is a gift we give ourselves.

I am blessed to have some wonderful people in

my life. The beautiful souls that lift you up and

shout your worth when the world seems too much to

handle and you forget who you are.

This is for you—friends, old and new.

Thank you for being part of my life.

And to my Matthew—who shouts loudest of them all.

One

Avery

"I SWEAR, AVERY, Ryan does this thing with his tongue . . ." Beth's voice trailed off and her eyes glazed over. "I came so hard I saw stars."

I glared at my best friend, dropped my fork, and held up my hands in supplication. "For God's sake, Beth, I'm trying to eat here."

Not at all worried over my reaction, she smirked. "I'm just saying."

"I know what you're saying." I lowered my voice as I looked around, feeling self-conscious. "You and Ryan have a great sex life. I don't. I get it."

She speared a forkful of salad and lifted it to her mouth, chewing as she regarded me thoughtfully. "When's the last time you got laid?"

I exhaled hard. "I think Justin Trudeau's father was Prime Minister."

"Since you weren't even born then, I doubt that."

I shrugged. "Let's just say it's been a while."

"You've been on a few dates since you broke up with Grant." She eyed me with concern. "That was over two years ago. Surely you've had sex since then."

I dug my fork into my salad with a little more force than necessary. It had been a long while. "A few dates, yes. But, no, I haven't."

"You didn't sleep with *any* of them?"

"No."

"What about that guy you said you hooked up with at the bar a few months ago? You even messaged me. No good?"

I squirmed a little in my chair and picked up my iced tea. I had texted her while slightly tipsy, thinking it was funny. "*Hook up* may have been too strong a word."

She narrowed her eyes. "What word works then?"

"Well, we did hook up. By that I mean, the key ring I keep clipped on my purse caught his sweater. I had to spend a couple moments unhooking the clip as he berated me for being so careless and causing his precious cashmere garment damage." I lifted one shoulder in embarrassment. "Strangely, he didn't ask me out after that happened."

Beth blinked at me, then threw back her head in raucous laughter.

I chuckled at her mirth.

For someone so outwardly elegant and classy, she had the most guttural, dirty laugh I ever heard.

She wiped her eyes with her napkin. "Oh, Avery. Only you. What am I going to do with you?"

I shook my head. "Nothing, Beth. I'm not like you. Sex, for me, is private and—" I waved my hand around, trying to find the right word.

"Non-existent," she finished.

"I'm okay with that."

She regarded me fondly, then shook her head. "I worry about you sometimes. You're such an introvert."

I smiled, brushing off her concern. "I get out, Beth. I'm not the social butterfly you are, but I don't sit in my apartment all the time."

"I know that. You take care of all your elderly neighbors. You run them around, take them grocery shopping, help them in their homes. But I'm not sure that is enough."

My throat tightened. "I like doing that. I'm comfortable with them. They make me feel needed."

"I know. But who is looking after Avery?"

"I'm fine." Wanting to get the focus off me and back onto less personal ground, I changed the subject. "How's work lately? You've been so busy, I've barely heard from you."

"I know. This latest assignment has been driving me crazy. There's a ton of paperwork and the interviews have been endless. I just want to get in there, then film and put it together."

"What is—" Her phone vibrated on the table cutting off my words.

She looked at the screen, mumbling a curse. "Sorry, I need to take this call."

I dug back into my salad while she answered the phone. I pushed through the lettuce and tomatoes looking for more of the grilled chicken, coming up with one tiny piece. Grudgingly, I speared it with some lettuce, ignoring the tomatoes. I didn't like tomatoes. And really, why call it a "grilled chicken salad" when there was scarcely any chicken? It should be called "big bowl of salad with a teasing glimpse of chicken." I pushed back the bowl, not wanting any more.

I studied my best friend as she spoke on the phone. Beth was tall, elegant, and refined; at least until she opened her mouth. Her long hair was a deep chocolate brown, hanging to her shoulders in smooth waves. Her makeup was perfect, her hazel eyes piercing and shrewd. She was passionate, driven, and talented.

However, at the moment, she was also incredibly pissed off.

"Fucking great," she mumbled, tossing her phone on the table. "I swear the stress of this shoot is gonna kill me."

"What's wrong?"

"Another volunteer canceled. We're set to shoot tomorrow and I'm down a person."

"Surely you have backups?"

"That *was* my final backup."

I patted her hand. "You'll figure something out. You always do."

She stared at me for a moment, nodding as if she had made a decision. "I need a favor."

"What?"

"I need you to be my replacement volunteer."

"What would I have to do? Help cart stuff?" I had done that for her on previous occasions. It was always fun.

"No. You'd be in front of the camera this time."

I blanched a little. "Oh, um, doing what exactly? I'm not an actress."

"I don't need you to be an actress. I need you to be Avery."

"And do what?"

"Kiss a stranger."

Two

Avery

THE SOUNDS OF the busy restaurant faded away as I stared at Beth in complete shock.

"You want me to do what?" I frowned at her calm face. She must be teasing.

"I need you to come to the studio tomorrow, and kiss a stranger."

"A kiss, like on the cheek? A quick, hello-type kiss?"

Beth huffed in exasperation. "No, Avery. Lips pressing." She grinned wickedly. "Tongues meeting, if you want. That type of kiss."

"With a *stranger*."

"That's the idea."

"You seriously don't have another volunteer you could ask?"

She shook her head. "No, I don't have the time to go through the application process. I know you. I trust you." She leaned across the table, clasping my hand, her hazel eyes pleading. "You're off work tomorrow—you have the time. I need this favor. Please?"

"Why are you doing it again? What is this for?" I asked.

"I was hired by a company to film this segment. It's a social experiment, to see how people respond physically and emotionally to a stranger in an intimate moment." She quirked an eyebrow in jest. "Hence the kissing."

"Well, I can save you a lot of trouble. I'll behave as if I was embarrassed—because that's exactly what I'll be. I won't even be able to speak. You know how nervous I am with new people."

Beth laughed. "Speaking isn't what I want your lips to do. C'mon, Avery. I need you."

I took a sip of my iced tea, stalling for time. I couldn't remember the last time I kissed someone. One of the few disastrous dates, I supposed. None of them left a lasting impression on me, that was for certain. I doubted I made it memorable for them either, since no second date had occurred. Now Beth wanted me to kiss a stranger? Simply the thought of meeting a new person was daunting, never mind kissing them.

Beth sat back, sipping her coffee while she waited for me to agree. Because she knew I would. I found it impossible to say no to my best friend.

"Is there, like, an age limit?" I shuddered. "I really don't want to kiss an old man. Or even worse, some young, pimply teenager."

"It's all mapped out," Beth explained, her voice patient. "We've matched up age groups and sexual orientation. My volunteer who canceled was your age and you'd be a perfect replacement."

"Do you know who I'll be, um, kissing?"

"Nope. Only that he's male, thirty-two years old, and likes females in his age category." She smirked. "Perfect for you. Maybe you can ask him for a date after. Or you know . . . *hook* up."

I scoffed at her teasing. It had been weeks—no, actually months, since I'd been on a date. I was sure it was less than a year—but I couldn't swear it.

"How long a kiss are we talking here?"

"Whatever you feel like."

"What if I don't like him? Or he has bad breath or . . . *oh God*, Beth, what if he's a clown in his spare time? What if he wants to go to the circus?" I hated clowns—they scared the shit out of me.

Beth threw up her hands. "It's not a 'hey, let's get to know each other' type thing! You don't have to like him, or get to know him. All you're going to do is kiss him and you can walk away. There'll be no clowns or circuses—I promise. And your pockets will be full of mints, so you'll be fine." She shook her head. "Please, all I need is a few moments of your life. You won't be the only one there. I'll be in the room too, and I'll make sure you're okay. *Please*."

I gave in. I could never say no to Beth and she knew that fact only too well. "Okay."

"Really? You'll do it?"

"Yes." I shook my finger. "If he's got a red nose, big feet, and halitosis, I'll never forgive you."

"Big feet are a plus. I keep telling you that."

I rolled my eyes. "Is it always about *sex* with you, Beth? It always comes down to, ah, *penises*—doesn't it? Large ones at that."

"Have you noticed the size of Ryan's feet, my friend? My man is packing. And it's a cock. Say it after me." She spelled it out by enunciating each letter. "C-O-C-K. You can't actually have sex without saying it, you know."

My face flushed. "I've had sex, Beth. It's just been a while."

She grinned in delight. "Well, maybe tomorrow will be the start of a new era for you." She pushed a card my way. "We're using a different studio than usual. Here's the address. Be there by eleven."

With a sigh, I picked up the card, holding it by the edges as if it were going to bite me.

What had I agreed to do?

I YANKED ANOTHER shirt over my head, tossing it on the ever-growing pile on my bed, huffing in frustration. What should one wear when they are about to kiss a stranger? Everything I tried on felt wrong. My turtlenecks said I was closed off. My blouses seemed too formal, and the last shirt I tried on made me look like a slut. Should I wear my hair up or down? Makeup? Perfume? What if he was allergic? Kissing someone sneezing and with watery eyes would not be fun. None of this felt fun.

I sat down, my head in my hands. I should never have agreed to do this for Beth. I was introverted. I became tongue-tied when I met new people. I never knew what to say, or how to act, so I remained quiet.

Beth told me to come as myself. Except, I wasn't sure what myself was when it came to the situation I found myself in. Standing up, I studied myself in the mirror. I looked unremarkable, to be honest. I had certainly been told often enough. The only people who had ever called me pretty were my parents and grandmother. I pushed aside the memories of being called "the ghost" at school by taunting classmates, or the teacher who'd muttered my pale hair color made me look like an old woman.

My hair was blonde—so blonde it was almost white, and hung past my shoulders in a mass of curls and ringlets. It had a mind of its own, and I'd given up trying to tame it. I was average—my eyes were my one positive feature. Large, wide, and a light shade of green, they were unusual. There was a beauty mark high on my cheekbone, next to my eye, and I had freckles. Silly little dots of color scattered across the bridge of my nose and the top of my cheeks like a small road map. I hated them, and I had tried every home remedy to get rid of them, to no avail. I was short and curvy—my figure an overall softness, not a well-placed voluptuousness I envied in others. Beth boasted Ryan could bounce a quarter off her hard abs, whereas a quarter would probably hit mine and roll off. If I could find my abs.

God, this was stupid. Why was I worrying?

I was going to walk into a room, kiss some man, and walk out. No doubt, he would forget about me as fast as I would forget about him. We'd never see each other again. He certainly wouldn't be looking at my abs—or lack thereof. I would probably be a blip on his radar. I simply needed to be comfortable.

Reaching into my closet, I pulled out my favorite, flowing gypsy skirt in black and teamed it with a white tank top. I grabbed my beloved shrug I had found at a vintage shop—vivid red with small flowers embroidered all over the neckline—and pulled my hair back from my face, leaving it hanging down my back. My shoes were my usual simple flats. Heels and I didn't get along. The only jewelry I wore was a pair of small, antique hoop earrings and my anklet with charms that tinkled and swayed as I walked. I never took either of them off because of sentimental reasons.

In the bathroom, I slipped in my contacts, blinking furiously at the pain caused by the right one. Confused, I slid my glasses back on, and grimaced when I saw a small tear on the edge of the contact. Checking the cabinet, I groaned—of course, it was my last pair. I had no choice but to wear my glasses or go in blind.

I added a touch of mascara and lip gloss, then looked in the mirror. I looked like me—maybe a little paler than normal, but me. I started to walk out the door, but turned back at the last minute and added a spritz of my perfume.

If he was allergic, too bad.

However, I did tuck my lip gloss in my skirt pocket and a few extra peppermints.

In case.

I STOOD ACROSS the street from the studio, hidden in a doorway, popping peppermints and tugging on the strap of my purse slung over my shoulder. I had seen quite a few people go in, and I wondered if any of them were the person I was supposed to kiss. A few looked around my age, but I wasn't sure. I knew Beth said there were four different rooms with crews taping people all day, so it was a busy place. I sucked in a long breath, wondering if there was any way I could get out of this without risking Beth's ire.

My phone buzzed with an incoming text and I pulled it from my pocket, causing my remaining peppermints to scatter over the sidewalk. Cursing, I crouched down to pick them up while looking at my screen.

> *I see you across the street. Your mystery man isn't here yet. Get your scared ass upstairs.*

Well, dammit, I thought I was being sneaky, hiding in the doorway. I should have known she'd be looking for me.

With a huff, I bent forward to get the last three wrapped

peppermints just as a boot landed on my searching fingers. I yelped in pain as the large foot pressed down heavily, crushing two fingers into the cement. Muttered curses filled the air as the foot pulled back and I fell on my ass, my glasses flying off. I held my aching fingers in my good hand, trying not to cry.

A figure materialized over me. "*Fuck*, I'm so sorry! I didn't see you there! Are you okay?"

I looked up at the tall man encased in black, looming over me. Without my glasses, all I saw was a blurry face topped with dark hair. I squinted a little, trying to bring him in to focus, but it didn't work. Between the tears I was fighting and no glasses, I didn't have a hope of seeing anything.

"I think you squashed my peppermints," I whimpered.

The unclear face bent closer, his voice low and concerned. "I'm actually a little more worried about your hand than your candies."

I looked at the sidewalk. "I needed those peppermints. I only have one now. I'll have to share if there is halitosis."

Mr. Blurry chuckled. It was a nice, friendly sound. "Um, okay. We'll figure something out. Can I look at your hand?"

I blinked as his soft, comforting voice enveloped me, its cadence soothing.

My phone buzzed, and I bit back a groan—I could feel Beth's impatience coming through the sound. I had no doubt she was getting impatient and would stomp downstairs any second to drag me upstairs to kiss my mystery man.

"No, it's fine. Really—I have to be somewhere." I stood, ignoring the proffered hand I could see waving in the air. "I have to go," I repeated.

Long fingers wrapped around my wrist, causing a curious warmth to run up my arm at the unexpected contact. "Please, let me look at your hand. I need to see how bad you're hurt."

I snatched it back, unsure why my skin was tingling. "No."

Mr. Blurry's voice took on a teasing tone. "I'll buy you a whole bag of peppermints, if you let me check it out."

That made me pause. I might need those candies. "The

spearmint kind?"

"Any kind you want." His voice was now persistent. "Please. I feel terrible."

He sounded so sweet, I couldn't resist any more, so I held out my hand. "Make it fast."

His gentle fingers probed and checked, the strange heat running over my skin. "They aren't broken, but they're going to be bruised and hurt. I'm *so* sorry." I winced as he moved the fingers again. "They're going to be extremely sore."

I pulled back my hand. "Too late—they already are. Now, my peppermints?"

He chuckled once more. I liked the sound.

"Impatient little thing, aren't you? There's a drugstore down the street. I'll get a finger splint, too. Wait here," he directed. "I'll be right back."

Then he was gone.

My phone buzzed again, and with a sigh, I kneeled down, found my glasses, and headed across the street.

I'd have to do without the splint and hope the peppermints weren't needed. If Mr. Blurry even bothered to return—which I highly doubted.

I wished I had seen the face behind the kind voice and gentle touch. Somehow in those few minutes, I had felt very . . . safe.

"WHAT HAPPENED TO you?"

"I dropped my peppermints and some guy walked on my hand." I held out my fingers for inspection. "He crushed the last ones."

Beth held up my hand, poking at my reddened, rapidly bruising fingers. Grimacing, I pulled back my hand to my chest. Mr. Blurry had been much gentler.

"Were his feet big?" she quipped.

I groaned. "When I fell, my glasses came off, so I couldn't see his feet or his face, so I named him Mr. Blurry. His foot felt heavy, though."

Beth snorted. "Only you, Avery. Go wash your hands and tidy up your mascara—you're in room four."

I swallowed, my throat dry. "Is he, ah, here?"

"He texted to say he was held up, but on his way. Go fix yourself up. I expect him any second."

I hesitated.

"Don't be nervous. It's fine. I'll be in the room."

"You're filming it?"

"I'll oversee. Cliff will do the filming. I thought you'd feel better."

I heaved a small sigh of relief. I would feel better with Beth there in the room.

She pushed me in the direction of the bathroom. "Go. We'll do this, and I'll get some ice for your hand after."

"Okay. I'll meet you there."

Three

Avery

I ENTERED THE room filled with nervous anticipation. Beth and another staff member were talking to a man whose back was to me. He was tall, towering over Beth. His shiny hair was a rich, chestnut brown under the bright lights, the bottom brushing the back of his collar. His broad shoulders were ensconced in a black leather jacket. Tight jeans clung to his long legs and framed a rather spectacular ass. He was laughing at something Beth said, his hands on his hips as he flung his head back in merriment. I hesitated as I watched him. He was incredibly tall. I wasn't sure I would even come up mid-chest on him. I was going to have to go on my tiptoes, and he would have to bend way down, if we had any chance of kissing. This already had disaster written all over it.

Beth saw me and waved me over.

My fellow volunteer turned around, and I almost fell flat on my face. He was gorgeous. His vivid, blue eyes glowed behind thick, black frames. His face was all angles, accented by high cheekbones and scruff—the entire package offset by his wavy hair. Those tight jeans hung low on his hips, and before I could stop myself, my eyes dropped to his feet. His *large* feet, which were encased by a pair of black, dusty Doc Martens.

His very large feet.

Color flooded my cheeks at my thoughts. It was as if I was

channeling my inner Beth. It was all I could do to look back up and meet his gaze. His eyes widened behind his glasses, a small smile playing on his full lips. Lips I would be kissing in a moment.

I swallowed, and unconsciously licked my own lips.

Somehow, I had the feeling I wouldn't need the last peppermint for him. My fingers fished around in my pocket. I had already eaten six, but maybe a seventh would be a good idea. I popped the candy in my mouth, realizing too late maybe we'd be kissing before it dissolved so I bit down, chewing frantically. He watched me the whole time, his lips quirking, as if he were trying to hide his amusement.

I knew, without a doubt, when he smiled, it would be like the sun filling the room. I wanted to see that. I wanted to make him smile. Why, I had no idea.

Hesitantly, I crossed the room to join Beth and the mystery man. Ever the professional, Beth held out a clipboard to each of us, instructing us to read and sign. I grimaced slightly holding the board, my bent fingers protesting. Twice, I peeked over my clipboard, only to find his intense blue gaze fixed on me, a curious look on his face. Each time I felt my cheeks flare with color, and I dropped my eyes back to the paper I was supposed to be reading. I had no idea what it said, so I simply scribbled my signature and handed it back to Beth.

"Okay." She grinned. "Here's what is gonna happen. You two—stand over there." She pointed to the empty area behind her. "Cliff will start the camera rolling. Do whatever you want. Talk, introduce yourselves, shake hands—whatever makes you comfortable. Or do nothing. You can kiss and leave, if that's what you want. You have half an hour, but at some point, during your allotted time, I need you to kiss each other. Clear?"

Mystery man spoke up, his voice surprisingly nervous and low, and strangely familiar. "You'll be filming the whole time?"

Beth nodded in affirmation. "We might use extra clips for the video. She held up the clipboards. "You gave us permission with these forms. Now, any questions?"

We shook our heads and moved to the center of the room

where Beth had indicated us to stand. Under the lights, his hair showed some red in the chestnut waves. It was tousled and messy—the look suited him well. I had the craziest need to bury my fingers in it and see if it was as soft as it looked. We stared at each other in silence, his hand cupping the back of his neck as our eyes held. I wanted to lose myself in his eyes; deep blue and rich like the color of the ocean on a sunny day. The image of lying underneath him as waves swept around us filled my head and once again, I blushed.

Where were all these thoughts coming from?

All of a sudden, he had his hands buried in the mess of hair on his head, tugging and pulling, creating even more chaos. Then he stood straighter, and a determined look came over his face. He tugged off his jacket, dropping it to the floor in a pile of smooth leather, leaving him in a simple, white T-shirt, which hugged his chest and torso to perfection. Ink peeked out from under the sleeve of his right arm, and I had the irrational need to see the design.

He took a step closer and held out his hand, palm side up, his fingers curling in a silent invitation.

"Hello," he spoke quietly, his voice a gentle caress to my ears. "I'm Daniel. Daniel Spencer."

I stared down at his hand. His palm was wide, his fingers long and graceful. Hesitantly, I placed my palm on top of his, my entire body feeling a familiar rush of heat as his fingers closed, encasing my hand with his touch.

"Avery."

"Avery," he murmured. "It is indeed a pleasure to meet you."

My legs started to tremble. Slow, torturous shudders ran through my spine as his hand tightened on mine.

"Can I kiss you, Avery?"

"If you want to," I breathed out.

God, I hoped he wanted to.

His hand drew me to him, the shudders increasing as I felt the heat, *his heat*, radiating from his body. "Yes. Yes, I want to."

His eyes never left mine as he bent lower.

Without thinking, I slid my hands up to his shoulders, and

fisted his T-shirt, despite the pain it caused my fingers, and rose on my toes to meet him part way. My eyes shut of their own accord, a small sigh escaping as I felt his lips brush mine.

His mouth was tender, his touch light, his lips as gentle as a summer breeze that teased your skin in the heat of the sun. It promised relief, but only to leave you wanting more—so much more.

He eased back, and my eyes flew open, disappointment flooding my senses.

That was it? A small whimper of protest escaped my mouth. I wanted more.

His voice was a quiet hum in my ear. "Avery, can I do something?"

I nodded.

He could do anything.

Daniel

I WAS ONLY gone five minutes. Seven tops. I raced through the drugstore, grabbed a splint, an instant ice pack, some Tylenol, and the biggest damn bag of peppermints I could find—the spearmint kind. I had no idea why she wanted peppermints so much, but because it was something she seemed to need, I wanted to get it for her. Standing in line, my fingers twitched with impatience. I needed to get back to the little Sprite I had trodden on inadvertently. I was in such a hurry, I hadn't noticed her crouched down in the doorway or seen her hand until it was too late and I heard her gasp of pain.

Nothing prepared me for the rush of incredible desire I felt when I hunched down and saw her for the first time. She was the most unique-looking woman I had ever seen. Riotous white-blonde curls hung around her face. Her eyes were green—so lightly colored they were luminous as she stared up at me. Her pale skin was dotted with freckles. Tiny flecks of sand scattered over the bridge of her nose and cheeks. A prominent beauty mark sat on the top of her cheek to the left of her eye.

She reminded me of a picture in a book I had been reading to my niece the other night called *The Woodland Sprite*. The resemblance was uncanny. She was beyond adorable; even with her huge eyes watery with pain. She was all stubborn and independent, refusing my offer of help. Instead, she scrambled to her feet on her own, her pretty skirt flaring around her legs as she moved. Her tiny chin jutted out defiantly at my offers, *my pleas*, to let me examine her hand, but eventually she relented. When she finally, *grudgingly,* placed her hand in mine, the shock of heat that went through me at her touch was astonishing. I was grateful her fingers didn't appear broken, and after some begging, she agreed to let me splint them— if I bought her some peppermints. Her bargaining tool amused me.

Except when I got back to the doorway, she was gone. All that remained were the crushed peppermints, the red and white swirls nothing but dust on the sidewalk. As I stood watching the breeze carry away the torn plastic and disintegrated candy, my phone buzzed, and I knew it was Beth from the studio questioning my whereabouts.

I had already texted her earlier to tell her I'd be late because of an emergency patient, and now I was even later because of walking over the woman hiding in the doorway.

Briefly, I wondered why she had been crouched there. Was she hiding from someone? Was she okay? Where had she gone? More importantly, how could I find her?

My phone buzzed again, and I pulled my glasses out of my pocket, sliding them on so I could tap out a message saying I would be there in a moment.

I should have never agreed to do this, but I had lost the last bet I made with my sister Caitlin, and participating in this study had been the wager.

She'd had the widest grin on her face when she pushed the newspaper my way, tapping on the advertisement. *"You lose, and you have to sign up for this experiment, Daniel."*

I had barely paid attention to the ad and agreed because I was certain I would beat her playing the latest version of the video game we liked to play. We'd been doing it for years, and it was rare she won. While the idea of kissing a stranger didn't appeal to me, it wasn't any big deal, since I didn't expect it to occur. If she'd lost, she would've had to arrive at an engagement party we were attending in a costume of my choosing—and it wasn't a costume themed party. My elegant sister would have hated it. All I had to do was drop a kiss on a stranger and walk away. I thought she'd back out when I laid down my terms, but she agreed.

As we started to play, it became obvious why she was so confident. She had been practicing, and even though I called unfair, she refused to budge, insisting I was being a sore loser. Reluctantly, I offered to accept any other wager, but Caitlin held firm, so here I was to make good on my promise.

What seemed unlikely beforehand was now too real.

I crossed the street, throwing another glance back over my shoulder. I would rather have been following through with my plans of convincing the stubborn little Sprite to join me for coffee. I wanted to wrap her fingers in the ice pack and talk to her for a while.

However, it appeared my idea wasn't happening. Tamping down my disappointment, I pushed the elevator button. I left on my glasses, remembering Beth told me I would have to sign a release form and I would need them to read the wording. I dug into the bag I held and grabbed a peppermint, popping it in my mouth.

I bought them—might as well make good use of them. I hummed at the sweet taste; they were very good. I stuck a couple in my pocket.

Maybe I would offer my kissing partner one.

WHEN I TURNED to see the woman I would be paired with entering the room, I was elated.

My stubborn Sprite stood in the doorway looking utterly nervous. She now had glasses perched on the end of her nose that highlighted her wide eyes and their unusual color. She bit her bottom lip, and it took everything in me not to cross the room and pull it away from her teeth.

I wanted to kiss that lip. Stroke it with my tongue, then dip inside her mouth and see if she tasted as sweet as I thought she would.

Her eyes grew larger and her gaze dropped to the floor. She seemed to be looking at my feet, and I glanced down, wondering if she recognized the boots that had stepped on her fingers. Looking up, I frowned, questioning why she blushed and fidgeted with something in her pocket. I fought back a smile as she popped a candy in her mouth and almost immediately began crunching away on it. I had to bite back a laugh recalling her mutterings about halitosis and sharing. I shook my head in amusement, realizing I had crushed the peppermints she meant to give me.

For the first time since I had agreed to this craziness, I was looking forward to what would happen.

I was going to enjoy kissing my Sprite.

That was, if she didn't recognize me first and kick me in the nuts in retaliation for stomping on her fingers.

I hoped that wouldn't happen. Kissing her would be so much better.

I signed the form without reading it, unable to keep my eyes off her. I saw her wince as she held the clipboard, her fingers still red and sore. The way she squinted at the form, even with glasses, I knew she didn't recognize me. I was sure she couldn't see much without her glasses, whereas I only needed mine for reading and close up work, but I had to tell her.

As soon as the kissing part was over, I would confess and wrap her fingers. I owed her that at least.

Every time her eyes met mine, she blushed—it traveled from the top of her cheekbones, to her ears, and down her neck. The color staining her cheeks only added to the immense attraction I felt for her. I wanted to touch the heat of her skin under my fingers; I wanted to know how far down her body her blush went.

Beth gave us our instructions, and we walked to the middle of the room in silence, staring at each other. I knew we didn't have to give our names. I knew we didn't have to say a word. I could kiss her and walk out of there in thirty seconds.

That wasn't what I wanted, though.

I wanted to know her name. I wanted her to know mine. I wanted her to know the man in front of her. Then, when I finished kissing her for the camera, I could take her somewhere and find out all I could about her, so I could kiss her again.

Nerves hit me when I looked at her, and I tugged on my hair. The tension dissipated at the tender look in her eyes as she gazed at me. I shrugged off my jacket as heat filled my body, and rubbed my damp palms down my jeans. Determination replaced worry, and I held out my hand, silently pleading with her to take it.

She startled a little when I introduced myself, hesitating before allowing herself to put her hand in mine. As I closed my fingers around hers, I paused in amazement at how right it felt encased by my larger one.

I moved closer, liking how her hands slid up to my shoulders. She was so short I had to bend low to be level with her face. Her eyes shut, the sexiest little sigh escaping her mouth as I tilted my head, barely grazing her lips with mine.

Blistering heat shot through me at the slightest touch. Our glasses bumped, causing me to frown and pull back.

"Avery," I whispered, "can I try something?"

Her eyes, those captivating pools of green, stared into mine—the same desire I felt, reflected back in wonder.

She nodded.

Avery

A SLOW SMILE, indulgent and sweet, curled Daniel's lips. The lips that had ignited a fire inside me so hot, I was surprised I wasn't a pile of ash at his feet. Those lips I wanted to feel back on mine. He stood up straight and pulled off his glasses, pushing them up into his hair.

"May I?" he murmured. "They were getting in the way." Not even waiting for an answer, he reached out and tugged off mine, folding the arms closed. He looked around, no doubt for somewhere to put them, and I opened the deep pocket of my skirt, letting him drop them inside.

He *wasn't* done with me.

Thank God.

He inched forward, his long fingers sliding up my neck and into my hair, caressing my skin with gentle, adoring touches. His minty breath washed over my face, igniting my passion. "I need closer," he murmured. "I need more." He bent his head, bowing his back to lower himself. My arms shot out, wrapping around his neck, bringing his mouth down to mine.

Time stood still.

The room disappeared around us.

There were no bright lights or camera filming.

No Beth.

Only him.

Only us.

Warm lips met mine. Full, firm, but gentle. His tongue swept inside, sliding over mine sensuously.

A small moan escaped my lips as he worked my mouth. His taste was overwhelming—sweet, hot, and something so unique— something so *Daniel;* I knew I would never get enough of it.

Slow and gentle became deep and carnal. Teasing and light became powerful and hot. He possessed me. Commanded me. Wrecked me.

I gave myself to him. All of me.

His hands descended in a slow path, running over my sides in a torturous circuit, wrapping around my back, crushing me to his body. Deep rumbles from his chest made me shiver. He groaned low and deep in his throat, his lips never leaving mine, never ceasing their exquisite possession.

I never wanted them to.

He straightened abruptly, one hand slipping under my ass and lifting me. I gasped in his mouth as I wrapped my legs around his waist. His other hand slid under my shirt, spreading wide across my back, fingers pressing and teasing, causing goosebumps to erupt on my skin.

Ignoring the pain in my fingers, I buried my hands in his hair, tugging the soft strands roughly.

His grunt of approval was muffled in my mouth.

Then I felt the cold, flat surface of the wall hit my back; I hadn't even felt us move. Daniel surged against me, his arousal now evident between us. Our lips separated as we gasped for air, but we remained close, our bodies melded together.

Our eyes met, blue versus green, want and desire merging and swirling. Swollen lips glistened under the lights, our chests heaved, and quiet pants of yearning passed between us. A look of understanding dawned, a silent, short conversation happening.

Our lives had just changed—we both felt it, *knew* it. There was no going back now—and neither of us wanted to.

My hands tightened on his neck, needing his mouth back. His head lowered, and I whimpered as his lips hovered over mine.

"Well, I think we got what we wanted." Beth's shocked voice exploded in the room. "We're done."

Daniel's head snapped up; his startled gaze meeting mine. We had forgotten we weren't alone. However, his grip didn't loosen and he didn't move away.

"Okay, good," he said roughly over his shoulder, barely sparing a glance her way.

"We'll, ah, just, um, leave you to, yeah, ah, finish up. Or whatever . . . you, ah, want. Yeah. Come see me before you leave, Avery."

Hurried footsteps and the quiet click of the door let me know I was now alone with Daniel. I shut my eyes, letting my head fall back to the wall with a small thud.

"Hey. Look at me."

I opened one eye, squinting at him.

His smile was wide. "Can you, ah, see me?"

"When you're this close, yes—well, mostly, anyway. Can you see me?"

His face moved closer, his lips a mere breath away from mine. The pulsating heat started moving up my spine again, small flames of desire burning through my skin.

"Yes." He dropped a gentle kiss on my mouth. "I didn't think you could be lovelier than earlier," he murmured.

"Earlier?"

"I thought you were beautiful when you walked in the room," he explained. "But now, seeing you look like this? You are exquisite."

"Like this?" I asked. I was, it seemed, unable to do anything, except repeat the words that came out of his mouth. His perfect, sexy mouth.

"Hmmm. The way you feel pressed up against me. Your lips all swollen from mine, your cheeks flushed, and the way your eyes are looking at me. You're a siren, Avery." He growled. "A fucking siren." He buried his face in my neck, his tongue swirling over my skin, trailing a hot, wet path up to my ear and tugging on the lobe. "I know we were only supposed to kiss, but I want you. God, I want you so much."

I groaned, arching toward him. I could feel how much he wanted me. I wanted him. I had never experienced desire like this until now. Until this man.

His mouth covered mine, and I was lost.

Lost to him and his kisses.

His warmth.

Him.

Something buzzed, startling us both.

Daniel pulled away with a curse, gently standing me on my feet. He slid his glasses back on, reached into his pocket, and grabbed his phone, answering gruffly with a "hello." He listened intently, his thumb grazing over my lips as our eyes locked. He groaned in frustration, tilting back his head.

"I'll be there as soon as I can." He slipped the phone back into his pocket.

"You have to go." Sadness filled my chest, and I was unable to look him in the eye.

"One of my patients isn't doing well."

"You're a doctor?"

Long fingers slipped under my chin, forcing me to look at him. Even blurry, I could see the frown on his face.

"I'm a veterinarian. I had to perform emergency surgery on a dog brought in this morning and she isn't doing well. I have to go." He paused and sighed. "But I don't want to. I want to stay here with you."

"Really?"

His arms wrapped around me, hugging me close. "You silly girl. Yes. I want to stay with you. I want to take you out and talk to you. Get to know you." His arms tightened. "Kiss you some more if you'd let me. No cameras this time."

"I'd like that, Dr. Spencer."

"You'd like to see me again? Or kiss me?" He teased, his lips nuzzling my head.

"Both."

"Can I see you tonight? Take you out?"

"On a date?"

"Yes, a date." He cupped my cheek. "But I need something to tide me over. Tell me three things."

I frowned in confusion. "Three things?"

"About yourself."

"Um, blue is my favorite color."

He grinned, ghosting his finger under my eye. "Green is mine." His inference why made me smile.

"Beth is my best friend."

He nodded. "One more."

"I'm an accountant."

"Smart *and* beautiful. That's an amazing combination."

I blinked.

Lovely. Beautiful.

I wasn't used to hearing those words when someone described me.

"You are."

Oh, God—I had uttered that out loud.

"See? We're getting to know each other. Now, tonight?" he repeated. "I have more questions. Lots more."

I tilted my head up. "Yes."

He kissed me. Long, slow, deep. Then again.

And again.

With a groan, he stepped back. "I have to go."

"I know."

Shyly, he handed me his cell phone and grabbed his coat, shrugging it on. "May I have your number, please, Sprite? And your address."

"Sprite?" I asked. I fished my glasses out of my pocket, putting them on so I could see the phone screen.

"Yeah, earlier . . ." His voice trailed off and a frown marred his face.

"Avery, I have something to tell you before I go."

"I don't like the sound of that." My heart beat a little faster at the sound of his voice. "Are you married?"

"No."

"Girlfriend?" I squeaked.

He chuckled. "No. Not when I walked in here, anyway." He winked.

My breath caught at those words. "What then?" I whispered.

He took in a deep breath. "I stepped on you."

"What?"

"Earlier. Outside. I stepped on you. I, ah, crushed your peppermints and your fingers."

"That was you?"

"Yes."

"But, your glasses—you weren't wearing any glasses!"

"I only need my glasses for reading and close up work, not

driving. So, most of the time, I have them shoved up on my head or in my pocket." He chuckled. "Otherwise, I leave them in the strangest places." He slid his glasses onto his head. "See?"

I shook my head.

With a chuckle, Daniel pulled off my glasses, as well. "See now?"

I gasped. Now I realized why his touch felt so right and his voice familiar. "It *is* you! Mr. Blurry!"

He laughed and slipped my glasses back on, kissing the end of my nose.

"I'm sorry. I was so worried about being late and nervous about being here, I didn't see you." He lifted my hand, ghosting his lips over my fingers. "I went to get you some things to help with the pain and when I got back, you were gone."

"Beth kept texting me. I honestly didn't think you'd come back."

"I did. I was very sad to see you were gone. I didn't know how to find you." His voice dropped. "And then you walked in here. You found me, Sprite."

There was that name again. "Sprite?"

"You look like a picture from a book I was reading to my niece the other night. A woodland Sprite." He caressed my cheek with the back of his fingers. "It suits you."

"Oh?"

He chuckled. "Mischievous, stubborn, and willful. You displayed all those traits in the few minutes I had with you, before you disappeared. Another trait you share with them. Disappearing. We'll have to work on you not doing that again."

I giggled.

Daniel opened a bag beside him and snapped a package in his hand, wrapping it around my fingers. Instantly, soothing cold soaked into my skin. "The ice should help the pain and the swelling." He passed me the bag. "There're splints if you need them, some Tylenol, and of course, your peppermints."

"Oh."

"Halitosis, Avery?" he asked, amused.

"I was worried," I admitted with a smirk.

Something pressed on my lips, and I opened them so Daniel could slip in a mint.

I rolled it around on my tongue, gasping as he kissed me deeply.

He eased back, looking mischievous, and opened his lips so I could see my mint now resting on his tongue. "So much sweeter now," he crooned.

Desire exploded in me. How did he make something like stealing a mint from my mouth so incredibly sexy? I was sure I whimpered.

Stepping back, he shook his head. "I dreaded coming here. And now I don't want to leave."

"I'll see you tonight."

"Can I call you this afternoon?"

"Yes."

"I'm sorry about your hand."

"You can kiss it better later."

His eyes darkened. "I'll kiss anything you want. Just promise me you won't disappear again."

"I promise."

His warm lips nuzzled my forehead. "Until tonight."

My eyes followed him to the door. He turned, winked, and pressed his fingers to his lips before he disappeared through the door.

I sighed and slid down the wall to the floor.

What just happened?

Four

Avery

I WAS SO lost in the mixed thoughts swirling in my head, that I was startled when another body slid down the wall beside me.

"Hey, Beth," I mumbled.

"Avery."

I peeked sideways at her.

Her hazel eyes bore into mine, and her brow furrowed.

"What?"

"What? You're seriously asking me *what*? You come in here unwillingly, looking as though you were facing the death squad, and fifteen minutes later, I almost had to use a crowbar to pry you two apart! And now you're asking 'what'?" Her head fell back, hitting the wall. "Jesus, Avery."

I gaped in shock. "Fifteen minutes? We were kissing for fifteen minutes?" It only felt like a minute or two. Certainly, not long enough, in my opinion.

She laughed. "Well, about twelve. You did sign some paperwork. After a fashion."

"After a fashion? What does that mean?"

"The two of you were so busy playing peek-a-boo with each other, neither of your signatures are legible or on the right lines. Both of them look like chicken scratch."

I couldn't help my grin. I had been rather distracted, and I liked knowing he had been, as well.

She tilted her head toward me, a huge smirk on her face. "That was one of the hottest things I have ever seen. I swear the camera almost melted."

"It felt pretty hot."

"I had to send Cliff out of the room."

"Why?"

"He was sporting a boner five minutes into the kiss. When Daniel shoved you onto the wall, I was afraid he was gonna come in his pants. Hell, I was afraid I might, too. I texted Ryan and told him to meet me for lunch. And it ain't no sandwich he's gonna be eating." She winked. "If you catch my drift."

I hid my face in my hands, embarrassed beyond words, but unable to stop laughing. I wasn't sure I could ever look at Cliff again—or Ryan, for that matter. However, nothing embarrassed Beth.

Beth bumped my shoulder, chuckling. "I thought I was going to have to turn the hose on the two of you."

My head fell back, and we shared an amused glance.

"Has, uh, that happened to anyone else?"

"Nope. We've seen some hot kissing, a few pecks, and some really uncomfortable attempts, but nothing, and I mean *nothing*, like the inferno we witnessed in here." She paused. "Do you want to talk about it?"

"It was him, Beth."

"Him, who?"

"Mr. Blurry."

"The guy who stepped on your fingers? It was Daniel?"

I nodded, touching my lips. They were still on fire from his possessive mouth.

"Avery, what's going on? I've never seen you like this—ever."

"I have no idea. I'm seeing him tonight, though." I drew in a deep breath. "There's something between us, something I can't explain. I felt it. He felt it."

"That's his cock. I've tried explaining that to you." She patted my knee. "I even spelled it out for you."

Another giggle burst out of me. I had felt his arousal pressed against me—hard and prominent. I arched an eyebrow at her. "Besides *that*, Beth." I hesitated, because I wasn't certain how to explain to her what I was feeling. "Something . . . profound. He made me feel so comfortable. I forgot to be shy. He made me feel safe. As if I was home." I swallowed the thickness in my throat. "I think he felt it, too."

"Holy fuck," she whispered. "Avery—you've never said anything like that."

"I know."

"You were only supposed to kiss him. Not fall in love."

I stared. I wasn't in love with Daniel. I only met him an hour ago. That was impossible.

Wasn't it?

Beth shrugged. "Stranger shit has happened."

Oh. True.

She chuckled. "Wait until Daniel finds out that you mutter out loud a lot. I'm sure it will amuse him."

"I think he already knows."

She laughed.

My phone buzzed.

I grinned when I saw his name appear.

He'd made sure we exchanged numbers before he left and he had my address. He told me he'd be googling it on his way to his truck so he knew where to pick me up later.

I never got your last name, Sprite.

Connor.

Avery Connor—it suits you. But I prefer Sprite. I am off at 6. I can pick you up at 6:45?

I replied quickly.

Looking forward to it.

Actually, if I take a shortcut I can be there about 6:41.

Please be safe. I would rather wait the 4 extra minutes.

OK. 6:45. I am adding 4 minutes onto the end of our date—I will not be denied 4 minutes of time I could spend with you.

I blushed at his words.

Okay. Duly noted.

If, in fact, the date ends at all. Just saying.

I shook my head at his words. He made me feel so . . . wanted.

You had better have a pocketful of those peppermints. You'll need them.

Done.

Beth grabbed the phone away and read our texts.

"Sprite?"

She started to grin as I told her why he called me that, and by the time I finished talking, she was smiling so wide, I was sure her cheeks had to hurt.

"He's already named you, Avery. He's an animal guy. You know what that means. Once they name you, they keep you. You are so done."

Before I could protest, my phone buzzed again. We both looked at the screen.

Is it 6 yet? BTW, dibs on tomorrow, too.

Sorry, I forgot my manners. My mother always told me to say please. So, please. Dibs on tomorrow.

"Oh shit," she muttered. Then she pushed herself up on the floor, pulling me up with her. "I had better get busy with research."

"Research?"

"Booking a church and all. Takes time, you know. At this rate, I have a feeling you're gonna need it."

I chuckled as I walked behind her. "Beth?"

"Hmm?"

"Did you *see* how big his feet were?"

She stopped so suddenly, I stumbled into her back, almost knocking both of us down. She started to laugh and flung her arm over my shoulders.

"I did notice, actually. I was certainly impressed. But for you to notice? Now *that* is impressive and I *know* it's serious—for both of you. C'mon, *Sprite*. We got some talking to do." She winked. "Maybe another trip to the drugstore is in order. Feet *that* big—we need some MAGNUMS."

I fanned myself.

Was it extremely warm in here?

AROUND THREE, I started pacing. My nerves had kicked in. Should I change into a different outfit? He said my skirt was pretty. Maybe he wanted me to keep it on. *Oh, God*—maybe he wanted to be the one to take it off.

Why was it so hot in here?

I didn't know what we were doing on our date.

Although, I hoped some of the evening involved kissing.

Lots of kissing.

It would be a shame if Daniel wasted the whole evening using that sexy mouth of his only for talking.

No. More kissing was needed.

Strains of music came from my pocket, and I dug out my phone, confused. I started to laugh. Beth had added a ringtone for Daniel: *If I Could Talk to the Animals* from *Doctor Doolittle*. She was vastly amusing.

I'd have to find one for Ryan and add it next time I saw her. I had passed him in the hall as I left the building. He told me with a huge smirk, he was there to have lunch, but there had been no bag in his hand. Recalling Beth's earlier words, I had to clamp my lips together in order not to laugh and hurry away. Maybe *Afternoon Delight* would work for her.

I was still chuckling when I answered the call.

Daniel's low, husky voice made me shiver. "You sound like you're in a good mood, Sprite."

"Beth was being funny."

"You're still at the studio?"

"No, ah, I'll explain later."

"Okay. Um, listen, Avery, I hate to do this—"

"No," I breathed, pain lancing through my chest. I sat down as my legs gave out. He was canceling. He had thought it over and realized how inane the whole situation was. He had come to his senses.

As if he could read my mind, his voice became louder. "No! No! Listen—please!"

"Okay."

"I don't want to cancel. That is the last thing I want to do. But the dog—Lucy—the one I operated on? She's having a rough time recovering. I can't leave her alone, so I have to stay. All I'm asking is if we could postpone until tomorrow." He paused. "Please?"

I exhaled as relief flowed through me. "Oh."

Daniel chuckled. "Did you honestly think I would call and cancel on you unless I had a choice? God, I'm so disappointed, I can taste it."

"So you'll just sit there all evening in the clinic and watch over her?"

"Well, sort of."

"Sort of?"

"My house is attached to the clinic, so I'll bring Lucy there and make her comfortable. But I'll stay with her all night, yes."

"You live at the vet clinic?"

"I own the vet clinic."

"Oh. I didn't know."

"There's a lot you don't know about me yet. It was one of my goals for tonight. I can't tell you how much I was looking forward to seeing you again. But, Lucy is—"

I interrupted him. "Daniel, it's fine. I understand. I think it's wonderful you care about your patients so much."

"I do. Tonight was important. I wanted to see you—more than I can say—but, I have to stay. Unless . . ."

"Unless?"

"Unless I could convince you to come here? I know it's not like a *date* date, but I could order in dinner, and we could talk while I make sure Lucy's okay? She'll probably sleep all evening from the pain meds, but I need to keep a close eye on her." His voice dropped to almost a whisper. "I'd make it up to you tomorrow. I want to see you, Avery. So much."

It wasn't a tough decision. I wanted to see him, as well. "Yes. On one condition."

"You want more peppermints?"

I chuckled. "No. I'll bring something and make dinner."

"You don't have to do that."

"I want to. I like to cook."

"What about your fingers?"

"They're fine. A little sore, but still working."

"Okay. I want to look them over again."

"Fine. So dinner?"

"As if I'd pass up the chance to see you? Dinner for sure. I'll text you directions."

"You want me to come around six?"

"Would you think less of me if I said I wanted you to pick up whatever you're making and come as soon as you can?"

"Really?"

"The thought of walking in my door and seeing you in my kitchen making dinner for us, is kind of, ah, doing things to me. So, yeah, I'd like that. A lot."

"Do I get a kiss hello?" I whispered.

"Hello, good evening, how are you, nice skirt, dinner smells great—any and all of them."

"I'll go shopping."

"Perfect."

"You didn't ask me if I was a good cook, Daniel."

"Doesn't matter."

"Maybe what I make will be inedible."

The sexiest chuckle came over the line. "Then I guess I'll just have to eat you."

I dropped the phone.

I SAT IN my car, looking at Daniel's clinic. It was a little way out of town, but still close enough to be convenient for his clients. Built to look like a general store, it had a homey, country feel to it. It was set back from the road with ample parking in the front and a simple sign that said *Veterinarian Clinic.* There was another sign labeling the side driveway *Private,* and I assumed Daniel's house was down there, behind the clinic. He told me it was attached to a big garage that made the clinic easy access for him.

When he texted earlier, he instructed me to park out front and he would drive around back with me. He would show me where everything was, then he'd return to work while I made dinner for us.

We'd have the evening alone.

The thought alone made me shiver.

There would definitely be some kissing involved, right?

My fingers fumbled as I pressed the button to lower the window. The temperature had suddenly risen in my body again. I wasn't sure I had felt anything but warm and flushed since I hung up from Daniel earlier.

When I picked up the phone, after dropping it, stuttering out an apology, he started chuckling. He snickered even harder when I asked him if he kept fava beans and Chianti on hand for eating guests. Once he stopped laughing, he assured me—in a very low, sexy voice—that was not the kind of eating he meant. He planned to devour me in an entirely different manner.

I dropped the phone again. He was howling so loud he could barely say goodbye.

A few minutes later he texted me, and I retrieved my phone from the floor.

Nom, nom, Avery.

Once again, the phone hit the ground.

I sighed when I picked it up. It wasn't going to last at this rate.

I left the window open for a few minutes, needing the cool air on my overheated cheeks. I popped another peppermint in my mouth and chewed it, savoring the sweet, minty taste. Finally calmer, I walked up the path and into Daniel's clinic.

I hesitated, stopping in the front entranceway. Should I ask for Daniel? Dr. Spencer?

Would they find it strange I didn't have an animal with me?

A woman came out, holding a carrier with a small cat inside, and held the inner door for me.

Unable to stall anymore, I walked into the clinic. The waiting room was empty, but from behind the reception desk, a tall woman with long brown hair and a friendly face, greeted me cheerfully.

"Hello! Can I help you?"

I stepped forward to ask for Daniel just as he came around the corner.

Our eyes met, and he hurried toward me, dropping a file on the counter. "Sprite." He breathed out my nickname, wrapping an arm around my waist, tugging me close. Without hesitating, he lifted me as if I weighed nothing, cupping my head as he captured my lips with his.

I was on fire in an instant. Wrapping my arms around his neck, I weaved my fingers into his thick hair.

Our glasses mashed together, digging into my skin.

I didn't care—neither did Daniel.

I whimpered at his possessive grip, almost weeping in relief at the feel of his mouth working mine. He tasted less minty now and more coffee-ish, and if possible, it was even more of a turn-on than earlier. He still tasted like Daniel. He must have liked how I tasted as well, since he groaned deep in the back of his throat, his hold becoming tighter.

A throat clearing behind him was like a gunshot in the room. I jerked back, my eyes panicked, remembering we weren't alone.

"Is that the new 'let's make the clients more welcome policy' you were talking about, Daniel? Or can I assume this is Avery?" An amused voice chuckled.

Not letting me go, Daniel turned around. "Avery," he rasped. "This is my sister, Caitlin."

"Hi," I squeaked, my face burning with embarrassment.

She grinned. "I think you owe me huge for this morning, brother."

"I do."

"Can I keep one of the ponies?"

"Yes. Take your pick from the stable. Any one you want is yours."

I gaped up at him. He had ponies?

I liked ponies.

"I'll give you one. Two if you want, Avery," he murmured, nuzzling my hair.

Oh. Had I said that out loud?

"Are you gonna put her down?" Caitlin queried, looking as though she were trying not to laugh.

I glanced down. I was wrapped in one strong arm, crushed close to his chest, my feet dangling mid-air. I had one hand buried in his hair and the other gripped his white coat. We had to look ridiculous.

Daniel seemed to disagree. "Nope. When's my next appointment?"

"Ten minutes. Mrs. Mueller is coming in with Sam. She wants him neutered."

I had to ask. "Sam's a dog, right?"

Daniel looked down, his eyes glittering under the lights. "No, Sam's her husband. We do that on the side for special patients."

My eyebrows shot up, and both Daniel and Caitlin laughed. Daniel pressed another kiss to my head. "Yes, Sam is her dog."

"Ten minutes?" he asked Caitlin.

She shrugged one shoulder. "Mrs. Mueller often runs late."

"A trait I love about that woman; particularly if she runs late today. I'm gonna show Avery my office."

Then, with my feet still dangling, he strode past his very amused sister. "Nice to meet you," I called over Daniel's shoulder.

"You, too!" she shouted.

Daniel walked into a room I assumed was his office. Hooking the door with his foot, it slammed behind us, and in one move, I was pressed between two solid surfaces for the second time that day.

Daniel and a wall.

I was okay with that.

"Take off my glasses," he instructed. "Yours, too."

I did as he asked with shaky hands, laying them on top of the filing cabinet beside us. "Nice office," I whispered.

"You know what the best part is?"

"No."

He moved his hand, and I heard a click.

"The door locks."

Then his mouth descended on mine.

Yeah. It *was a great office.*

Avery

A QUICK RAP on the locked door startled me, and I pulled back from Daniel's sexy, talented mouth.

His head moved forward, following my movement, as his hand tugged my face back to his lips.

"No, not yet," he whispered, his breath washing over my face. "More."

"Daniel, Mrs. Mueller called," Caitlin's voice rang out, her laughter barely hidden. "She is running a little late, but I think you need to show Avery where things are? At your *house*?" She paused. "Right, big brother?"

Daniel muttered a low curse, and his head fell back. "Yeah, thanks, Caitlin. I'll take Avery to the house."

I smothered a giggle at his disgruntled voice. Stretching up, I grabbed our glasses, sliding mine into place. Once Daniel set me on my feet, albeit grudgingly, I stood on my tiptoes, and I slipped his on to his head.

"I need to cook us dinner." I tapped his chin. "And you need to get to work, Doctor."

His expression changed, his frown melting into a sincere, affectionate smile. "What must you think of me, Avery?" He shook his head. "I can't seem to keep my hands off you."

"I think you're the most amazing man I've ever met," I

responded. "I don't want you to try to stay away."

Cupping my face, he gazed at me with an expression so filled with emotion and tenderness my eyes became misty. "How did I get so lucky?" He touched his lips to my forehead, sweetly ghosting my temple, drew back, and held out his hand. "C'mon, Sprite. Let's do the making-out walk of shame in front of my sister. No doubt she has Steven waiting with her."

"Steven?"

"My partner and brother-in-law."

"Oh."

He wrapped his large hand around mine, smirking. "Don't look them in the eye. They'll sense fear and pounce. Just keep walking."

I ducked my head, trying not to laugh at his instructions.

He unlocked the door. "Ready?"

"Ready."

I SHIVERED A little, trying to warm up my feet. The ceramic tiles in Daniel's kitchen were cold on my bare feet, but when we had walked into his house, he had removed his shoes, so I did, as well.

He checked out my fingers, assuring himself they weren't broken, then insisted on wrapping them up to protect them while I cooked.

Our making-out walk of shame, as Daniel called it, turned out easy, because a client had walked in to pick up food for their pet and Caitlin was busy. Steven had grinned knowingly at us, waggling his fingers, but Daniel pulled me along and we never stopped.

Once at the house, he gave me a quick tour of his large, state-of-the-art kitchen. He told me to make myself comfortable and help myself to anything I needed.

Then he left me—but not before bestowing my mouth with another one of his blistering kisses, this time with me lifted to the counter, him standing between my legs. It was a perfect height for him, and he showed his pleasure in a most generous fashion.

I sat there long after he left, trying to calm myself down. Never had I met a man like Daniel. Never had someone kissed me the way he did. It felt as though every time his lips touched mine, he stole another little piece of my heart and took it with him.

He possessed me, completely.

I shook my head at my strange thoughts and looked around his kitchen in awe. Rich, mahogany-stained maple cupboards, quartz countertops, and stainless steel appliances all shone under the recessed lights. Cool tones of taupe and cream showed off the deep satin and black surfaces. His stove made me want to weep, thinking of my small one, and I could hardly wait to use it. I was making spaghetti, hoping Daniel liked pasta, as well as salad and my garlic-cheese bread. Luckily, it had been my turn to bring baked goods to work last week, so I had cupcakes in my freezer, and I brought those along, as well. Men always liked cupcakes. They were my dad's favorite.

After preparing the spaghetti sauce and leaving it to simmer, I was a little chilly. I had removed my shrug, to avoid a random tomato sauce accident, so with bare arms and no shoes, I was cold. I padded into the living room, taking in the sizable room and clean lines. The oversized window seat was inviting, and I sat down carefully, offering my hand to the big, gray cat sitting in the sun. Daniel had introduced us earlier.

"This is Dex." He bent down to pick up the large cat weaving around his legs, demanding attention. The cat's fur was short, with a few patches almost bare, part of his tail was missing, and the tips of his ears were gone. He looked like an alley cat that had lost more than his share of fights, but his golden eyes were gentle and he let me pat him.

"Hello, Dex," I murmured, running my fingers over his back.

"I found him one night on my way home from school. There was a storm, and he was lying in the snow, obviously hurt. I took him back to the apartment I was living in at the time, and nursed him back to health,"
Daniel explained. "He's been with me ever since. He sort of owns the place."

I laughed. "I'll remember that."

Daniel chuckled as Dex licked my hand and allowed me to scratch his head. "He likes you."

"Is he not a people cat?"

"I think he was mistreated before I found him. I assume he was abandoned and left to fend for himself, which is why he fared so poorly. He is a bit cautious of other people aside from me. Somehow, I don't see that as an issue with you."

The way he spoke, I knew how fond he was of the creature who lay so content in his arms.

"He's lucky you found him."

Daniel nodded. "He's been a great companion."

Dex let me stroke him as I took in the details of the room.

A huge sofa and matching chair in a deep green filled the space. I ran my hand over the curved back of the sofa, touching the lushness of the weave in the fabric. The same color palette as the kitchen, made the room feel inviting and cozy. A massive fireplace graced one wall, a large TV hung over it.

After a final pat to Dex's head, I stood and studied the fireplace, but had no idea how to use it, or if I should be so forward. The thick rug in the center of the room offered some respite to my cold feet, yet I was still chilly. I hesitated, not wanting to snoop around Daniel's house, then pulled out my phone and texted him.

> Do you have a pair of socks I could borrow?

His reply was swift.

> Top drawer in dresser. R U OK?

I could sense his concern in the short message.

> Feet are chilly. I didn't want to snoop.

> Bedroom at end of hall. Snoop all you want.

> Thanks.

I stood in his doorway, breathing in the room. Daniel's room. It smelled just like him.

Warm. Citrusy. Clean. Sexy.

The whole room was dark blue and cream. It was huge and airy, and like the rest of the house: neat, tidy, and well cared-for. The king-size bed situated in the middle of the long wall was covered in a plush duvet. I swallowed deeply, thinking of Daniel sleeping in it, of me sleeping in it with him—or maybe not sleeping. The image of Daniel pressing me down into that deep mattress, his toned body covering mine, his sexy mouth doing wicked things to me everywhere . . .

Suddenly, I wasn't as cold as I had been a few minutes ago.

Shaking my head, I crossed over to the dresser, opened the top drawer, and giggled as I stood on my tiptoes to be able to reach a pair of his socks. The man was ridiculously tall—and so was his dresser.

As I turned, I gasped in pleasure. A set of double French doors, centered on the end wall, showcased the view. As if pulled by an invisible string, I drifted toward them and looked out onto Daniel's back property. Rolling hills, woods, and open fields met my eyes. In the distance, an expanse of shimmering water glistened in the sunlight. Closer to the house, a red barn and paddock were to the left, and a couple horses grazed in the fields. He really did have ponies. The whole scene resembled a charming painting—scenic, peaceful, and lovely.

I stood there mesmerized. I could envision a future here.

A small table and two chairs sat on the attached deck, and I could see myself sitting beside Daniel, sipping coffee, on lazy summer mornings. I shook my head at the peculiar thoughts as my gaze drifted back to the beautiful vista in front of me. What a wonderful place to live. It suited Daniel with its open, serene ambience.

I was startled when warm arms wrapped around my waist and pulled me back to a firm chest.

"You like?" Daniel murmured into my ear, his lips grazing over the sensitive curve.

"It's breathtaking. So peaceful," I whispered, not wanting to break the silence.

"I love it here."

"Is it all yours?"

"Yes. I had an inheritance from my grandfather, which I used it to buy the property and start the clinic. I love to ride, and when I bought the land, the barn and paddock were already here. I tore down the old house and built the clinic and this house. I breed horses and stable them for people. Sort of a sideline."

"Wow."

"Do you ride?"

"No. I've never even been that close to a horse. They're, ah, kinda big and intimidating."

"I'll take you out and show you soon." He squeezed me. "I can teach you to ride, if you want—you'll love it." He turned me in his arms. "Now, about you being cold. Can I do anything to warm you up?"

"I found some socks."

"Holding them won't make your feet warm, Avery." He smirked. "You need to put them on for them to actually work, you know."

I grinned. "I was going to do that, but the view caught my attention."

He drew me to the bed, lifting me up on the mattress, taking the socks. "Let me help."

Kneeling in front of me, he tsked as he felt how cold my feet were. He rubbed them briskly, then slipped the socks over my toes, smiling as I sighed at the instant relief they offered. They were too big, but he rolled them around my ankle a few times.

I felt warmer already. Although, I wasn't sure if it was the socks or the fact he was kneeling in front of me, his hands still on my legs.

His fingers traced a pattern on my skin.

"So soft, Avery," he crooned. "Your skin is so soft." His hands crept higher, slipping over my knees, caressing.

Our eyes locked, and the passion and desire I saw in them

caused a wanton, almost pleading groan to escape my lips.

He was on his feet in an instant, towering over me, dragging me up to his chest as he kissed me.

Deep.

Wet.

Hard.

I clung to him, wanting more.

He gave it to me.

Sinking together into the mattress, he felt better than I had imagined.

He claimed me, branding me with his touch. His hands were everywhere, stroking my arms, slipping under my tank to caress the skin, ghosting up my side, making me shiver and my body hum in ways it never had with anyone else.

His phone vibrated, and we pulled apart, gasping for air. He dropped his face into my neck, his hot, heavy breath on my skin, then pushed off me and answered his phone.

"On my way."

We stared at each other.

A tender, loving expression crossed his face, while the sweetest smile curved his lips. He leaned down, pressing a series of light, affectionate kisses on my face. My cheeks, nose, and forehead all were swept with his full lips, then he brushed three tender kisses on my mouth. He slipped my glasses back in place—I hadn't even noticed him taking them off.

"Forgive me. I can't seem to stop myself where you're concerned. I see you and all I want . . . all I need, is to feel you against me."

"I feel it, too, Daniel."

"Good. But, I'll try to behave like the gentleman my mother taught me to be and less like a raving sex-starved Neanderthal when I come back, okay?" His fingers danced across my cheek. "I want to know you. All of you. It's not just about this intense draw I have to you." He inhaled. "I've never experienced anything like this in my life. Ever."

"Me either."

He lifted me up so I was standing in front of him. He frowned and rubbed my arms. "You're still cold. Where is your little jacket thingy?"

"Oh. It's rather old and delicate so I didn't want it stained. I took it off while I cooked."

He disappeared through a door and came back holding a beige knitted sweater. He helped me shrug it on and laughed as he rolled up the sleeves. "That will keep you warm. Plus, I turned on the fireplace in the living room. Since I'm not home in the day, I didn't think about how chilly it would be in here."

"I feel much better now."

"Good. Now before I leave, I need three—"

He didn't need to finish his sentence. I peered up at him, knowing what he wanted.

"I love watermelon."

He beamed and nodded for me to continue.

"I love animals, but never had a pet growing up."

"Your parents didn't like them?"

"No, they were fine with it, but that sort of ties into number three. My grandmother lived with us, and she was allergic."

"Ah. Is she . . . ?" He let the question hang in the air.

I shook my head. "She died when I was fourteen." I swallowed the lump in my throat I always got when I thought about her. "I still miss her."

"I'm sorry."

I shrugged, unsure what to say next.

"I didn't mean to make you feel sad."

"I'm not. She was wonderful and a huge part of my life."

"You can tell me about her later."

"I'd like that."

He pulled me in for a quick, tight hug. "I'll be back soon."

He crossed the room, pausing at the door. "Help yourself to anything you need. Look around, find whatever you want." He reassured me with a wink. "I plan on you being here a lot, so settle in, Sprite. Make yourself comfortable. By the way, you look adorable in my socks and sweater. I like it."

Then he was gone—leaving me feeling cared-for, adored, and anxious for him to return.

I HEARD THE side door open and slid the garlic bread into the oven to heat through. Daniel had texted to say he would arrive soon, and he only needed ten minutes for a quick shower.

He walked in, pushing a cushioned basket on a trolley. He beckoned with his hand for me to join him. "Come meet Lucy," he spoke quietly.

Curled up inside was a lovely Collie dog, who let me stroke her with a small thump of her tail. "How is she?"

He pulled his glasses off his head, tossing them on the counter. "Doing better. I'm pleased." He heaved a sigh. "And relieved."

"Good."

He hugged me close. "Hello."

I glanced up, feeling shy. "Hi."

"I think I owe you a kiss with that—do I not?"

I slid my hands up his chest and around his neck. With a low groan, his lips met mine tenderly.

"How are you?"

"Good," I whispered. "Better now."

"Excellent." His lips touched mine again, this time with more pressure.

"Find everything?"

"Yes."

His tongue dipped in, teasing and light.

"Warmer now?"

"Much."

"Perfect."

And I was lost.

His mouth moved, molding itself to mine. His taste overwhelmed me, making me moan low in my throat. With the lightest of caresses, his hand cupped my cheek, his fingers dancing on my skin. When he leaned back, he tucked me under his chin and held me close. His heart was thumping in his chest—its accelerated rhythm matching mine. "God, what you do to me," he murmured. "It's so intense."

I snuggled closer in silent agreement. Never had I experienced such a connection with someone until now. His touch felt like home to me.

Finally, he pulled back, beaming down at me. "I thought it smelled good in here earlier, now, however, it smells incredible."

"It's only spaghetti."

"I love spaghetti. I suck at making the sauce, though. Mine comes from a jar."

"Hungry?"

His tongue traced over his bottom lip as his eyes narrowed. "Starving."

My breathing faltered. I sensed he didn't only mean for dinner.

I might have whimpered.

"Do I have time for a shower?"

I nodded, unable to speak.

"I'll get Lucy settled and be back in a few minutes."

"How will Dex feel about a dog being here?"

"Dex is an old mother hen. He'll sit close to Lucy all night and watch over her, just as I will. He always does when I bring injured animals home with me. I think, because he was hurt, he just gets it. It's as though he senses their pain." Daniel shrugged. "Or maybe not. He is very gentle, regardless."

"That's amazing."

He dropped another kiss on my head. "Yeah."

I watched as he took Lucy into the living room, settling her basket by the fire where she would be warm. Dex jumped down, investigating the basket, and Lucy lifted her head, the two animals sniffing warily at each other. Lucy snuffled and laid her head back down, while Dex curled up on the floor beside the basket as Daniel murmured to them both, stroking their fur.

I smiled and turned to the stove to stir the sauce. My own Doctor Doolittle, talking to the animals. He reappeared in the doorway, and I noticed his grimace as he reached around and rubbed the center of his back.

"Are you okay?" I asked, feeling guilty. He had picked me up a lot today. "I'm not the lightest of things to pick up."

He shook his head. "You barely weigh anything. You fit perfectly in my arms, so stop thinking like that. I love how you fit around me."

His words caught me unaware, and I stared at him. No one had ever told me I was perfect.

"You are."

Oh.

Obviously, I spoke out loud.

"But, you're sore?" I asked, still worried.

"I'm good—just a little stiff. I am by the end of the day, bending over the exam table so much—a drawback of being tall. It has nothing to do with picking you up. That has been the very best part of my day—so far." He winked. "I hope I don't drop my shampoo, though. I'm not sure I could bend down and pick it up." His face broke into a wicked grin. "If I did, would you come and . . . *help* me in the shower, Sprite?"

A strange noise came out of my throat, even as my face grew hot.

Help him?

In the shower?

He'd be naked.

Wet and naked.

In the shower.

"I–I . . ." The only words I was able to gasp out.

My gaze flew to his amused, mischievous expression. He winked again, turned, and sauntered down the hall, laughing the entire time. He was only teasing me.

Cheeky, sexy man.

Unable to resist, I stepped in the hall. "Yes, I would!"

It was my turn to chuckle as his steps faltered.

Gotcha.

"AVERY, DINNER WAS awesome. You made too much, though."

"I thought you could have some leftovers."

"Great." He bent over, kissing my cheek. "Thanks, Sprite."

I giggled.

I giggled every damn time he called me Sprite—or teased me—or kissed my hand, cheek, or temple. I was like a schoolgirl, yet I couldn't help myself.

Daniel sat back, taking a sip of wine. He had enjoyed his dinner thoroughly, eating two platefuls of spaghetti, plus salad, and a frightening amount of garlic bread.

"Did your mother teach you to cook?"

"No. My mom could cook, but it wasn't her forte. My grandmother taught me. After my grandfather died, she came to live with us. My parents were worried about her being alone. I was about six when she moved in. She loved to cook and bake. It was how she showed her love for everyone."

He smiled over the top of his glass, his eyes crinkling. "And how you show yours now?"

I nodded in agreement. "We'd spend hours in the kitchen. She'd be waiting when I got home from school, and I would do my homework and she would cook. When I finished, I got to help. It was my favorite thing to do—then and now."

"Your mom worked, too?"

"She was a financial planner. She worked from home a lot. I loved to sit and listen to her talk about market trends, interest rates, and investments. I found it fascinating. I think that was where I got my love of numbers."

"So you became an accountant."

"Yes."

"You were very close to your grandmother."

I sighed, thinking about her and all we did together. "She was a force. I don't think there was anything she couldn't do. If she didn't know how, she would teach herself. She was petite, a ball of energy, and always on the go. She had a kind word for everyone, and everyone who met her loved her." I tapped my beauty mark on my cheek. "She had the same beauty mark, and she was blonde and fair-skinned. She used to call me her twin—except she was open and beautiful."

Daniel frowned. "You are, too."

I let his remark pass. I lifted my leg, the charms of my anklet twinkling. "This was hers. She wore it long before anklets were even popular. I never take it off."

He reached down, fingering the silver, his touch warm on my skin. "It suits you." He glanced up, meeting my gaze with a tender look. "You're very sentimental."

"I am."

His grip on my ankle tightened. "I like that, Avery. That suits *me*."

My gaze fell to my plate as my cheeks flushed.

I liked suiting Daniel.

LUCY WAS SLEEPING with Dex curled up in the same basket, watching over her. She was doing much better, and Daniel relaxed.

We cleared the table together and I made coffee, which I brought to the living room with the cupcakes.

His eyes lit up when he saw the small treats, and he eagerly reached out for one, popping it in his mouth. Daniel, it turned out, was a huge cupcake fan—especially, red velvet ones with cream cheese frosting.

I was well rewarded for my efforts.

He drew me close, kissing me thoroughly. The sweetness of the cupcakes heightened his taste, making me moan with desire.

He kissed me senseless.

To the point, I was dizzy with want.

Want for him.

We were moving so fast, my head was spinning.

He groaned at one point and moved me off his lap. "I promised to behave like a gentleman and I'm not doing such a fuck-hot job, am I?"

I lifted one shoulder and winked. "I dunno. I'm feeling rather hot myself."

He laughed. "I'll be good. I want to know about you. I want you to know me." He ran his fingers over my cheek, his touch gentle. "Let's talk."

We spent the rest of the evening alternatively talking or making out. Sometimes, both at once. He asked more questions about what I did as an accountant and about the office where I worked. He admitted he found numbers and spreadsheets way over his head. He smiled a little too wide when he innocently stated he might be looking for accounting advice for his clinic. Ignoring his little hint, I asked him about his practice. I was eager to learn how he decided to become a vet.

His face lit up as he explained he knew he wanted to work with animals when he was only seven years old. He spent every weekend and summer from the time he was ten, volunteering at animal shelters and clinics, soaking up everything he could learn from the staff and vets themselves, when they had time to spare. Shyly, he confessed he had always been a favorite at the places he volunteered, which allowed him to learn freely. He was first in his class at vet school, and he never once wavered on his career choice.

I could see how much he loved his clinic and all his patients. His face glowed as he talked about his practice.

"You spent all your time in clinics?" I teased. "No time for dating? The girls must have been heartbroken."

He shook his head at my teasing. "I was too tall and awkward for girls when I was a teenager. I was all legs and long arms, tripping over my own feet. I wore glasses and studied too much."

"I bet you were cuter than you think."

"I grew into my body late in senior high. I discovered the gym and I liked to work out. Dating didn't really happen until I was almost seventeen."

"Wow."

"What about you? Tell me more about teenage Avery."

"I wasn't allowed to date until I was sixteen. I was a bit of a surprise to my parents, and my father was pretty strict."

"A surprise?"

"My parents tried for years to have kids with no success. They sort of gave up and my mom got pregnant with me when she was forty-four."

"Surprise, indeed."

"She thought she was going into early menopause, but she got me instead."

"A good surprise."

"I think so. They're great parents—older, but very active."

"Do they live here?"

"No, they're retired and live in British Columbia now. The winters are easier to deal with there. I see them a couple times a year." I paused, wistful. "I miss them a lot."

"Names?"

"Mom and Dad."

He chuckled.

"Janett and Doug." I spelled it out for him. "Janett with two 't's. It's pronounced Jeanette, but spelled differently. It's a family name."

"Huh. It is different. I like that." He relaxed, crossing his ankles. "And Janett and Doug were quite protective?"

"My dad especially. He was a principal at the local school and pretty tough. All the kids were scared of him. My mom was more lenient. But, they were fair and loving, even if my dad went overboard at times."

Daniel chuckled. "Principal, heh? I imagine that was rather intimidating for any boy who was interested."

"I could do group outings, that sort of thing, but no dates. He always had to know where I was and who I was with." I chortled at the memory. "The first boy I went on a date with, Tommy Forsyth, was so scared of my father and the interrogation that happened, he didn't even try to hold my hand. He walked me to the door at exactly ten o'clock and literally waved goodnight and took off."

"No second date?"

"No. I didn't date a lot until after high school. I come from a small town up North, and everyone knew my dad. He *was* a bit much for the boys to handle, I guess." I shrugged. "I had some good friends and we all hung out together."

"And dating in university?"

"There wasn't a lot of that either, never really has been."

"I find that difficult to believe."

"I've never really connected with anyone easily." I picked at a small thread hanging from my skirt. "I–I'm a little shy and I tend to hang back. It's off-putting to some guys, I think."

"How so?"

"I get tongue-tied and nervous. Some people see it as me being snobby, but sometimes, I simply don't know what to say."

"I noticed the shy part." He lowered his voice. "I find it appealing, to be honest."

"Oh."

"All anyone has to do is look at the depth in your eyes, and they would know you aren't snobby."

I stared at him. "Maybe no one has looked hard enough."

"Your soul is in your eyes, Avery. When I look in them, all I see is warmth."

I shook my head in wonder. *Who was this man?*

He chuckled. "You don't seem shy with me."

He was right. I didn't feel the same overwhelming shyness with Daniel. "You make me feel . . . different. I feel very comfortable with you."

He lifted my hand, kissing the knuckles. "Good."

"Tell me about your family."

He scowled a little at the change of subject, but let it go. "Well, you met my sister Caitlin. She's two years younger than I am." A thought must have crossed his mind. "How old are you, Avery?"

"You don't know?"

"No, we weren't given any personal information about the person we were matched to."

"Twenty-seven."

"I'm thirty-two."

"Beth told me your age when she was asking me to step in," I confessed. Then I waggled my eyebrows. "An older man. I love older men."

He laughed at my teasing. Leaning forward, he kissed the end of my nose. "You are adorable."

I rolled my eyes.

Sitting back, he crossed his legs, watching me with an amused expression. "My parents live about twenty minutes from here. My dad, Sean, is a patent lawyer and my mom, Julie, runs her own daycare."

"You're close to them?"

"I am. My family plays a big part in my life."

"That's lovely."

He lifted my hand and kissed the knuckles, his gaze intense. "They are gonna love you."

Then he continued as if what he said wasn't as deep and meaningful as it seemed.

"I had a fairly normal childhood and teen years. I wasn't perfect, by any means, and we had our share of fights, but they were, and are, great parents." He paused. "I wasn't always as close with my dad as I am now. He wasn't around a lot when I was younger, and I acted out some."

"Oh?"

"He was a football player with the CFL. So he was away a lot with games, and when he was home, he was at practice or meetings, and often participating in some sort of media event. Even in the off-season, he was busy. He did player stuff plus went to school and worked."

"Wow. That seems impressive. Although I don't know a lot

about sports. Should I have recognized the name Spencer?"

He laughed. "No, it's fine. It was years ago. Your dad might recognize the name if he liked football."

"I'll have to ask him. Why did he work if he played professionally?"

"Players in the CFL aren't paid the way NFL players are. You have to work and play to make a living—especially back then. Plus, he was going to school, so he was a busy man. My mom was the glue that held us together." He shifted a little in his seat. "I missed him a lot and I acted out."

"I think that's probably normal."

"I suppose. Still I feel bad when I think about how I behaved at times."

"I'm sure your parents understood."

"They, particularly my mom, were really patient. She was always there for me. When I was eight, late in the season, my dad took a hard hit. He blew out his knee and had to retire—it was a career ending injury."

"How awful!"

"Yes and no. He was sad for a while, but he liked being home more. He found a great job with a respected firm and has been there ever since. I loved having him around; well, we all did, but I really loved it. I settled down and not long after, found my own place in life."

"Your dad never wanted you to become an athlete like him?"

He shook his head. "No. I liked sports and I enjoyed playing at school, but I never had the drive he did. He told me later he was glad I never had."

"Why?"

Daniel paused, looking sad. "His body is old beyond its years. He walks with a limp because of his knee, his hips cause him pain, and the baby finger on his left hand was broken so often, it sticks out at a right angle. Professional sports are tough on the body."

"Oh dear."

"We work out together, and he sees therapists. He tries to stay ahead of it and look after himself. Some of the newer technology helps him a lot. Seeing how it's affected him, I'm glad I stuck to animals." He winked at me. "Lifting cats, dogs, and the occasional woodland Sprite is far easier on the body than a three-hundred-pound man driving you into the hard ground constantly."

I laughed at his analogy. "How did your parents meet?"

"My mom went to a football game with some friends. She didn't know much about sports, and after the game was over, they bumped into some players at a bar. She had no idea who he was and paid no attention to him. But my dad noticed her, and by the end of the evening, they were a couple."

"It would seem spontaneity runs in the family."

He smiled. "My dad always says 'you know when you know.'" His smile became wider. "I'll have to admit to him now he was right."

Unable to resist, I shared his amusement. "Tell me about your practice?"

"My brother-in-law and I own the clinic. He specializes in farm animals while I handle the domestic ones."

"That makes for a diverse practice."

He nodded, draining the last of the brandy he'd been sipping. "I met Steven while at school. We became fast friends, and I brought him home one break." He grinned at the memory. "My parents liked him right away, but he and Caitlin didn't hit it off."

"Really?"

"The two of them seemed to disagree about everything—all weekend. After dinner on Saturday night, they got into a heated debate on some environmental issue. Watching each of them argue their side was like a ping-pong match. It was worse than two cats fighting, and at one point I thought I was going to have to separate them. I was sure it was the only visit home he'd ever be making with me."

"Obviously, they worked it out."

"I apologized on the way back to school, and he looked at me as if I was crazy and told me he hadn't had such a good time in years. He loved disagreeing with Caitlin. When we got back to campus, he hit the library and dug up even more information. They emailed back and forth for weeks, arguing. Finally, Caitlin admitted he was correct, and he informed her she owed him a date. They've been together ever since."

"Wow. That's some story."

"They complement each other. She's very outgoing and he's very laid-back. The argument they had was the first time I'd ever seen Steven riled up." Daniel chuckled. "She is the only person to this day who can do that."

"So they had their own sort of connection right away."

"I suppose." He stroked my cheek with one, long finger, his light touch bringing with it so much warmth. "Not like ours."

We had shared our stories earlier over dinner of how we ended up in that studio today. I did it as a favor to Beth, while he had to do it because he lost a bet. I laughed as Daniel talked about the wagers he and Caitlin made all the time. He made a face when he described having to eat blood pudding, and how funny it had been watching Caitlin drink hot sauce, and the way she ran around fanning her face and gasping for air as she tried to cool off her mouth. I snorted when he told me about having to wear a dress one day at the clinic, including heels. He laughed just as hard talking about the wagers he had lost as the ones she had. They were obviously close.

"I think I'll forever be grateful I lost that bet," he said. "I actually won big time. I got to meet you."

I wasn't sure how to describe our connection, but it was there, like a living, breathing thing between us—pulsating and surrounding us.

Daniel kissed me, his lips soft against mine. Our eyes held, and I could feel my cheeks redden under his gaze. With a grin, he grabbed the last cupcake off the plate and sat back.

He continued, telling me how Caitlin now managed the clinic, billings, and together, they ran the stable. The three of them made a good team, each bringing a different strength into the business.

Watching him talk about his parents, sister, and his patients was inspiring. When he spoke of his beloved niece, Chloe, Caitlin and Steven's daughter, his eyes and voice were filled with tenderness. Love literally rolled off him when he discussed those he held most dear.

His voice was quiet when he asked, "Do you want children?"

"Yes."

He wrapped his hand around mine and squeezed it. "Good. That's good."

Another one of those strange, silent conversations flowed between us.

I want them with you.

I drew in a deep breath. "I can't believe—" I hesitated.

He pulled me back onto his lap, tucking a piece of hair behind my ear in an affectionate gesture. "Ask me," he implored.

"How are you not taken? Already married with a house *full* of kids and some adoring wife? You're too wonderful for that not to be the case."

Not to mention how incredibly drop-dead sexy you are.

I huffed and sighed. "And the way you kiss? I mean *really*, how are you still single?" Then, realizing what I had blurted out, I slammed my mouth shut.

Daniel cupped my face, bringing me close and kissing me. Tiny, light brushes of his lips. "I could ask you the same," he murmured. "How the hell did I get so lucky to meet you today? I know you said you haven't dated much, but I still can't believe it."

"I've never had a serious relationship, or even particularly long ones." I shrugged. "Aside from the obvious, I think I might be too boring. I was always the shy, studious girl, easily passed by."

"The obvious? What does that mean?"

I played with my hair, holding up a strand for his inspection. "My odd looks. My eyes and my hair are so light that I almost look albino. The only color on my face is the infernal freckles I can't get rid of. I've always known I'm no great beauty, or even normal looking, so I've been told, but—"

His hands dropped and tightened on my hips. "Wait. Odd

looks? Who said that to you?"

I shrugged. "I've heard it my whole life."

"From? Not your parents, surely."

"No. They always told me I was perfect. I sort of stuck out at school, with the white hair and light eyes. Kids, you know. They liked to tease. My hair, if you can believe it, was even lighter when I was young. The kids called me Ghost. I heard a teacher once say I looked like an old woman with a kid's face. It all stuck with me."

"She shouldn't have said that, and you can't dwell on what kids say. Little buggers are full of it. They spout off to make themselves feel better."

I sighed ruefully. "I know, but others think that way, too."

"Who?"

"It doesn't matter. He was right. I'm—"

He interrupted me again. "Who?"

"My last boyfriend, Grant. When we broke up, he told me he always found my unusual looks distracting—and not in a good way," I admitted, embarrassed.

He slid his hands up my arms, and tilted my chin up with his finger, forcing me to look at him.

"Your face," he stated slowly, his eyes never leaving mine "is beautiful. All of you is perfect. You are not, in any way, *odd*. Unique, yes. Exquisite, yes. I thought it the instant I saw you. Beautiful," he repeated in a firm voice. "Understand? Ignore whatever inane comment that loser had to say. He was obviously fucked in the head."

His last sentence made my lips quirk. I started to chuckle and he joined me, his broad shoulders shaking with mirth. His thumbs ran small circles on my cheeks. "Don't listen to him, okay?"

"I should listen to you?"

"I am a doctor. That means I'm smart—so, yes. Listen to me."

"Okay," I breathed out. "I'll try."

A wicked smile spread on his mouth as he drew my face nearer. His intoxicating scent surrounded me as his lips hovered over mine.

"Good. And thanks, Sprite. I think you're pretty drop-dead sexy, too."

I gasped as he crushed me to his chest.

Damn mutterings.

Avery

BREATHLESS FROM DANIEL'S passionate kisses, I drew back, pushing myself into the corner of the sofa. He ran a hand through his hair and sighed.

"Did it again, didn't I? You get close and I want you closer."

"I don't mind, it's just . . ."

"I know," he assured me. "We only met today. I'm not expecting anything. I do like kissing you, though."

"I like it, as well. Maybe too much."

He winked. "I'll keep that in mind."

"You never really answered my question earlier," I began, "how are you not taken?"

He sat back, crossing his arms behind his head, stretching out his long legs. "I've had girlfriends. I'm not a player, though, and I haven't had many relationships. I'm more of an all-in guy, I suppose. None of them were long-term or serious. My last girlfriend, Karen—we were together for over a year."

"What happened?"

He shrugged. "Nothing really. No huge drama or anger. She was a wonderful woman. Pretty, fun, and we got along well. My family liked her, and we had many incredible times together. Everything was good. She's an amazing person, actually."

My stomach twisted at his tone, the unfamiliar feeling of

jealousy emerging. He spoke so fondly of her.

He continued with a wry smile. "But we had one problem."

"Oh?"

He tilted his head, studying me. "How do you feel when I kiss you, Avery?"

"Breathless. Achy." I thought back to our first kiss. "Wanting more. So much more."

"That's how I feel. I can't get enough. I *can't* get close *enough*. Karen and I never had that all-consuming spark. We were great together as friends—it was how we should have stayed. One day, I realized we hadn't been *together* for over a month and I had no desire to ask her to be with me. We sat down and talked and she confessed the same thing. So, we broke up—over a year ago."

"I'm sorry."

He laughed. "Don't be. Neither one of us was particularly upset, so we knew we made the right decision. Life is too short to settle. We remained close and we're still friends. A couple of months after we split up, she met Buck, and a month later, she was married. She told me the first time she shook his hand she couldn't let go and it was the same for him. She found her soul mate. She's happy, and I was, and am, thrilled for her."

"Does, she, ah, live here?"

"No. They moved not long ago. He's a lawyer and had a great offer in New York. Karen loves it there. She is more of a big city girl. We keep in touch—she is very happy."

"Oh." I breathed a sigh of relief. I wasn't sure I wanted to meet his ex-girlfriend he still spoke so highly of even after a year of ending their relationship.

He grinned. "Don't be jealous. How I felt about Karen is vastly different from how I feel about you. It's like comparing a lake to the ocean." Reaching for my hand, he brushed a fast kiss on the knuckles. "And in case you aren't clear? She's the lake, and you're the ocean."

"*Oh.*"

"I saw her not long after she got married and watched the two of them together. They were ideal for each other. After seeing that, I knew I could never settle for anything less. She told me she had never been happier, and when it happened for me, I'd know it." He lowered his voice. "I didn't really believe her—until today."

My heartbeat sped up at his words.

"I feel it. I felt it the first time you let me touch your hand. It was as if I'd found the one missing piece to my puzzle. The one thing I'd been waiting for to make me complete."

He tugged on my hand, pulling me back to his lap. "Do you feel it, Sprite? That draw? Do you feel how strong it is between us?"

"Yes."

He shifted closer, the heat of his body sinking into my skin.

"Can I keep you, Avery Connor? Will you be mine?"

"Please."

His smile was brighter than the sun in mid-July. "Good answer."

DANIEL EXHALED OUT a low sigh, his head burying farther into the cushion on my lap. Talking had ceased a while ago after he checked on Lucy. When he returned to the sofa, he lay down with his head on my lap. As my fingers slipped through his hair, loving how silky the strands felt, we continued to talk until I noticed his eyes drifting shut and his body becoming heavier. He was in the middle of a question about my favorite hobbies when his voice stuttered, paused, then stopped, his breathing evening out and his grip lessening. He never let go completely, though.

I looked down at him in wonder. Even in sleep, he was striking—perhaps even more so. Relaxed and at peace, the lines that creased his forehead were smooth and his full lips were pursed as if waiting for a kiss.

God, kissing Daniel.

What an experience.

I'd been kissed, but never the way Daniel kissed. I had never experienced anything like the fire that erupted when his lips were touching mine. I never wanted a man the way I wanted him. The way I reacted to him now, I could only imagine the inferno we'd feel when we made love. Just the thought made me shudder with anticipation.

I had never felt this sense of rightness when it came to being with another person. I had never experienced a yearning to care for someone and have him care for me in return. Talking and getting to know him better, had only cemented my feelings further. Our likes and goals were similar—it was as if we were part of the other person. I knew I wanted to be the one Daniel turned to in his times of need. I wanted to know he'd catch me when I needed him.

In the blink of a moment, I saw an entire life with Daniel. It felt as easy as breathing. I saw our future: evenings like this cuddling on the sofa, weekends exploring the world around us. Nights spent in his arms. I saw it all with him: children and pets; laughter and loving, even tears and heartaches.

I kept stroking his head. Common sense told me I was being ridiculous—there was no way I could possibly feel all this, having only met him today.

But I did.

And by every indication, so did Daniel.

I should be scared and wary of how he made me feel.

Yet, I wasn't.

Instead, I felt whole.

I didn't want to lose that feeling.

Daniel shifted, his body curling into mine, as if he knew what I was thinking.

I held him close, hoping in his sleep, he knew I was there.

TENDER KISSES WOKE me.

Daniel's voice was a gentle hum in my ear. "Come to bed, Sprite."

Confused, I looked up at him, then over to the clock. It was past two in the morning. "I have to go home!"

He shook his head. "It's late. I don't want you driving." He kneeled in front of me, tucking my hair behind my ear. "Some date I was—falling asleep on your lap."

"You were tired—it's fine. Besides, I liked it."

"I did, too. Stay, please, Avery."

When I hesitated, he wrapped his hands around mine. "Nothing will happen, I promise. I'll even sleep on the sofa. I need to know you're safe. Please."

"You don't have to sleep on the sofa. I trust you."

He scooped me up in his arms, carrying me down the hall. I snuggled into his chest, loving how it felt to be near him.

His lips brushed over my head. "You better keep the sweater on," he muttered. "Otherwise, I'm not sure I *can* be trusted."

"For tonight." I agreed.

"Yeah. For tonight."

Daniel

WAKING UP WITH Avery tucked beside me was an incredible experience. She had barely moved all night, despite the fact I slipped in and out of bed to check on Lucy, who was steadily improving. Every time I came back to bed, Avery curled into me with a sigh of contentment. Holding her close, I felt the same way. Content. Happy. Complete.

Looking down at her, I was in awe. The very second I had touched her something inside my chest had relaxed. I'd never experienced a reaction like that in my life. Somehow, in the short span of time since then, it had grown—exponentially.

When I returned to the clinic the previous afternoon, I couldn't stop thinking about her. Images of her in my kitchen, making dinner for us kept floating through my head, distracting me. Recalling the feel of her mouth underneath mine, the way she felt in my arms made my body tighten. I wanted to feel her close again—taste her sweet lips and feel her body mold itself to me. It hit me when I sat at my desk that I had left a stranger in my home. Someone I didn't know at all, apart from her name. Except, somehow I knew I could trust her—totally. Still, my behavior was out of character for me. I was the steady one—Caitlin was the impetuous one.

I scrubbed my face wondering what I was thinking.

When, in fact, I knew I *wasn't* thinking. I was feeling.

Caitlin poked her head in my door.

"Hey . . ." Her voice trailed off. "Daniel, what's wrong?"

"What am I doing?"

She sat down across from me. "Avery, you mean?"

"I left her in my house. Alone. I don't act like this—I'm never careless or impulsive."

"Are you worried?"

I shook my head. "No. That's what I'm worried about. I should be concerned."

Her brow furrowed. "You're worried about not being worried?"

"Yes."

She studied me for a moment. "You know you sound like Dad, right?"

"Shut up."

"You do. He talks about the way Mom bowled him over in seconds. You sound exactly like him."

I flicked my hand. "Get out of my office."

Her laughter drifted down the hall.

She was right, I did. Avery had bowled me over, so to speak. It shocked me how much I already felt for her and how well she seemed to fit into my life. Knowing she was there while I was at the clinic had made me anxious to be done for the afternoon. Normally, I was never in a hurry to leave, but I couldn't wait for the day to end, and be able to spend more time with her. The excuse to help her find some socks was all I needed to hurry over and see her. Leaving her had been a difficult thing to do, even though I knew I had responsibilities waiting. I had to remind myself I would see her in a couple short hours.

Those hours seemed to drag, though.

Thoughts of her drifted through my mind between patients,

and more than once Caitlin had to repeat herself when we were talking. She had laughed, teasing me about my unusual lack of concentration. Then she made a list of gifts I should buy her to say thank you. I ruffled her hair as I went past and tossed the list in the trash to piss her off, and she yelped, slapping my hand away. She hated having her hair messed up. I felt, as her brother, it was my right to drive her crazy—even if she was spot-on in this instance. The list reappeared on my desk later, and I tucked it in my drawer. She did deserve something. Maybe I'd have Avery help me pick out a surprise for her.

Even my clients noticed my mood; one elderly woman told me I had "that" look on my face. I laughed with her, not commenting, since I didn't know what to say. It was a mystery, but I liked the feeling. Avery certainly brought forth something in me, and our connection was strong, even if it was still new.

Seeing her in my kitchen last night made it feel as though I was truly home. Waking up with her this morning felt so natural—her wild hair loose and flowing over the pillow, her hand fisted in my T-shirt.

Everything about her was a gift. Her sweet smile, expressive eyes, and her shy demeanor were all delightful, but it was her spirit—open and giving—that was truly amazing. Watching the emotions flit through her eyes as she talked about her grandmother or the sadness when she spoke about missing her parents made me long to erase her pain. Listening to her laugh when she shared more stories of her grandmother and growing up—I knew how deeply Avery felt about the people in her life. I also knew I wanted to be one of those people.

I was grateful to have been the one lucky enough to meet her, and be able to have her in my life. Now, I wanted to be the man she needed, one she could look up to, and who would always love and care for her. I wanted to be hers. As fast as this had happened, I was certain about that one thing. It was the same as knowing what I wanted to do with my life years before—a sure, unwavering conviction. We belonged together.

Carefully, so I didn't wake her, I kissed her brow, and slipped out of bed to get ready for the day. I wished I could stay with her, but knew if I did, I wouldn't be able to resist her tucked close to me, warm and sleepy.

As it was, my cock was hard and aching for her, and I knew she wasn't ready for such a huge step. I was content to take it at whatever pace she chose to set. As long as she was beside me, it was all that mattered.

I looked back before I left the room to go downstairs and work out. She was so small burrowed under the covers.

My little Sprite.

I grinned as I descended the steps.

Yeah.

Mine.

WHEN I CAME out of the shower, the bed was made and she was gone. I threw on my jeans and hurried down the hall, relaxing when I could smell coffee.

I leaned on the doorframe, taking in the sight of Avery in the morning. She stood, feet crossed, fingers drumming on the counter as she watched the coffee drip into the glass container. I shook my head in amusement at her impatience. She had told me about her addiction to caffeine and her deep love of coffee. She was still in my socks, wearing an old jersey of my dad's I had given her to change into last night, SPENCER in large letters across her back. It was worn and thin, and I loved seeing her in it. She looked adorable and very sexy. I liked having my name on her. My dick twitched a little in my pants in agreement.

I cleared my throat, and her head snapped up, a heartfelt smile lighting up her face. I sucked in a fast breath. If I thought she looked right last night, this morning she was perfect in my kitchen. Her hair was long and messy, like a burst of sunshine around her shoulders. Her eyes were sleepy but they held such warmth, my chest constricted.

"Hi." She appeared wary. "I, ah, made coffee. I hope that's okay."

"More than okay."

"I woke up earlier and you were gone. I had thought you went to the clinic, but Lucy was still here, so I assumed you were, as well."

"I was downstairs. I have a small gym and I work out every morning." With a sly grin, I flexed my arms. "I do a lot of lifting in my line of work. Gotta keep up my strength."

Her gaze roamed my torso, her stare open and frank.

I met her gaze with one of my own.

"It's working," she praised. "Whatever you're doing. Keep it up."

I almost told her I would have no problem keeping it up for her, then decided action was a better plan.

I strode across the kitchen and had her on the counter in about two seconds flat.

She let out a little squeak when her legs hit the cold stone, but it turned into a whimper as soon as I tucked her against me and kissed her. Long, slow, and deep, my tongue explored her mouth, and I lost myself to the sensation of holding her close.

"You look so right here, Avery." I kissed her again. "In my kitchen." *Kiss.* "In my clothes." *Kiss.* "I want to see that every morning." *Kiss.* "Every." *Kiss.* "Morning." *Kiss.*

She held me closer, her arms tightening around my neck. "It feels right, Daniel."

I liked starting my morning this way.

"WHAT'S IN THE container?"

"Oh, I made your lunch. It's just the leftover spaghetti. I didn't know if you took it with you or came home . . . So yeah, I, ah, just got it ready."

"Thank you. I'll take it with me. It's another busy day."

"Okay." She took a sip of coffee. "There's enough left for dinner for you tonight, as well."

"Great. Wait . . . Are you not having dinner with me tonight?" I frowned. "I called dibs yesterday." A thought hit me and I stared at her, as my stomach clenched. "Unless you already have plans?"

"No! I, um, just didn't want to assume anything. I didn't want you to think you had to . . ."

I reached out and took her coffee cup from her hand, hunching down so our eyes were level. "Dibs. Tonight, tomorrow, the weekend. Any time you want to give me, I want. As long as it's what you want, as well. Understand?"

"Really?"

"Oh, Avery." I smirked and ran my fingers through her messy hair. "I don't even know how I'm going to let you go this morning. I kinda wish you were a woodland Sprite." I kissed the end of her nose. "Then I could put you in my pocket and keep you all day." I chuckled wickedly. "God knows the havoc you'd wreak in my pocket though. I might scare people."

"How do you do that?" she whispered, her eyes wide.

"Do what?"

"Make me feel so . . . wanted."

I wrapped her up in my arms. "You are wanted. So very much."

Avery

I WAS IN a daze all morning. More than once I had to recheck figures in reports I was working on, and twice in our morning meeting, my thoughts had wandered.

All I could think about was Daniel. His gentle gaze, the tender way he cared for Lucy, how he had treated me all evening—as if I was special. I wasn't used to feeling that way, but I liked it immensely.

One other thing I couldn't stop thinking about was his mouth.

His talented, wicked, *wicked* mouth.

Soft, full, pouty lips that teased and smiled. Laughed

and puckered. Muttered curses, then crooned the sweetest of endearments into my ear.

And when they touched mine . . .

My cheeks flushed as I sat at my desk, thinking of the goodbye kiss he laid on me before he disappeared around the corner into his clinic. He left me a panting mess, leaning against my car, weak-kneed. I watched him walk away, Lucy beside him, recovering well and able to walk the short distance with him. He paused only once to throw another air kiss my way, which I pretended to catch, giggling the whole time. We were sickening sweet with the constant affection, but neither of us could help it.

I was amazed at the way he made me feel about myself. For the first time in my life, I felt beautiful. To him, I wasn't unusual, or distracting. Daniel's serious words, his intense gaze, and the way his powerful body reacted to me. He wanted me—just the way I was. It was a heady feeling.

I wasn't sure what would happen tonight when there was no Lucy to distract us. It was probably a good thing we were going out to dinner.

"Avery?"

I looked up at Denise, grinning at me from the doorway.

"Hey."

"Delivery for you up front."

"Oh, okay. It's probably the Simpson file. They said they would send it over this morning."

She shook her head, her grin getting wider. "I don't think so."

Mystified, I walked into reception and gasped in delight. A lovely bouquet of flowers sat waiting for me. There was no doubt about who sent them—all my favorites were there. It had been one of Daniel's "getting to know you" questions.

Roses, lilies, carnations, freesia, and alstroemeria spilled out of a huge vase, their fragrance filling the room. Pink, yellow, purple, white and red blooms filled the container; an explosion of color for my eyes.

I carried the heavy vase into my small office, smiling at the fact they took up a large part of the tiny space. I pulled the card out of the envelope, my eyes misting as I read the words.

One kiss changed my life.

Dibs on the rest of yours.

~ Daniel

Once again, he left me breathless. He was a remarkable man.

I dialed his number, biting my lip in nervousness, especially when he answered in total professional mode.

"Dr. Spencer."

"Hi, Daniel."

His voice warmed instantly. "Sprite."

"I don't mean to interrupt. I only wanted to thank you for the flowers. They're so beautiful."

"Can't possibly be as beautiful as you."

"I . . ."

He snickered. "I love making you speechless. Although, I prefer using my mouth to do that rather than words." His voice lowered, rasping and gritty. "I do love feeling your sweet mouth under mine."

"Daniel." I whispered his name as desire shot through me.

"Avery?"

"You need to stop. I'm—I'm at work."

"So am I."

"You have a big office. With a door, you can shut. Stop it."

"You don't have a door?"

I laughed. "Well, there is a frame, but no actual door to shut. We have small *spaces*—the walls don't even go to the ceilings. Kind of an open-concept thing."

"Hmm, well, I won't come to visit then. Totally inadequate."

"Inadequate?"

"I can't kiss you if I can't shut the door, Avery. Not the way I like to."

"Oh. *Oh*."

He hummed in agreement. "Yeah. Like that."

"Daniel—" I warned.

"Stopping now," he sang, still chuckling.

"Tease."

"I love teasing you. Now, listen, I was wondering . . . I know it's going to rain later tonight, but I heard it was going to be hot tomorrow. Would you like to go riding with me?"

"Are you sure you don't want to wait and see how the date goes tonight?"

"No need. I already know it'll be amazing. I'm just being proactive."

"Okay. I don't know how to ride, though."

"I'll show you. Promise."

"Do you have, um, small horses?"

"I'll pick the gentlest one for you."

I looked up to see my boss in the doorway. "Okay. But, I have to go."

"All right. Six forty-one, Sprite. Be ready."

I laughed. His four-minute shortcut. "I'll see you then."

After my boss left, I picked up my phone and sent Daniel a text.

> *Would you like me to make a picnic for tomorrow? I thought maybe we could have lunch in the sun?*

Half an hour later, I was in a meeting when his reply came back.

> *I love you*

I almost swallowed my tongue.

Daniel

THE DAY WAS going great. Avery loved her flowers. I would see her tonight for our date and I was taking her to my favorite restaurant.

Plus, she agreed to go riding with me. She sounded nervous, so I had a feeling my idea of having her ride with me on the same horse would please her. I could hold her nice and tight. That would please me.

Her text made me happy. Lunch in the sun with Avery. A picnic. That usually involved a blanket. Avery lying down on a blanket in the sun. Me beside her. Close.

Yeah, that was a great idea.

I quickly texted her back confirmation.

Caitlin called my name, and I hit send, then headed out front to see what was going on. After helping her with the supply delivery, I returned to my office, surprised to find no reply to my text.

Scrolling up, I almost choked. My text of *I love your idea of a picnic* had been cut off. All the text said was:

I love you

I sent Avery a text telling her I loved her a day after we met. A low curse came out of my mouth as I stared at the screen.

What must she think of me?

And why did the thought of saying I love you to her not bother me more?

I dropped my head into my hands. From the lack of reply, she no doubt thought I was some sort of loser who went around declaring his love to women he had only met the previous day.

Which I wasn't. Until Avery.

Caitlin walked in my office. "Daniel, what do you want . . . ?" Her voice trailed off as she took in my distraught face. "What's wrong?"

Wordlessly, I handed her my phone. For a moment, there was silence.

"You sent this to Avery?"

"Yes."

"Did you mean to? Or is this the work of your subconscious?"

"What? No! I meant to say I love your idea! You called for me and I hit send too quickly!"

She chuckled. "And she hasn't responded?"

"No. She's undoubtedly too busy changing her number and booking a moving van to run away from my overeager, needy ass."

"Stop being such a drama queen. Call her and explain. I'm sure she'll laugh it off."

Caitlin was right. Mistakes happen all the time with texting. I was sure Avery knew that fact.

It was only a mistake. I didn't mean it.

I was sure I didn't.

"Get out, sister of mine."

Still laughing, she left with a wave over her shoulder.

Hesitantly, I called Avery's number. She answered in a quiet voice.

"Hey, Sprite. I, um, yeah, sometimes I'm an idiot, okay?"

"Oh?"

"I was texting you earlier and I hit send in a hurry. I wanted to tell you 'I love your idea.'" I stressed the words. "Not you. But Caitlin called me to help her—I was rushing, so I didn't look before I hit send. So, you got that message, which no doubt made you wonder about me, and . . . yeah. Like I said—idiot."

"Oh. So you didn't mean it?"

I pulled the phone away from my ear. She wanted me to mean it?

"Um."

"That's okay, Daniel. I'm sure I can get the deposit back."

"Deposit?"

"On the church. Luckily, I hadn't picked the menu yet for the reception. The money would have been a bugger to get back."

Silence. There was utter silence on the phone. It was as if my voice had disappeared. I cleared my throat.

"Um, Avery?"

"Yes?"

"You're . . . pulling my leg, right?"

Her endearing giggles filled my ear.

I slumped forward in relief. "Nice. And you call me a tease."

"Sorry."

"I don't think you are." I lowered my voice. "I think maybe I need to make you pay for that little stunt."

"What're you going to do about it?"

I grinned into the phone. "Brace yourself."

"You started it."

"And I'll finish it. Tonight. Six forty-one."

I hung up to her laughter.

I WAS EARLY, and she was ready.

Dressed in another pretty skirt, with her hair down, I wanted to jump her as soon as she opened the door.

So I did.

Her mouth was perfect moving with mine. Pressed against the closest wall, her curves molded to my body as she wrapped herself around me. Muffled groans and whimpers mixed with muttered hellos and low gasps as my hands explored, her body arching in to my touch. My dick ached to bury itself into the warmth that was so close—the heat of her burning through the thin material separating us. Finally, panting, and regretful, I pulled away, dropping my head to her shoulder.

"*Fuck* . . . what you do to me," I moaned against her skin, swirling my tongue on her neck. "You drive me crazy." I pulled her lobe in to my mouth, tugging with my teeth as she whimpered. "I want you."

Her fingers pulled on my hair, drawing my face back to hers. "Me, too," she whispered, our gazes locked. "So much it scares me."

Those few words stopped me. I stepped back, gently setting her feet on the floor. Cupping her face, I kissed her with as much adoration as I could. "I don't want you scared. I'm coming on too strong, aren't I?" I murmured against her lips.

"No," she insisted. "*You* don't scare me. I'm afraid of how much I feel for you." She inhaled a long breath. "I'm afraid of how much

I liked it when I saw your message earlier. Even though I assumed it was sent in error, I still liked it."

I slipped my fingers under her thick hair, caressing the back of her neck. "Caitlin informed me she thought I sent it subconsciously. Because I wanted you to know."

"Kn-know what?"

"That I'm feeling . . . *something*. Something I've never felt for anyone. I'm not ready to use the word love yet, but it's strong. It's real."

"It's not . . ."

"What?"

"Just, um, lust?"

I had to laugh. "Well, there is, without a doubt, lust involved. But it's more than that." My mouth brushed hers. "When you're ready we'll explore it all—together. Until then, I'm happy to get to know you on every level."

"You won't stop the kissing though, right?"

I pulled her to my chest. "Never." Lifting her hand to my mouth, I kissed her knuckles, and examined the fingers I had trodden on the day before. "How do they feel?"

She waggled them with a grin. "Much better. I keep icing them."

"Good. I still feel bad for hurting you."

She shrugged. "It was an accident. You've more than made up for it."

I pressed another kiss to her skin. "Good. I'll keep doing so."

"Are we crazy? I mean forty-eight hours ago I was worried about kissing a stranger, and now . . ."

"Now we're not strangers anymore." Smiling, I rubbed the end of my nose against hers affectionately. "Does it make us crazy?" I shrugged. "Maybe. But I like it."

"Me, too."

"Good." I pressed closer again, my mouth hovering over hers. "Now, about that kissing—"

Seven

Daniel

"C'MON, SPRITE. YOU'RE perfectly safe."

She shook her head, holding tight to the top of the fence. "You don't have a saddle, Daniel. That's just a blanket."

I laughed quietly, patting Zen's neck. "He is used to me riding bareback. It's the best way to . . . *ride*." I winked and extended my hand. "Hold on and I'll swing you up. It's this or I saddle you your own horse."

That did it. As I suspected, she was too nervous around the large animals to sit on one by herself. With a look of determination, she raised her arms, and I easily lifted and situated her in front of me. Zen's ears twitched, but otherwise he stood still, patiently waiting for my direction. Avery let out a shaky sigh and I leaned forward, running my lips up and down her neck, my tongue darting out to taste her. Sweet, slightly salty, and simply Avery.

"Do you really think I'd let anything happen to you? Zen is a gentle giant." I nibbled on her lobe, smiling at her shiver. "Just like me." I grabbed the picnic basket that she had packed off the top of the fence. "Now, are you ready? We'll start off slow."

She drew in a deep breath and exhaled loudly. "Yes."

With gentle pressure of my heels, we were off. Her little squeaks of excitement, mixed with terror were amusing. I nestled her tight to me as we broke into a trot, her hands covering mine holding the reins. "I've got you."

She tilted her head, grinning up at me. I kissed her as we broke into a faster gait. Another squeal escaped her lips and she pressed herself back into me.

So far, I liked the bareback riding lesson.

Very much.

THE SUN WAS warm on my face as I lay on the blanket, munching on an apple; the delicious picnic Avery brought with her, now devoured. The leaves overhead were bursting into life, the long grasses and wildflowers bloomed everywhere. It had rained in the night, and the air was fresh and fragrant.

I watched Avery wander around, picking up leaves and stones, examining them closely. A happy smile would break out on her face when she found something she liked and the odd stone would disappear into her pocket. I loved seeing her delight in the simplest of things around her, and I looked forward to spoiling her and making her feel that way, as often as possible. I had the feeling she'd never been spoiled much, and I was going to enjoy doing it a great deal.

The sun reflected on her hair, turning the light color a white-silver around her face. She had discarded her plaid shirt, her arms bare and pale in the sunlight.

I had laughed when she got out of the car; we had matching attire: jeans, white tanks and plaid shirts. She was much sexier in hers, though. Somehow, the sight of her in jeans and a simple tank top was even more appealing than her pretty skirts. The way the jeans hugged her hips, and I could see the small sliver of skin on her back over her waistband every time she bent over. Yeah, I liked the jeans more and more. I wanted to run my fingers over that small expanse of skin. Then follow it up with my tongue. I wanted to taste her—everywhere.

The most amazing part of all was the fact she had no idea how sexy she was. It was an artless, unaffected sexiness, which drove me crazy. I knew she compared herself to Beth and her tall, overall voluptuousness, but to me there was no comparison. Avery's soft curves and tiny stature appealed to me in a way Beth's could never touch—or any other woman. She was my idea of perfection. Her body flawlessly fit against mine when I held her in my arms. Her hand fit snugly in the cradle of mine. Her sweet lips were shaped for my mouth only. She was meant to belong to me.

I stifled a laugh as she warily approached Zen, offering him the last of her apple, her tiny hand outstretched and shaking. My favorite horse, ever gentle, nuzzled her palm before taking the proffered treat. Stretching up on her tiptoes, Avery stroked his nose, giggling at his contented snort.

Another male who liked her attention, which was hardly a shock to me; although, I knew she would be surprised.

She was amazing. Dinner, and the entire evening last night, had been too short. Time flew by as we talked and ate, our hands rarely apart. The corner booth was private and secluded; our waitress smiled in understanding when we sat on the same side of the booth so we could stay in contact. Everything with Avery was so natural: exchanging bites of our dinner, sharing dessert, sipping wine, and laughing. It all felt as though we'd been doing it for years, not hours.

"Give me three." I grinned at her.

"What is it with you and three?"

I bit into my dinner roll, chewing as I thought about it. "When I was younger, and I'd get upset over a project or something, my dad would tell me to stop thinking about the whole picture. To break it down the way they did in football practice. So I found that if I broke it into smaller pieces, things didn't overwhelm me as much."

"And three worked for you?"

"Yeah. I'd pick the three things I needed to concentrate on and work with them. Then the next three and so on. I also use it in my practice, as well. People come in and they're upset or have too much information, so I ask them for the three most important things they need to tell me, and we go from there."

Her eyes were worried. "Am I overwhelming you, Daniel?"

I leaned over and brushed her mouth with mine. "Only in the best way. But I love getting little facts from you."

She relaxed and picked up her wine. "I met Beth my first day at university. She was coming around the corner and ran smack into me. Then she stood up, berated me for not looking where I was going, and helped me up."

"But she ran into you."

"I know. I told her so, in a snarky voice I might add, and she started to laugh. Then she dragged me out for coffee to say sorry, and we've been friends ever since."

"I met my best friend at university, too. Noah Cooke. Brilliant mind. He became huge in the marketing industry in Toronto."

"Are you still close?"

I sighed. "We sort of drifted apart. He went through some difficult times, and I got back in touch. We are close again. He gave up marketing and runs his family's business now. I'll take you to meet him soon. They have an organic produce store in the Niagara region, and their own winery. You can buy stuff and cook for me."

She rolled her eyes.

"Second."

"I'm addicted to mints."

"I already knew that. I'm not sure addiction is the right word. I'm not sure there is a word to describe the relationship you seem to have with mints."

"My grandmother always had a pocket full of them. My dad bought them for her all the time. I think I'm carrying on the tradition. After she died, he started getting them for me."

"And now you have pockets full of them?"

Her cheeks colored. "And my purse. I keep bowls of them on my desk and at my place, too," she admitted. "They're my weakness."

I hesitated, then said what was on my mind. "You use them to cover your nervousness, as well. You can't talk if your mouth is full of candy."

She traced the edge of her plate, not meeting my eyes. "I suppose."

"I'm not judging," I assured her. "It's just an observation. We all do

things when we get nervous."

"What do you do?"

"I pull on my hair and my hands sweat." I winked. "If it's really bad, I grab pretty girls with silvery-green eyes and kiss them senseless."

She giggle-snorted, picking up her wineglass, taking a sip.

Needing to reassure her, I pressed a lingering kiss to her forehead. "I guess since your dad is so far away, I'd better take over making sure to keep your supplies up."

She looked pleased.

"One more."

Her brow furrowed. "I hate clowns."

I bit back my smile. "Any particular reason why?"

"I was never a big fan. I always found them scary. But my dad took me to the circus when I was young, and somehow I got lost."

"Oh."

"I wandered around, and I ended up in the clown tent."

I could feel her tensing up, relating the story. I slipped my arm around her shoulders, rubbing circles on her silky skin. "What happened?"

"They were all in various stages of getting ready for the show. It was all a bit much for me. The makeup, the wigs, the costumes—some with their faces half-done." She shuddered. "They were trying to be helpful, but a few of them were just too close and tried too hard. Laughing, teasing, making balloon animals, and pulling things from their pockets to try to keep me entertained. They were terrifying to a little girl," she informed me, dead serious, adding, "and loud. Ugh. Scary, scary little buggers."

I glanced away, trying not to laugh; even though I knew it was a painful memory for her. I cleared my throat.

"But they found your dad?"

"Yes."

"And you've never got over it."

"No." She shook her head, regarding me knowingly. "You can laugh. I know it's funny."

I let out a chuckle. "I'm sorry."

"I was worried the day we met . . . about that."

"About what?"

"That maybe you were a closet clown or something."

This time I couldn't stop it. I began to laugh, my chest aching from suppressing the sound. I loved the way her mind worked.

She laughed with me, rolling her eyes at her own silliness.

I kissed her hard. "I guarantee you I am not, nor ever will be, a closet clown. I'm not overly fond of them myself, so you're safe."

"Good to know."

"I promise to keep any wandering clowns away from you, Sprite, and I will never take you to the circus." I lowered my head, meeting her gaze. "And for future reference, we won't have any of the scary buggers at our kids' birthday parties, okay?"

At my remark, her mouth formed an O in surprise, but it earned me another of her kisses.

The waitress appeared with our food, setting it down in front of us.

Avery thanked her warmly, smiling kindly when she asked for more water.

After the waitress left, I picked up my fork.

"You're very polite."

"I'm sorry?"

"Well, in general you are, but to wait staff, especially."

She had chatted to the hostess, thanked the wine steward, was very friendly with all the staff in the restaurant. I found it endearing.

"My parents instilled manners and being polite into me from a young age. They felt everyone deserved a pleasant smile or a kind word. My grandmother used to tell me that you never know what another person is going through, and sometimes your smile might be something that makes a difference in their day."

I stared at her, my respect for her growing even more. I fully agreed with her, and I admired her for that quality.

"I was a waitress at the local coffee shop when I was a teenager," she added. "I know how tough a job it is, and people should respect them for their effort."

"Did you like it?"

She scrunched up her nose. "Like would be a strong word. In the small town where I lived, there wasn't an abundance of jobs. I babysat when I was younger, but I needed more money toward school, and I got the chance, so I tried it. During the school year, I worked weekends and in the summer, I got more shifts. It served its purpose, but it gave me a healthy respect for people who do it as a career."

"Your parents didn't pay for school?"

"They contributed, but I wanted to pay for as much as I could myself. It was important to me."

I nodded in understanding. I felt the same way when I was going to school, so her declaration didn't surprise me. I knew she was independent and stubborn. I liked both those traits.

Every trait I discovered, every story she told me, the harder I knew I was falling. I loved finding out all the things that made Avery so special. Her gentle voice was like a balm to my soul. Her quiet chuckle made me happy, and when I made her laugh loudly with some of my comments, the sound was so infectious that I had to laugh with her.

After dinner, we'd taken a walk along the river, not talking much, but enjoying the shared silence. She fit effortlessly under my arm, tucked into my side as if she belonged there.

I watched her fondly as she slipped some money into the hand of a homeless person, stopping briefly to speak to him. My affection grew as she pulled me into a bakery and bought cookies and bread to share with her elderly neighbors. Then she stopped on the return walk to give some to the same man, who thanked her with tears in his eyes. I tugged her closer, dropping a kiss to her head in silent approval, marveling at her kindness. She obviously was a caregiver, and loved to look after people—even those she didn't know well. Her compassionate heart overflowed with love.

She took care of others, and now, I decided, it was time someone took care of her.

And that someone was me.

Leaving her at her door had been difficult; it took all my restraint not to beg her to pack a bag and spend the entire weekend with me. Once again, our kisses had turned deep and frantic. It seemed every time Avery was in my arms and a wall or door was close that was where she ended up—pressed between it and me. I told her I had no choice but to lift her up when kissing her, otherwise my neck would get stiff. She laughed as she arched into me, saying one stiff thing to deal with was enough. I almost dropped her I laughed so hard, but I managed to keep her close and kiss her once more.

The night had seemed endless without her in my bed. How one night with her sleeping beside me could possibly change my sleeping pattern, I had no idea, but without her, I was restless. The pillow she slept on smelled like her, honey and flowers. The only way I could fall asleep was to wrap around it and pretend it was her; all the while knowing I was totally and truly a goner.

I'd been pacing the driveway when she drove in, waving as she pulled to a stop. She barely turned off the engine when I had her out of the car, lifting her up and kicking her door shut, pinning her against it, eager to feel her lips beneath mine. We groaned as our mouths fused together, a sense of completion settling over me. From the sweet smile on Avery's face, I knew she felt it, as well.

She was especially adorable in the stable. Nervous and trying not to show it, she followed quietly as I showed her around, standing well back from any of the horses, except the three small ponies that were currently under my care. Those she reached out to stroke and pet with her tender hands. When I introduced her to Goldie, the gentlest horse in the stable, and offered to saddle her up, her nervousness had showed in the twisting of her fingers and the way she tugged on her shirtsleeves. However, she greeted my suggestion she ride with me with far more enthusiasm.

Now, seeing her reach out to Zen, I had a feeling I would soon get her up in the saddle and riding herself. I hoped so, anyway. I loved riding and wanted to share that with her.

I wanted to share everything with her.

When she glanced my way, I sat up, leaning against the tree, and patted the space between my legs. She'd been gone away from me for too long. I tugged off my shirt, using it to cushion my back from the rough bark of the tree. When she settled against my chest, I wrapped my arms around her, holding her tight.

Neither of us said a word, happy to be close.

Closing my eyes, I relaxed, resting my chin on top of Avery's head, feeling her heartbeat under my forearms and occasionally nuzzling the top of her head.

She idly stroked my arm with her fingers. "You have a tattoo."

"I have two."

"Will you tell me about them?"

"This one—" I tapped my arm "—is a veterinary one I had done after I became an official vet."

She turned, studying the design, running her fingers over the image. "It's very cool."

"I like it. A friend designed it for me," I explained. "It has all my favorite animals in it."

"Horses, dogs, and cats?"

I touched one of the smaller images. "Elephants, too. I think they're amazing animals."

She peered up at me with a mischievous grin. "Is that allowed? Should vets have favorites?"

"I don't let the birds and ferrets see. They might get upset."

She laughed, still tracing the ink. "You have big arms. Strong," she added with a whisper.

"I lift weights and work out. I need the upper body strength to work with the bigger animals."

"Yeah, I, ah, noticed how massive your chest is."

With a low growl, I bent down and nipped her neck. "It's not the only massive thing I have, Sprite."

With a small gasp, she turned back in my arms, facing away.

Laughing, I tucked her close and lowered my lips to her ear. "I think you'll be pleasantly surprised."

"Not so surprised," she muttered. "I've felt your, ah, *package*, a few times."

My package.

My chest shook with amusement. She was funny.

"Where is your other tattoo?"

I shook my head with a grin. "You'll have to discover that one on your own."

"Ah, a mystery."

"Think of it like a treasure map." I dipped my head, pitching my voice low. "And there's a prize at the end for you, Avery."

Her hands tightened on my arm. "X marks the spot?"

"Oh, I'll mark it, all right."

She shivered, her flesh pebbling under my fingers.

I dropped another kiss on her neck and leaned back. I liked her reactions. I liked them a lot.

The playlist on my iPod ended, the quiet strains of the music dying off.

Avery turned her face up to me. "Why do I hear the sound of waves?"

I rose to my feet, pointing to the thick row of evergreens that hid my secret. "I saved my favorite part for last. Come with me."

I tugged her up, grabbed the blanket, and led her through the thick trees, then down the rough path, making sure she didn't fall. When we reached the bottom, I swept out my arm. "My own private oasis."

Avery moved past me, beaming in delight. A small inlet of water, the lazy waves dancing in the sun, reflected a multitude of colors at us. The small beach was grainy, the sand thick with tiny pebbles and crushed rock. Some larger boulders edged the one side, forming a private area.

She turned to me with wide eyes. "Is this yours?"

"It is. We're way at the back of my property. The water you can see from the house is the big lake; this is just a little bay."

"It's lovely!"

"I did a lot of work on it. It was quite overgrown. We cleared the beach, and I had some sand moved from another area to make it a little nicer, but otherwise, it's the way I found it."

"Can you swim here?"

"It's a little cold, but yes. I do on occasion later in the season." I laid the blanket on the sand that was still damp from the earlier rain. Avery sat down and I sat behind her, trapping her between my legs. I wrapped my bare arms around her, closing my eyes and letting the peacefulness surround us. She eased back with a sigh, her body relaxed and supple.

The sun felt good on my face, the breeze drifting over my skin, lifting my hair off my forehead as it blew past. It swirled up the scent of the water and sand; the pungent aroma of the washed-up pieces of driftwood and kelp were heavy and rich in the air.

Drawing in a deep lungful of air, the honeyed fragrance of the woman in my arms overwhelmed me. I buried my face into her curls, nuzzling the silky strands, breathing in her soothing scent. When her fingers reached up to play with my hair, I hummed in happiness, tightening my arms.

Her heartbeat picked up as I nudged her hair over her shoulder, grazing my lips down the column of her neck, flicking my tongue along the warm skin. She whimpered, and pressed back against me, causing my cock to swell as her grip tightened on my hair, keeping me close.

Leisurely, I dragged my hand over the bend of her arm, elbow to wrist and back down, a continuous circuit of gentle, teasing strokes. Another whimper escaped her mouth and goosebumps broke out on her skin when I slid my hand closer to her shoulder. I ghosted my fingers over the curve and down her side, to graze the edge of her breast, only to start again at the wrist.

Her nipples puckered against my arm that held her secure.

My dick hardened further in response.

Turning my head, I traced my tongue over the crease in her elbow, dipping and tasting, leaving a trail of moisture that made her shiver. Her breathing quickened; little pants of desire that increased as I teased and stroked, my fingers dancing and moving in a constant pattern, touching and tickling, but never settling. I pulled her tighter to my chest. Her hand clamped around my forearm as she let out a low, sexy moan, pushing her head into my shoulder, exposing more of her neck.

I ran wet open-mouthed kisses on her fragrant skin, nipping and tugging at her earlobe. "You like that, Avery? You like me touching you?" I growled in her ear.

"*Yes.*" She panted. "*Oh, God . . . yes.*"

I drew in the soft skin of her neck and sucked lightly. "Do you want more?"

She gasped, pushing herself into me, trapping my raging hard-on between us.

I groaned. "Do you?"

"Yes. Daniel, *yes*."

I wrapped my hand around her hair, tilting her head back. Her eyes were wide and filled with desire. I brushed my mouth against hers, trailing my tongue over her bottom lip, tasting the apple she had eaten. "How much more?"

"You. I want *you*. *Please*. Now . . ."

Our eyes held.

"Are you sure, Avery?"

I wanted to make her mine. If she was ready, so was I. It was fast, but I didn't care—it felt right. We'd already covered the subject of our pasts and protection in our talk the previous night, and we were safe. There was nothing stopping us if she was sure about this—about us. But it was her choice. Always her choice.

"Yes," she said, breathless. "I'm positive."

In a second, I had her under me on the blanket, a mass of entwined limbs and warmth. The small square of cloth did nothing to protect us from the beach, but neither of us cared. The damp of the sand soaked into the cloth and denim, the rough grit of the beach clinging to everything.

It didn't matter.

I couldn't get close enough. I couldn't taste her enough. Nothing existed but her. Us.

Our passion erupted, finally allowed to explode. I weaved my hand into her hair, holding her face close as I ravished her mouth. Sand clung to the dampness of our arms and feet, the coarse grains scratching against our bodies. I slid my hand under her tank, running up her stomach, ghosting over her skin. As my palm covered the curve of her breast, she gasped, bowing closer, her hand digging into the sand. She dug her other hand into the small of my back, sliding her fingers under my waistband and gripping my ass. I grunted my approval into her mouth, thrusting forward.

Clothing disappeared fast—every inch of new skin uncovered, explored and tasted. The material of her tank tore easily under my fists, and I pulled away long enough to yank mine over my head, wanting to feel the touch of her silky skin. Her mouth was so sweet and wet, and her taste wrecked me forever. I didn't want to be without it now. The feel of her was like nothing else on earth.

She moaned and gasped as I traced swells and dips, learning them with my hands and memorizing with my mouth. Avery's hands tugged at my shoulders, frantically caressing and stroking, as her nails pressed into my skin, the slight sting making me hiss.

Sliding my hands up her arms, I pinned them over her head. "I want you, Avery."

"*Yes.*"

"Tell me to stop and I will. Tell me to take you home and make love to you in my bed and not outside on the sand and I will."

"No, I want this, I want you." She made it clear by slipping one hand free, and wrapping it around my cock.

"*Fuck!*" I hissed, looking down at her hand on me, then moved my gaze upward to take in her whole body. She was a vision lying underneath me in the sun. Her skin glowed like the finest piece of ivory—smooth and iridescent in the light. Tiny clusters of freckles were dotted over her skin like small trails to be discovered. I wanted to taste every inch of her, touch every soft curve and tautly covered muscle with my tongue. Trace the circle of freckles by her left nipple. Kiss the triangle of dots behind her ear until she whimpered. I wanted to plunge my hands into her thick curls and pull her face to mine, then kiss her until she couldn't remember anyone else's lips but mine. I wanted to possess and claim every single inch of her.

"I want you so much," I admitted, my voice thick with desire. "I don't know if I can be gentle. I don't want to hurt you."

"I want you just as much. You won't hurt me." She arched up against me. "You won't."

Still, I hesitated—this was such a huge moment for us.

Her silvery-green eyes met mine, filled with longing and determination. "Be gentle next time. Be with me just like this, right now. *Please*, Daniel."

I couldn't say no to her. I would never be able to say no to her. I slid inside her slick, welcoming heat. Groaning against her neck, I stilled at the incredible sensation of being surrounded by Avery.

Her legs wrapped around my hips, pulling, urging, as she gasped my name.

I lost myself to everything that was *her*. Her taste, her scent, the way she felt beneath my body—her form melted into mine as we rocked and moved. Damp skin slid together. Long, deep, passionate kisses shared. Low murmurs and keening whimpers escaped from our lips as our hands gripped, stroked, and clutched as we loved and fucked.

I drove into her, mindless and aching, feeling her clench and writhe under me. She met me thrust for thrust, her body molded to mine; accepting me, as if I were made for her and her alone. Nothing had compared to this moment—nothing ever would. My spine snapped with electricity as I thrust hard inside her, our bodies surging and ebbing as we moved like storm waves pounding against the shore. Each movement, every deep plunge rolled and retreated, hard and fast, flowing and building into our frantic release.

I fisted one hand around her hair while the other twisted deep into the sand as she rode out her orgasm. Color exploded behind my eyes as I shouted out her name, finding my own release, spilling deep within her body. When I finally stilled, and the peaceful release soaked into my skin, I collapsed into her arms.

Blissful and sated, I rolled to the side, tucking her against me, drawing the edges of the blanket around us so she wouldn't get cold, but still small shivers ran down her spine.

I wrapped her closer, running my hands up and down her back. "Are you all right?"

She nuzzled her face into my neck, kissing my skin with light, airy brushes of her mouth that made me want to purr.

"I'm good," she hummed. "So good, Daniel."

I smiled against her hair. "Yes, you are. I, ah, didn't hurt you?"

"No. My insides feel like jello, and I don't think I could walk right now, but I'm not hurt. In fact, I can't remember the last time I felt this . . . unhurt. Maybe never."

I chuckled. "I feel a little jello-ish, too. Are you cold?"

"No, I'm quite content. A little gritty feeling, but good."

I had to agree with the gritty feeling. I was certain I had sand in places sand should never be found.

"Making you mine on a blanket, in the middle of nowhere, wasn't part of the plan today."

She tilted up her head, her hair wild and tangled around her face. "Am I yours now?"

I smoothed back her hair from her face, cupping her chin and kissing her. "Totally."

She curled back up with a sigh, and I relaxed as we basked in our new intimacy.

Her curious-sounding voice broke the silence. "What *was* the plan for today?"

"I thought I'd teach you to ride a horse and spend some quality time with you. That was all, really."

Her tiny hands tugged my head down to her mouth. "I like the addition to the plan."

Groaning, I tightened my hold on her, already feeling the stirrings of new desire.

"I need to take you home. I want you in my bed, so I can take my time with you."

"So the riding lessons are done for the day?"

"For now." I sat up, pulling her with me so she straddled my lap. "But maybe you'd like to ride a different stallion." I arched against her, smiling at the moan that came from her mouth as I grazed her pussy with the head of my rapidly swelling cock. The sound was erotic; a small panting noise that made me even harder. "Ever heard the term 'bucking bronco'?"

Her head fell into my neck, and it was my turn to groan as she nipped and laved at my skin, pushing herself down on my erection.

I wrapped the blanket tighter around her.

We weren't leaving just yet.

Eight

Daniel

WE LEFT THE beach, climbing to the cliff with our fingers entwined.

I had helped her dress, apologizing for her torn tank and the sand clinging to her skin, even while I tried to brush it off.

She laughed, pushing away my hands. "I'm fine. I need a shower, but I'm fine."

I yanked my shirt over her head and kissed her brow, trying not to think of how she'd look in my shower.

Wet.

Naked.

My steps hastened as I tugged her behind me. We needed to get home soon.

We gathered our things, and I helped her up onto Zen before swinging myself up behind her. We were quiet on the way back, both of us lost in our thoughts.

I knew everything had changed.

I had changed. Our relationship, albeit brief, had changed.

I already adored Avery. I had from the very instant I met her.

Now it was deeper. It was more. It was everything.

When we got back to the stable, she was more comfortable. She even helped me groom Zen and settle him for the night. My stable hand had already looked after the other horses, so with a final pat to Zen, we locked up the gate.

Hand in hand, we walked back to the house, peaceful and content. When I noticed her shiver, I dragged her against me, hurrying her to the house.

Once inside, I directed her into the shower, wanting to warm her up and help soothe her aching muscles. I knew her legs had to be sore since she'd never even sat on a horse, and our lovemaking had been rather vigorous. My lower back felt a little achy, so I could only imagine the effects that her poor little body was feeling. Add in the fact we smelled of horse, sand, and sex, a shower was in order.

Pulling her into the bathroom, I saw the look of longing she gave the huge garden tub that sat, unused, in the corner. I'd never been a bath guy, but when I was building the house, the architect assured me one day I would be grateful I had it installed.

"Easier to do now than later. You'll thank me, Dr. Spencer," he stated *with a wink. "My wife loves the one I put in our house."*

From the look on Avery's face, I would say today was that thankful day.

I kissed her cheek. "Shower first to warm up and get the, um, sand, and grass off," I teased, pulling some bits out of her hair. I trailed my fingers down her thighs, tapping at the dampness. "Not to mention me. I'm all over you, Avery. Sexy as that is to me, I'm sure you'd rather it not stay that way."

She blinked, her mouth opened and closed as she glanced around the room, her gaze bouncing everywhere. "Merciful God, what you do to me," she muttered, and I knew she didn't realize it was aloud.

I chuckled. I did enjoy saying things that made her flustered, and hearing her inane mutterings in response. I found them amusing.

"Shower," I repeated.

Her excited eyes stared at the empty porcelain in the corner. "Then the bath?"

"Yes. You'd better start filling it up now. I think it might take a while." I looked around. "I'm not even sure where the drain plug is."

"You've never used it?"

Wrapping my arms around her, I shook my head. "Nope. The tub and I have never been close. In fact, the tub and I will be virgins, meeting for the first time." Nudging her hair away, I brushed my mouth over her ear. "Will you be gentle with us, Sprite?"

"I'll do my best." She cleared her throat. "You never, ah, I mean—"

I knew what she was asking. "I've only been in the house for about eight months. I built the clinic first." I tightened my grip on her. "You are the first and only woman I have ever had here, aside from my sister or mother."

Diffused color rushed over her cheeks as she smiled. "Oh."

She looked pleased.

I ONLY MEANT for the shower to warm and clean us. That was all. But as I watched her tilt her head to rinse out the shampoo, back arching, pushing out her breasts, making them look so perky—so inviting—that tiny circle of freckles beckoning, any and all ideas of what *should* happen in the shower became what was *about* to happen in the shower.

The soap I held fell out of my hand when I stepped forward, one arm going around her waist as I drew her to my body. My mouth closed around one pink, tempting nipple, pulling and teasing the flesh with my tongue and teeth.

Avery whimpered as her hands grasped my shoulders for support. The softest, sweetest, sexiest sound I had ever heard.

Without a thought, I'd lifted and pinned her against the wall, my cock already surging, every molecule of my being, wanted to be inside her.

Avery gasped as the cold tile pressed into her back, and I braced my arm against the wall, struggling to hold her up. My mouth met hers in a series of frenzied, messy kisses, noses bumping, teeth hitting, and lips sliding as we grappled and slipped in the wet.

"Fuck," I muttered. "This looks so much easier when I watch porn. They never seem to have gravity issues."

Avery started to giggle, light, gasping little puffs of laughter, as I tried to stay upright, now laughing myself.

"Not the most romantic thing to say, I guess, eh, Sprite?"

She pulled me closer, her legs tighter, and I groaned as my cock slid, rubbing against her wet folds.

"*Jesus*, Avery. I want you so damn bad again, but I'm afraid if we continue this here, one of us is gonna end up needing a new hip." I thrust forward warily, testing out my balance, cursing as my feet slipped on the smooth bottom of the shower floor. "I think I need to install a bench in here." Then I groaned at the thought of what I could do to her while sitting on said bench. What she could do to me. "Fuck sake!" I growled. "*That* mental image is not helping me right now."

Her giggles became outright laughter as her head fell back against the tile. "A shower virgin as well, Daniel?"

"Yep."

She shifted and I slipped deeper, her heat surrounding me. I flicked my tongue against her ear. "I bet the tub is roomy. Less dangerous. Maybe we can work up to the shower."

Her arms locked around my neck. "Bath. Now."

I shut off the water.

THE TUB WAS damned slippery too, but we figured it out. With less chance of hip replacement surgery, we were more adventuresome. I showed Avery my wet version of a bucking bronco, while she grasped tight to the sides of the tub, riding me hard, crying out my name. Water splashed over the edge of the tub, creating a large puddle on the floor, spreading toward the door. I didn't care about that or anything else. Only the woman riding me as I groaned and cursed, straining upward to bury myself as far inside her as I could, my hands like vices as I gripped her hips and shouted her name.

I held her after, the warm water swirling around us. I made a mental note to pick up some frothy stuff women liked, so I could lure her back in here again soon, and to call the contractor who built the house and have a bench installed in the roomy shower. When I spoke the thoughts aloud, Avery informed me you could buy non-slip bath mats. I decided I needed to pick one of those up tomorrow—maybe we could retry the shower porn. I was certainly willing to give it a go.

When we were finally out and drying, she discovered my other tattoo. Inked on my shoulder blade, the Celtic tree of life was a blaze of color. Her touch was light as she ran her fingers over the ink, then pressed her lips to it. I slipped a shirt of mine over her head and tucked her beside me in my big, cozy bed, urging her to sleep for a while. She had to be exhausted. I knew I was, and I happily slept for a short while with her beside me.

Now awake and holding her, I teemed with emotions. I had never experienced so many feelings for one person. What I had thought was a good relationship with Karen had nothing on what I already felt for Avery. I wanted to share everything—every part of my life with her. I could see her beside me, making my house *our* home, filling up the empty hours with her presence. I knew how much my parents, my mother especially, would adore her. I knew Caitlin was looking forward to getting to know her more. She had always liked Karen, my whole family did, but Avery fit me effortlessly. I had a good feeling she'd fit in with my family the same way, and with her parents so far away, Avery needed that, as well.

I traced my finger over her cheek, tucking a curl behind her ear. I should be scared of how strongly I already felt for her. But I wasn't. It felt right. I knew she also felt something intense for me. We wouldn't have made love, otherwise. I had told her there hadn't been anyone since I broke it off with Karen over a year ago, and she admitted she hadn't been in a serious relationship for over two years. From the little she had told me, it didn't sound as if she had much luck with any of her previous partners. I planned to change her views on relationships.

I knew we'd been waiting for each other.

"Hi," she whispered.

Startled, I looked down. "You're supposed to be asleep."

"I woke up." She frowned. "You're thinking awfully hard up there. I can see the forehead crinkles from here."

I rolled, hovering over her. "I'm thinking about you. About us."

She grimaced, her expression anxious. "That's making you frown?"

"I'm worried."

"Is it too much?" She wondered. "I know this is all happening so fast."

I slipped my hand under her head, lifting her to my mouth. Long minutes passed as I assured her with my caresses that *nothing* to do with her was too much.

I stayed close after drawing back so she could see me and not doubt my sincerity. "I'm worried how you'll feel when I tell you tomorrow is Sunday—which means my weekly brunch with my family. I want you to come with me and meet them. I want to introduce them to the woman I know is going to change my life. Who already has changed my life."

Her light green eyes glimmered with tears.

"I want to spend the rest of the weekend with you, Sprite. I want you with me every second until you have to leave for work on Monday. Then I want you back here as soon as you can be. I want it all—your time, your kisses, your laughter—" I paused. "Your heart."

She gasped low in surprise.

I shrugged in apology. "That's what I'm worried about. I feel so much and it's so *solid*, so real, and I'm worried it's too fast for *you*. I'm worried you couldn't possibly feel the same way." I cleared my dry throat. "Yet, I hope you do. I want it more than I've ever wanted anything in my entire life. Because–because I'm falling in love with you, Avery. Given the intensity of my feelings now, how I'm going to feel about you next week or next month, astonishes me. I had no idea I was even capable of feeling anything this powerful."

Restlessly, I rubbed my fingers on the silky skin of her neck as her beautiful eyes stared at me, tears running down the side of her face, disappearing into her hair. For the first time since I met her, I couldn't read the emotions in those normally expressive eyes of hers.

"Please tell me those are tears of happiness," I begged. "Tell me you feel this. Please."

Avery

I STARED INTO Daniel's eyes. No one had ever looked at me the way he did. The way he was right at this moment. His blue eyes overflowed with warmth, need, desire—love.

And it was all directed at me.

There was another emotion swimming in the depths of his gaze.

Fear.

He had opened his heart to me and wasn't sure his feelings would be reciprocated.

There were no words to describe adequately how I felt about Daniel.

His quiet confession and final plea left me dumbfounded. I had known last night, as I tossed and turned, my head filled with nothing except him, that I was falling in love. Hard. Making love with him today had only proven it to me. Together we were right. We fit together like two pieces of a puzzle.

Our time together the previous evening had shown me even more of the tender man within Daniel. At the restaurant, it was as if only I existed for him. He listened with rapt attention to everything I said, asking questions, making comments, or observations which showed me he was listening. Really listening. Grant told me once he usually tuned me out since I never had anything interesting to say. Daniel thought differently.

His impeccable manners showed in the way he acted toward me. Opening doors, having me slide into the booth first, making sure I was comfortable, worried I was warm enough in my shawl, and offering his jacket if I needed it. He wasn't putting on an act, or trying to show off. It was simply Daniel being Daniel.

After dinner, during our walk, he kept me tucked tight to his side, guiding me around obstacles, making sure I didn't trip over curbs. I felt protected in his embrace. When I stopped to talk to the homeless man, he kept his hand on the small of my back as I bent over, in a shielding stance. We stopped every time someone approached us with a dog, and he'd kneel, allowing the animal to sniff his hand before he would stroke its fur, talking quietly to his new furry friend. When I bought the baked goods for my neighbors and told him how I liked to bring them treats, he murmured about how he thought I was an amazing person. The look in his eyes when I stopped to give the homeless man some of the baked goods warmed me to the core. The pride and tenderness I saw in them stole my breath away. He saw me in a different light.

The same way I saw him.

I knew people would think we were crazy, and that there would be whispers and stories. I knew there was a chance his family wouldn't like me. I didn't want to come between him and his family. However, I was already in too deep.

I didn't care.

I cupped his worried face, tracing over the small 'V' between his eyes, and soothing the puckered skin.

"You have all of me."

His expression was beautiful, filled with light, as one slow tear ran down his cheek. "I can keep you, Avery?"

"For as long as you want."

"Then I'm calling dibs on the next ninety years."

CONTENT AND WRAPPED in Daniel's arms, I snuggled into his chest, kissing his damp skin. His lovemaking had been beyond sweet, his touches and kisses deeper and adoring. He surrounded me with his affection, drenching me in love as he moved unhurriedly, claiming me even more profoundly than his more vigorous exertions earlier. His touch branded me, his lips possessive, as his body made me his in every way possible.

I could never belong to anyone else again. Daniel was it for me.

His fingers moved in lazy circles on my bare shoulder. "Can I convince you to move in tomorrow?"

Most of me wanted to throw my arms around him crying *yes!* The more reasonable part shook my head in regret.

"Soon?"

It seemed inevitable. I wanted it. However, I knew I needed to try to be rational.

"Why don't we get through meeting your family tomorrow before we discuss that?"

"I have no doubt they will love you," he assured me.

"Do your mom and dad know about me?"

"I'm sure Caitlin has filled them in. Brunch is at her place, and I know she was dying to tell Mom."

"Ah."

"What is it? Tell me what's going on in that head of yours."

"What if they object? Or don't like me? I can't come between you and your family, Daniel. I can't do that."

His mouth was warm on mine. "You won't. They will like you. I have no doubt."

"I—"

"Don't, Avery. The fact you are so worried about it tells me everything. I won't have to choose." He tugged me closer. "And if I did, I'd choose you."

"No, you can't say that."

"You. Us. First. Always," he insisted. "And my family would understand, but it isn't going to be an issue. There isn't a person on this planet who could meet you and not love you."

I snorted. "Well, I can name a few. I think you're biased."

"Okay, then. No one I love, though, couldn't love you. Better?"

"Better."

My stomach chose that moment to growl, and Daniel laughed

as he sat up, dragging me with him. "Come on, Sprite. I need to feed and water you."

"Feed and water me? Like Zen? Do I get a feed bag?"

He pulled on his sweatpants, handing me a long shirt, his shoulders shaking with laughter. "Sorry. Wrong terminology. Usually, on the weekends, I only have to feed whatever animals I'm looking after in the clinic or stable. I like having another person to care for—it's different." He bent low, his lips brushing mine. "I especially like looking after you."

"Thank you," I breathed out. "I like it, too."

"Good. Because it's my new favorite job."

Then with a laugh, he picked me up and flung me over his shoulder, snickering all the way to the kitchen.

I grabbed onto his ass and held on.

For safety.

It had nothing to do with the fact I liked how tight his ass felt under my fingers; how the muscles flexed and moved as he walked.

Not at all.

Nine

Daniel

IF I THOUGHT Avery looked nervous when we met at the studio—or yesterday in the stable—it was nothing compared to the way she looked at this moment. She was positively green, and I wondered if she was going to throw up in my truck. I glanced behind me at the blanket on the backseat, wondering if maybe I should put it in her lap. Not that there was much to throw up—she had barely sipped her beloved coffee earlier, but it might come in handy. Stretching my arm, I snagged it off the seat and draped it over the console. She didn't even move.

She was so tense, I was certain if I touched her the wrong way, she would shatter to a million little Avery pieces right there in front of me.

I turned in my seat, sliding my hand along the back of her neck as carefully as possible, as I called her name.

Her eyes remained locked ahead, her body rigid. Cars already lined the driveway of my sister's place. I knew my parents had arrived, Steven was home, and Caitlin's beloved Jeep was parked out front. I tried again, my fingers kneading the back of her neck a little more firmly.

"Avery . . . *Sprite*. Look at me."

Her eyes met mine—anxious, silvery-green so filled with panic, my heart ached for her.

"Hey. My parents will like you. My sister already does. *Please* don't look like that. It's gonna be fine. I promise."

"Is it her birthday?" she gasped out.

"What? Who?"

"Your niece—is it her birthday?"

I shook my head, completely confused. "No. Why?"

Avery's shaky finger pointed out the van I hadn't noticed parked on the road. I bit back the laughter threatening to escape. Glancing down the street, I indicated the house two doors down, the front gate covered in balloons. "That is the Wilson's house. Caitlin told me it was their daughter's birthday today. I'm certain that's where Rusty the Clown's traveling circus is. Don't worry."

"Not–not at your sisters?"

"No. *Not* at Caitlin's."

"Oh." She offered me a weak smile as a shaky sigh escaped her lips. "I don't think I could handle a clown *and* your family today."

She looked at me again, panicked. "You don't think he'll do any door-to-door sales stuff, do you? The clowns won't wander the neighborhood?"

I buried my hand into her thick curls, leaning over the console. "Do you think I'd let a clown come near you, Sprite? That fucker would find his big red shoes up his ass and be face first on the road before I'd let him close. No door-to-door. No clowns. Period."

"Really?"

I kissed her. Hard. "Really." I kissed her again. "Better?"

"Yeah."

"Now, are you ready to come meet my family? I assure you, they may act like clowns, but none of them look the part."

Reassured of no ninja clown attacks, she relaxed a little, the color returning to her cheeks. I exhaled in gratitude that the blanket probably was not needed.

She reached into her purse and dug out a mint, popping it into her mouth. "Okay. Ready."

I had to laugh. I wasn't sure what made her more endearing, her strange aversion to clowns, or her addiction to mints anytime she was nervous.

I kissed her once more, almost pulling her over the console and onto my lap. I wanted a mint as well, but not one from her purse. The one she had in her mouth would taste much better, and it was highly enjoyable to seek it out. I loved kissing my girl.

I grinned as I drew back, my prize caught between my teeth.

"You took my mint again." Avery huffed. "You could have asked. I have plenty."

I tucked the candy into my cheek. "Not with Avery flavor added." I winked.

A slow, rosy blush infused her cheeks as she unwrapped another candy, but the curve of her lips let me know she was fine with my candy-stealing tactics. Good thing, since I didn't plan to stop.

Now with color back in her face and her greatest fear laid to rest, she looked much better. Glancing down the street, I decided it was time to go inside before the clown appeared to get something from his van. I wasn't sure how Avery would handle that situation. I didn't want to have to take someone out for wearing too much makeup and a costume, but for her I would.

"Ready?"

She squared her shoulders. "Ready."

AVERY'S EYES WERE huge with apprehension as I introduced her to my family.

My parents looked relaxed and happy, and they beamed at Avery in welcome. My mother's short hair was still dark with a touch of gray scattered through it, and her blue eyes sparkled behind her glasses. She had passed on her bad eyesight to me. There was still a youthful air about her; her gentle humor and patience were evident in her expression. Beside her, my father's shoulders were still broad, his hair, more salt than pepper, gleaming under the lights. His eyes, a darker shade of blue than my mother's, were friendly, his gaze open.

Only those of us who knew him could see the underlying pain

in his expression, or would notice the furrows in his brow when he walked or moved a certain way. He was strong and stubborn, and I had inherited both of those traits.

My mother hugged Avery far too long, and my father stepped forward.

"Let the girl breathe, Julie." He smiled at Avery. "I'm Daniel's dad—Sean Spencer. Sorry about my wife—she's a bit exuberant."

Avery held out her hand. "Nice to meet you, Mr. Spencer."

He shook his head. "Just Sean and Julie." Then he took my mother's place, engulfing Avery in a hug that lifted her feet right off the floor.

I had to roll my eyes at their enthusiastic greetings. It wasn't as if I'd never brought a girl to meet them until today.

Luckily, Steven behaved himself, smiling and welcoming her with one of his firm handshakes. Until he spoke. "Happy to see you again, Avery," He winked. "You're looking a little less rumpled than the last time I saw you."

Caitlin burst out laughing, and even my parents snickered.

I knew the teasing today would be nonstop.

So far, it was a normal brunch.

As everyone went down the hall, Avery glanced up at me. "I feel as though I've stumbled into the land of the giants. All of you are so tall!"

I had to laugh. She was right. My mother was the shortest of us all at 5'7". Caitlin was three inches taller than she was, and my dad and I were both 6'4", and Steven a couple inches taller. Avery was only 5'3", she had told me, so no wonder she felt as though we towered over her. I slung my arm over her shoulder, escorting her to the kitchen. "It's okay, Sprite. Chloe's shorter than you. By a lot."

She turned her head and pressed a kiss to my arm, right over my tattoo. "She's nine months old."

"Yep. Think about it. You'll tower over her for years."

Her low laughter made me smile, and we joined my family.

I WAS WRONG. They didn't like her. They moved right past that to adoring her completely. She had them under her spell in less than ten minutes. All of them. I liked watching her interact with my family and seeing how they had taken to her. It warmed my heart.

An hour after we'd gotten there, Chloe was on her lap, Avery cooing at her, as they played peek-a-boo.

My sister was so busy patting herself on the back she burned the pancakes, causing Steven to run around, opening windows to let out some of the smoke.

My mother sat beside me, asking in a not-so-quiet voice, when Avery and I could give her another grandchild, since we'd make beautiful babies.

My father leaned back, smirking, as he informed me I got all my moves from him, and no wonder Avery had been unable to resist me.

There was laughter and teasing, and in the midst of it all, Avery glowed.

"Daniel tells me your parents live in B.C., Avery," my mom stated. "You must miss them?"

Avery nodded, her eyes misty.

I slipped my arm around her shoulders in comfort. I knew how much she missed her parents and how lonely she was at times.

"I do. They visit every year, and it's where I go on my holidays, but it isn't the same as having them close all the time."

My mom patted her arm in sympathy.

"The climate suits them, and they love it there."

"I am sure they miss you, as well."

"They do, but they are happy, and that's all that matters."

My mom caught my eye, her eyebrow lifting slightly. I had a feeling she would be happy to fill the void Avery felt in her life. I could already see how easily she would slip into that area of my life as well, and become a part of us. She had already slipped into my heart.

My parents knew how we met. The wagers Caitlin and I made with each other had grown bigger every passing year. Avery laughed the hardest when Caitlin told her of the bet I had lost, and the fact I had to attend an all-male review, sit in the front row, and tip some of the performers. Caitlin sat beside me the entire time laughing uncontrollably and shoving money in my hand, pointing out the next moment of embarrassment for me.

Then Caitlin told her the story of the bet she lost. "I had to hold a snake and a spider." She shivered. "They scare me."

"Don't you have to deal with them at the clinic, as well?"

"No," Daniel explained. "There's an exotic pet veterinarian closer to Toronto. I recommend him for people with unusual pets."

Avery's eyes were sympathetic as she gazed at my sister. "So what happened?"

Caitlin chuckled over the memory. "Daniel took me to the shop, all prepared to make me go through with it, except when he saw how scared I was, he held them. I did touch them though, and he called it done."

Avery gazed at me tenderly. "You're too sweet."

I shrugged. "It wasn't fun when I saw how scared she was—I mean, so petrified she was shaking. I thought she was going to pass out just having to touch them. I made her eat a jalapeno popper at lunch though. She hates spicy food."

Avery leaned close, kissing my cheek, her lips lingering. "You're a good man, Daniel Spencer."

I ducked my head and grabbed my coffee. I liked knowing she felt that way.

My dad cleared his throat. "I think this is perhaps the best wager of them all, yeah? I think we all won." He gave Caitlin and me a stern look. "Maybe it's time to call an end to the wagers."

I reached for the coffee pot. "Dream on, Dad."

He laughed, deep and rumbling in his chest.

"Worth a shot."

"Good try."

Everything was going great, aside from the embarrassment that was my family, until Caitlin set down the plate of remade pancakes on the table. "Oh, Jeanne and Chris invited us over after. It's Emily's birthday—they have a whole circus set up in the backyard! We can go over after we're done eating!"

In one smooth move, I was down on my knees in front of Avery, catching Chloe before she could drop her, gripping her hand. Everyone stopped what they were doing and watched as I shook my head at Avery. "No clowns," I assured her in a hushed voice. "Not happening."

Avery nodded, remaining calm but pale.

My mother leaned over, stroking Avery's shoulder sympathetically. She looked at me, brow furrowed. "What is it, Daniel?"

"Avery, isn't, ah, *big* on clowns. You guys can go. We'll hang here."

My mother looked between Avery and me, and she shook her head. "I'll stay with you," she whispered conspiratorially. "Those little fuckers are creepy. They're sort of like the devil in drag with all that makeup. God only knows what they'll yank out of their pocket next!" She shuddered a little. "Your father loves them. He can go." She kissed Avery's forehead and took Chloe from my arms, walking over to Caitlin.

My father chuckled and raised an eyebrow at us as he shrugged.

Watching the adoration that crossed Avery's face, I'd never loved my mother more than at that very moment.

I also wasn't sure I'd ever get over hearing her say the words "little fuckers."

WE SENT EVERYONE over to the Wilsons' while we cleaned up the kitchen. Listening to my mom and Avery chat and laugh as they did the dishes kept me smiling. My mom had a way of drawing things out of Avery without her even realizing it. I groaned as I wiped down the table while she advised Avery of her availability for babysitting services, and of course, daycare when he or she was older, once we had children.

"Give us a break, Mom," I grumbled. "You'll scare her away."

Tossing the cloth on the counter, I tucked Avery into my side, kissing her forehead. "I just found her."

Avery looked up at me, her eyes filled with emotion. "She's not scaring me away. It's all good."

"Yeah?" I tried not to grin like a madman. I had no idea why I wasn't running away scared. I had only known her for a few days, and yet, somehow, the thought of Avery glowing, carrying my child—*our child*—made me almost giddy. With her, everything seemed to fall in place with such ease, and I could see it all. Living, loving, and growing old together in the house I built that would become a home once she was there with me. I could see children running around in the open fields, teaching them to ride a horse, telling bedtime stories, and kissing chubby cheeks.

I wanted it. All of it. *With her.*

And with the way she gazed at me, I thought she wanted it, as well.

WITH FRESH CUPS of coffee in our hand, we sat talking to Mom at the table, waiting for the others to return from the mini-circus.

Avery's phone rang, and she slipped it out of her pocket with a frown. Glancing at the screen, her eyes grew large with distress. "Oh, shit," she whispered.

"What's wrong?"

"It's Beth." She shook her head. "I forgot. I totally forgot!"

"Forgot what?"

"I was supposed to have coffee with her today." She stood up. "Please excuse me; I have to take this call." She slipped out the door, closing it behind her with the phone to her ear and apologies already spilling from her mouth.

I ran my hand through my hair, knocking off my glasses. I grabbed at them, setting them on the table. "Oops," I muttered.

Mom grinned at me. "I think you've clouded her mind."

I watched Avery pace around, talking fast, her free hand gesturing wildly. I hoped her friend wasn't too upset with her.

"Ugh, yeah, it's my fault. She came over yesterday for a horse ride, and I couldn't let her go." I glanced sheepishly at Mom. "I had to drive her to her place this morning so she could change. She didn't want to come over dressed in my stuff." I waggled my eyebrows. "Not that I would've objected."

"You've fallen hard, Daniel."

I didn't deny it, only nodding as I sipped my coffee.

"I've never seen you act like this with another woman."

I pointed toward the door and the woman I couldn't take my eyes off. "I'd never met her."

"Do you think you're moving too fast?"

I met her gaze—tender, loving eyes that had been there my whole life. They were filled with understanding and patience. The corners crinkled deeply when I shook my head.

"No. We're moving exactly right for us."

"You sound like your father. He bought me an engagement ring a week after we met."

I laughed, knowing the story. "He waited two weeks to ask, though."

"Yes, that man has the patience of a saint." She chuckled with a wink. "I thought Caitlin was my impetuous child. You've always been the more cautious of the two."

"I can't help it with her, Mom. I can't control it; it's like a freight train." I paused to think about everything that was going through my head, and my heart. "I've never felt anything like it—with anyone. It's right, and it's real, and I don't want it to stop."

She covered my hand with hers. "Then don't."

I glanced back to see Avery had stopped pacing. Her head was down and she appeared to be listening intently to whatever Beth was saying to her. I stood, worried.

"I'm just going to go check on her."

If Beth were angry with her, I would take the phone and make sure she understood that it was my fault. I didn't want Avery taking the blame. I knew I had overwhelmed her. We had overwhelmed each other. She'd made a simple mistake and forgotten. I'd drive her to meet Beth, if it was what she needed. I would hate giving up the afternoon with her, but I'd do it.

I slipped out the door and walked behind Avery, who was talking and shaking her head. "No, Beth. I won't." She sounded more exasperated than upset. I hesitated, wondering if I should leave her to sort it out between them. "I am *not* saying it."

She listened for a few seconds, then suddenly threw her hand in the air. "Fine! *Yes!* Yes, okay? Daniel's big feet live up to your expectations! She lowered her voice. "His . . . *penis* is huge! Is that what you wanted to hear?"

I stepped back in shock, while I grinned with a touch of pride at the declaration. I had to clap my hand over my mouth to stop the laughter at her next statement.

"Okay, fine. His *cock*, Beth. Is that the word you wanted? His cock is huge. He filled me like no one ever has and I came so hard I saw stars!" She huffed. "Now, are you satisfied?" I could hear Beth's laughter from where I stood, and Avery shook her head. "I'll see you tomorrow for lunch." With an impatient sigh, she ended the call and whirled around, stopping dead when she saw me there. Her cheeks bloomed with color, her eyes huge.

"I, ah, came to see if you were okay. I was worried Beth was angry with you," I offered, trying desperately not to laugh.

"Um, no, she's fine. I'm meeting her for lunch tomorrow."

"Good."

"How long have you been standing there?"

I shrugged. "I only came out as you were hanging up."

"Oh, okay." Her relief was evident.

I held out my hand. "Ready t-to," I stuttered, the laughter starting to escape, "*come* inside, Avery? There aren't any stars to look at right now."

"You heard!"

I covered the distance between us in two long strides and yanked her into my arms. Burying my hands into her thick hair, I pulled her mouth to mine and kissed her. Hard. Deep. Wet. Until she was panting, clinging to me as though I was the only thing keeping her upright.

"I need to take you home . . . *now*," I insisted through another kiss. "Me and my *cock* need you alone. We want you to show us how hard we can make you come again."

"Your family—"

"Is fine. Home. *Now*, Avery."

"Okay."

"WE NEED TO go to bed, Sprite," I groaned and stretched. "It's late and we have to work in the morning."

"We *are* in bed, Daniel."

I pressed my mouth to her neck, flicking her damp skin with my tongue. "Right. I meant sleep. We need to sleep."

"Then stop doing that." She moaned as my fingers drifted up her leg, slipping between her thighs to her warm center.

I caressed her, teasing and stroking. "I can't."

She arched her back, a small gasp of want escaping her mouth. "You could . . . if you tried."

"I can't. I'm addicted," I admitted as I slid one finger in her softness, reveling in her desire.

"*Oh . . . God . . .*"

"More, Avery?"

"Yes, yes!"

I added another finger, pumping slowly as I pressed my thumb against her bundle of nerves. I lowered my head to her rosy nipple, drawing it into my mouth as my tongue skimmed the hardened peak. Another keening moan spurred me on, my already hard cock pressing in the mattress, wanting, *needing* to be back inside her.

After hearing her confession to Beth, I had been desperate to get her alone. It took all my patience to take her back inside and explain to my mother that I had to drive Avery somewhere to meet a friend. My mother didn't know the friend was already there, desperately trying to get out of my pants and into Avery. There'd been hugs and promises of next week's brunch at their place. Then

I got her in the truck, kissing her senseless, before I drove us back to my place as fast as I could without being pulled over.

We barely made it in the door when I had her pressed against the wall. Our clothes disappeared fast and I took her roughly, her gasping my name as I filled her. She dug her fingers into my shoulders as I slammed into her hard and fast, unable to stop myself. After, I carried her to the tub for another soak, and we'd ended up back in bed, where we spent the rest of the day.

We made slow love, later that afternoon, and once more after dinner, yet, it wasn't enough. It would never be enough when it came to Avery.

"Tell me what you want," I pleaded.

"You . . . inside me . . . *please*, Daniel. I'm so close." She moaned as her hands frantically grasped at my shoulders.

I gave her what she wanted—what we both wanted.

One thrust and I was deep inside her. We rocked and moved in unison, pressed as tight together as possible. Our mouths molded together, our breaths shared. I cupped the back of her head, twisting the long strands of her hair around my fingers as my tongue tasted and commanded her mouth. Avery's legs wrapped around me, hands splayed across my back, and her fingers dug in as she moaned and whispered my name.

The headboard slammed against the wall rhythmically, growing louder as we lost ourselves in each other. The bedding moved and twisted around us. At one point, Avery's arm flung out, knocking the clock off the bedside table, somehow activating the alarm, its beeping noise persistent. I didn't care. Nothing mattered. Only her. Only us.

My spine rippled with fire as my orgasm built. The heat exploded as I cursed and begged her to come with me. Her body shuddered, her cries became louder, and she pulsated around me, gasping my name. I drove into her deep, coming hard, her name a raging plea as I quaked over her.

My chest dropped to hers and I lay, panting and satiated, wrapped in her arms. She peppered tender, loving kisses on my head and down my cheek as her fingers stroked the back of my neck. I shivered at the warmth of her touch, loving how right it felt.

I rolled over, gathering her up. She fit against me perfectly; the same way she fit into my life.

I pressed a lingering kiss to her forehead. "I can't let you go now."

"I don't want you to."

I stroked the soft skin of her shoulder. "I have a big house."

"I know that."

"Lots of room to share—" I kissed her lips "—and to grow."

Other than a quick intake of air, she was silent.

"How attached are you to city living and your apartment?"

"Daniel—"

"I know," I assured her. "I know it's reckless."

"It's crazy."

"It is. I don't care."

She sighed. "My lease is up in three months. I have the papers on my desk to re-sign."

I lifted her chin and stared into her beautiful eyes. "Don't sign."

"I . . ."

"I know it's fast. I know it's crazy. It's right. We're right. Tell me you feel how strong this is—how strong *we* are."

"I do."

"Don't sign, Avery," I pleaded. "Think about it. Please."

"I will."

I tugged her back to my chest.

"And Avery?"

"Hmm?"

"Soon, I'm probably going to send you a text. One that says I love you again." I blew out a long breath. "Only this time, it won't be a mistake."

I felt her tears on my chest. "I'd like that," she whispered.

I pressed a kiss to her head.

"Good."

Ten

Avery

BETH SMIRKED AT me knowingly as she arched an eyebrow. "I am not wearing some off-the-rack, ugly green dress when you get married, Avery."

"It's a little soon to be talking about a wedding, Beth." I huffed, dropping my fork, picking up my glass of wine.

"You spent the whole weekend with him. You forgot about me. Your best friend."

"I'm aware."

"You had *sex* with him."

"Yes."

"Numerous times."

My lips quirked at the memories flitting through my brain. Daniel's wandering hands. His wicked, talented mouth. His strong, muscled body. His massive . . .

I swallowed heavily, trying to calm my increase in breathing. "Yes."

She tapped my phone. As soon as I sat down, she had grabbed it, scrolling through our text messages, crowing in delight at them. "He adores you. He says so—repeatedly. He's building up to the 'L' word."

"I know."

She studied me for a moment. "You love him."

I sighed. "I think maybe I do." I shook my head. "How is it even possible, though?"

"It happens."

"In fairy tales, and maybe, to other people. Not to me."

She studied me over the rim of her glass. "Why not you?"

"I haven't had the best of luck with relationships."

"Hmm. You have had a run of bad luck—especially, the last one. I know Grant ended up being a complete ass, and I know he wasn't very nice to you. I'd like to knee him in the nuts for what he said to you." She covered my hand with an affectionate squeeze. "But don't you see? Daniel is different. Everything about him is different."

"I know. He's amazing. It seems too good to be true."

"Or maybe, your luck is changing. Grab it, Avery. I've never seen you look so happy."

"I am. He makes me feel special."

"How?"

I shrugged, unsure how to describe it. "When he looks at me, the expression on his face, it's as though everything he sees is perfect. All the things I think are wrong, he finds right." I sighed. "He makes me feel beautiful."

"I think there's more."

"More?"

"You're holding yourself differently. You aren't hiding. I think he's bringing out your confidence."

I thought about it, and had to agree. I did feel more confident. Daniel made me feel that way. Beautiful. Confident. Enough.

Beth beamed at me. "You have always been enough, Avery. I've told you countless times you're beautiful. If Daniel makes you feel that way, hold on to him."

I had obviously spoken aloud—again. I smiled at my friend. "I plan on it."

"Good." She winked and lightened the conversation. "I don't even need to ask how good he is in bed. You're walking a little funny today."

"You've already asked. Many times."

"And you keep changing the subject."

"How's work?"

She rolled her eyes. "Throw me a bone here. I know you're private and I understand, but something—anything!"

I stalled, twirling my pasta around my fork to buy me a little time. I *was* a bit stiff today. Still, I couldn't hide my happiness. I was dying to tell her everything, but I was less forthcoming than Beth.

Beth leaned forward, her voice low. "He's an animal in bed, isn't he?"

I drew back my shoulders and met her gaze. "If we make it to the bed . . . Daniel has a thing for walls." I winked. "He's like a sex machine, too."

Her jaw dropped, then she began to laugh. "I knew you had it in you."

"Several times, actually."

"Woohoo!" she exclaimed. "That's what I'm talking about!"

She picked up her wine. "No ugly green dress."

I gave in. "You can pick whatever dress you want."

"That's all I'm saying."

We grinned at each other, clinked our wine glasses, and drank.

I ROLLED MY shoulders, glancing at the clock in my living room. Another hour and Daniel would arrive.

The past two weeks had been hectic for both of us—even the weekends. Steven and Caitlin were on vacation, and although he had a temporary vet who filled in and another receptionist, it was one of the busiest times of the year at the clinic.

"With the nicer weather, pets are more vulnerable. They are outside more, get off their leads, or indoor pets sneak out and get lost. Dogs and cats that have never been out of their yard, get hit by cars or wander away," he stated sadly. *"I've seen too many cases of that. Or too many incidents of owners forgetting to make sure their pets are hydrated or have a cool place to get shade."* He shook his head. *"Some days are harder than others."*

He had shown up at my door last night, looking tired and

upset. Once I got him something to drink, he told me about losing a dog because the owner had "forgotten" to let him in during the heat of the day, and neglected to fill his water bowl.

"I did all I could," he told me with tears in his eyes. "I couldn't save him."

I held him tight, allowing him to let go of the pain. He worked tirelessly for all his clients, but I knew some pet owners were better than others when it came to their care. For someone like Daniel, it was a mystery. To him, if you loved your pet, you took care of it. Unfortunately, that wasn't always the case. He took it very hard when an animal died, although he was strong at the clinic. I had already seen the more vulnerable side of him, and I was glad he felt comfortable enough with me to allow me to care for him when it was too much to handle.

He still seemed upset and tired when he woke this morning. He held me close all night, but I knew he didn't sleep much. Every time I woke up, his fingers were running over my skin, drawing abstract patterns across my flesh. When I looked up at him, he pressed a kiss to my forehead or mouth, then cradled my head back to his chest.

"Sleep, Sprite."

"But you—"

"As long as you're here, I'm fine. Just let me hold you."

I studied him as he pulled on his clothes in the dim light of the morning. "Do you want me to cancel tonight?"

He rested his arm on the bed, cupping the back of my neck as he bent close. "No. I'm fine. I'm looking forward to a night out with my girl and meeting her friends. Don't change our plans." He kissed me gently. "Are you still planning on driving to my place tonight and we'll come in together?"

It was the most logical thing to do. Then my car was at his place for the weekend and I could drive myself in on Monday morning. "Yes."

He studied me for a moment. "You know, if you just moved in we wouldn't have to have this discussion every weekend." He sighed. "We'd be together every night."

I tried not to sigh. It was getting harder to say no to him every time he asked. "Daniel . . ."

A frown marred his features. "Too soon, I know. I'm going to keep *asking, though."*

"I know."

"Think about the kitchen. You love the kitchen."

I pushed him away, unable to stop my smile. "Yes, I love the kitchen. You love what comes out of the kitchen."

He bent forward, his face so close, I could feel his breath wash over my skin. "I love having you in my kitchen. In my house. I want to make it our house. Our home."

"I need a little more time."

"The offer is open-ended, and there is a generous early signing bonus."

"Oh?"

He yanked me to his chest, kissing me hard. "Me." He promised. "Any time, anyway, anything you want."

"Even the shower?"

His eyes darkened, sadness fading. We'd used the bench he had put in the shower a few times already. "Especially the shower."

"I'll think it over."

"Think hard."

Spreading my hand wide, I cupped his erection. "I think you've got hard covered."

He yanked his shirt over his head. "Let's see about covering you."

I shivered thinking about the way his body had covered mine and filled me. He was certainly persuasive.

Tonight, I would be officially introducing Beth and Ryan to Daniel. I was nervous and excited—much the way I felt when I met his parents. I wanted them to like him; although if they didn't, it wouldn't stop me from seeing him. Beth was right; I was already in love with him. Even my mother commented on how cheerful I had been the last two calls. While I had admitted to meeting someone, I kept it fairly low-key. My much older parents were very protective, and they would be horrified to know how deeply I already felt for Daniel. It was a conversation best left for their next visit, which would be in the fall. Of course, if Daniel had his way, I'd already be living with him by then.

My phone rang with Daniel's ring tone and I picked it up.

"Hey."

His voice was weary. "Hey. I'm going to be late. I have a last minute emergency."

"No problem. I'll let Beth know. Want to just meet there?"

"Why don't you drive out and bring your stuff, then we can go in together. That way you aren't driving in the dark."

I tried not to roll my eyes at his protectiveness, but I failed. I knew he did it because he cared.

"Sure. I can leave now."

"You have your key?"

"Yep."

"Okay. I'll see you at home."

I hung up, thinking about what he said. His place did feel like home. I wondered how much longer I would resist the lure of his house, bed, and constant company. Probably not much longer.

WE PULLED UP in front of the restaurant. It was later than anticipated, but Beth was insistent they were still fine, and Daniel wanted to go. He was quiet, the weariness etched on his face, and I knew without asking he had lost another patient. I let him collect his thoughts, while I hung on for dear life as he barreled toward the city.

He shut off the motor and glanced my way, a frown on his face.

"You can let go of the handle, Sprite. We've arrived, perfectly safe."

I pivoted in my seat. "*That* was your shortcut?"

"Yes."

"You drove like Mario Andretti!"

He tried to suppress his laughter, failing badly. "I was barely going over the speed limit. It seemed fast because we didn't have to slow down, and there were no other cars around, that's all."

I shook my head. "No, you were going way too fast."

"I realize, to someone like you, it seemed fast, but I assure you, it wasn't."

I didn't like his tone. It was almost patronizing. "Someone like me?"

He got out of the truck, came around to my side of the vehicle, and opened my door, extending his hand.

I ignored it and scrambled down from the truck on my own. I had to admit, it was a lot easier when I let him lift me down, but I was trying to make a point.

I glared up at him. "Someone like me?" I repeated, crossing my arms. "You mean a woman?"

He mimicked my actions. "A ninety-year old woman, named Gladys, yes."

Gladys?

"I do not drive like a ninety-year old woman."

"Avery, you do."

"I'm a cautious driver, unlike you."

He narrowed his eyes. "I *am* cautious. Your driving is far more dangerous than mine. Don't even get me started about the way you handle reverse."

"And what, exactly, is wrong with the way I reverse?"

"Nothing, if you're ninety, can't see well, and like to hold up traffic."

"You've driven with me twice! How can you say something like that?"

He shrugged his shoulder. "It only took me once to pick up how tense you are behind the wheel, which is why I offer to drive when we go out." He cocked his head to the side. "Were you in an accident at some point? Is that why you dislike driving?"

"I have never been in an accident!"

"Who taught you to drive?"

"My mom."

"Ah, well that explains it."

"Excuse me?"

"You said yourself your mother was older. She passed her nervous habits on to you."

"Take that back! You don't know my mother, and you can't just be spouting shit!"

He arched his eyebrow. "*Shit*, Avery? You shoulder check at least six times before changing lanes, you go under the speed limit, and it took you a full five minutes to reverse from the parking spot last week—and there were no cars around. It's not shit—it's true fact." He shook his head with a frown. "You turn into an old woman behind the wheel. An overly cautious stick-in-the-mud. You need to learn to relax. Or else you're an accident waiting to happen behind the wheel. A real hazard."

A memory stirred of Grant standing in front of me, sneering. "*You're so dull, Avery—a real stick-in-the-mud. Old before your time. Besides your odd looks, frankly, you bore me. I'll be glad when I don't have to deal with you anymore.*"

Tears pricked my eyes. Daniel felt the same way?

"I'm sorry I'm so much trouble to you."

"Don't twist my words. I didn't say that."

"Yes, you did." I sucked in a shaky breath. "I'll call Beth and tell her we need to cancel. I think it may be for the best."

"Is that so? You want to leave?"

"I want you to leave."

"Now you're being childish."

His words stung.

"Well, then, it's for the best if you aren't stuck with my childish, hazardous behavior this evening, isn't it?"

"And how will you get home? Walk?" He dragged a hand through his hair, no longer smiling or teasing. His eyes narrowed in anger as he glared. "I suppose you'd get there quicker than driving." He added in a sardonic tone.

That was it—I was done with this conversation. "That isn't your concern. Beth will make sure I get home safely. You take your shortcut, go home, and pat yourself on the back for saving your precious four minutes in such a manly fashion." I spun on my heels, heading toward the restaurant. I half expected for him to shout my name or come after me, but all I heard was the slam of the truck door, and the tires peeling on the asphalt as he tore out of the parking lot.

I turned in time to see his truck disappear around the corner. I blinked at the tears in my eyes. How had that happened? One moment we were fine, and the next we were being ugly toward each other. I had never heard Daniel so critical. It made my chest tighten at the thought of his opinion of me changing.

I took out my phone with trembling hands to text Beth and cancel, but it was too late. Her car pulled in, and she waved at me, looking perplexed when she saw I was alone.

She parked the car, and her and Ryan came over. She pulled me in for a hug. "Where is Daniel? Did he go in to get the table?"

I steeled my features. "No. I was just texting you. There was an emergency—he had to go. He sends his apologies. It's been a bad week at the clinic."

"Oh no!" She frowned and glanced at Ryan. "I was looking forward to getting to know him."

"You guys go have dinner. I'll just walk home and we'll reschedule."

She linked her arm with mine. "No way. You have to eat, too. We'll have dinner and run you home. The four of us can do dinner next week. Right?"

I let her drag me toward the restaurant, nodding. I wasn't sure how to tell her there might not be a next week for Daniel and me.

I SLID INTO my chair after returning from the restroom. I had checked my phone, disappointed but not surprised there wasn't a message from Daniel. My fingers hovered over the keys. I wanted to send him a message and make sure he arrived home okay. I hadn't been kidding when I told him that I disliked his shortcut. The road was narrow, twisted, and full of deep ruts—more like a country lane than a road. I could only imagine what it was like on a wet day, and considering the mood he'd been in when he left, I got the impression he gave the speed limit no consideration at all. I stared at the screen, then slipped my phone back into my purse. If he didn't text, maybe I needed to leave it for now. Let him cool off, and allow my hurt feelings to settle.

I picked up my wine, taking an appreciative sip. "Where's Ryan?"

"He had John pick him up. They went for beer and wings."

"What? Why?"

She gave me a knowing look over her glass. "An emergency, Avery? From the devastated look on your face, I'd say more like a big fight."

"Oh, um . . ." I stumbled over my words. "I thought–I thought I'd hidden it."

Reaching across the table, she grabbed my hand. "Maybe from other people, but you're my best friend. You can't hide from me."

I squeezed her fingers. "Ryan didn't have to go."

She shrugged. "He was fine. There's a game on tonight and he's just as happy to hang with John and watch it while stuffing his face with wings and beer. He figured there wouldn't be much eating happening here."

"We can leave."

"Not until you tell me what happened."

"I don't know what happened. One minute he was teasing, the next . . . he wasn't. He hates my driving apparently." I met Beth's sympathetic gaze. "He compared me to a ninety-year-old woman—with very bad habits."

I expected her instant denial, or a gasp of outrage on my behalf. Instead, she looked down at the table, her finger tracing the design on the tablecloth.

I gaped at her. "You agree with him?"

"You are, ah, overly cautious."

"He said I was a stick-in-the-mud."

Her gaze flew to mine. "That's what Grant said to you when you broke up."

I wiped an errant tear off my cheek. "I know it's silly . . ."

"No," she interrupted me, "it's not silly. He said something that reminded you of a painful time, and it hurt you." Her voice softened. "It hurt you because his opinion matters."

"It does." I sniffled. "I told him I didn't want to have dinner anymore and he said I was acting childish."

"I'd say he was the one acting childish."

"He's tired," I insisted. "He's lost some animals this week, and it upsets him. He's working long hours and with Steven and Caitlin away, it all falls on him . . ." My voice trailed off at the look on Beth's face. "What?"

"Listen to you, defending him. You're upset and hurt, yet you won't say anything bad about him."

"He was an ass?" I offered, though it didn't sound very convincing.

She threw back her head and laughed. "You don't sound like you mean that."

"I do. But I know how difficult things have been for him. He drives in to see me at night, and he looked so tired this week. I guess I shouldn't be surprised he wasn't himself."

"So, he's forgiven?"

I rubbed my hand across my head. "No. We need to talk, and he should apologize. If he calls, that is."

"He will. I'm sure he's as distressed as you are."

"My car is at his place."

"I'll drive you there to get it. You can stay at my place tonight, then we'll go early tomorrow and get it before he wakes up. Let him stew a bit, okay?"

"Ryan?"

"He'll be out most of the night with John. We'll have all weekend. Tonight, it'll just be us. Let's get a pizza and trash-talk about our men and commiserate. We'll go back to being sweet girlfriends in the morning, okay?"

Another tear slipped down my face. "What if—?"

"It's a fight. A disagreement brought on by bad moods, exhaustion, and wrong words. It's not the end."

"We started so hot, maybe it was . . ."

"No. It will be fine. It's one bad day. You'll see."

I picked up my wine. I hoped she was right.

BETH GLANCED OVER at me with a frown. "I'll drive you up to the house."

We were sitting at the entrance to the clinic, just off the highway. "No. It will wake him up and disturb any animals in the clinic. I'll walk in and get my car."

"What about your stuff?"

"It's just my overnight bag. I'll either have to come and get it when I give him back his key, or I'll use it next time if we clear this up."

"Which you will."

I sighed, tired and distraught. Despite the amount of wine I drank, and the laughs we shared as we "trash-talked" our men, I hadn't slept well. The truth was I had little to trash-talk about, and even Beth stretched to find too many things to complain about when it came to Ryan. We ended up talking the way we always did when we were together. Although, I did have enough alcohol that I shared a few more intimate details than I normally disclose.

Back at Beth's apartment, I kept checking my phone. Several times, I began to text Daniel, but then erased what I wrote, stretching back on the sofa, only to start the process over a short while later. There were no messages from him, either, which alternatively made me angry, then resigned. My phone died around one o'clock, and my charger was in my bag at Daniel's, so I was going to have to plug it in after I got home with my spare.

I opened the door and slipped out. "I'll be fine. We'll talk later okay?"

She sighed in resignation. "Fine. You sure you don't want me to wait?"

"No. I'll get my car and head home."

"All right. Call me later."

I watched her drive away with a wave, then turned, trudged down the driveway and past the vet clinic. It was early, the air was still, and not a soul was around. I should have remembered Beth's inane need to be up at the crack of dawn, no matter what time she went to bed, before I agreed to stay over last night. Since it was so early, I would have a long day ahead of me, and I decided I would maybe go into the office for a while. It was a busy time, and with no one else there, I could get a lot done.

I rounded the corner and stopped. My car was parked where I had left it, but Daniel's truck was now parked behind it, angled in such a way I couldn't back up. I marched forward, walking around my car, cursing under my breath. That *bastard*. He trapped my car, and the only way I could get out was to ask him to move his vehicle. I huffed out an angry breath of air. He had the nerve to call *me* childish!

Frustrated, I looked in his driver's window, surprised to see the keys in the ignition. He usually left them in if he parked in the garage, but took them if he parked outside.

How lucky for me he forgot them. I would move his truck, then get my car and be gone. He was no doubt asleep or working out—he'd never know.

Easy.

Eleven

Avery

I SLID INTO the driver's seat, shut the door, and surveyed the cab. Next to my small Corolla, Daniel's truck seemed massive. I glanced in the rearview mirror and took in a calming breath. I searched around the edge and found the mechanism I needed to bring the seat closer to the steering wheel. Daniel had extremely long legs.

"You can do this, Avery," I muttered.

I turned the key, grimacing at the sound of the loud engine roaring to life. I squared my shoulders, adjusted the mirrors, and put the truck in gear. As I lifted my foot off the brake, the large vehicle lurched and I gasped. This was a more powerful vehicle than what I normally drove, and I prayed I wouldn't smash into anything trying to move Daniel's truck.

A tap on the driver side window startled me, and my hand flew to my chest. I turned to see Daniel's weary face outside the window, staring at me. He stepped back, holding up his hands in supplication. He was shirtless, his broad chest strong in the early morning light. A pair of sweatpants hung low on his hips. His eyes were no longer stormy and angry, and silently we stared at each other through the glass. He tapped again, and I shifted back into park, then hit the button to lower the glass.

"Training for a new career, Avery?" His voice was flat with

fatigue. "Grand theft auto in case accounting doesn't work out for you?"

"I wasn't *stealing* your truck," I replied. "I was just moving it to get my car out."

"I knew you weren't stealing my truck. I came out here to see if you needed some help."

"Right, because I couldn't possibly move your truck without your help." My anger started to build again.

He sighed and scrubbed his face. "Do you really want to fight over this again?" he asked softly.

"I didn't want to fight about it in the first place."

"Neither did I. I only meant to tease . . . and suddenly we were arguing. Then you sent me away."

"I didn't think it was a good idea to meet my friends while we were angry."

"Probably not." Opening the door, he leaned into the cab of the truck, his muscled body pressing into mine, his face so close I could feel his hot breath on my cheeks. "But I didn't like it."

"I wasn't very happy either."

He narrowed his eyes. "Where were you last night?"

"I was with Beth."

"I came looking for you."

"You–you did?"

He nodded, his gaze locked on mine.

I could see the exhaustion etched on his face, dark shadows under his eyes.

"I came back to the restaurant to look for you, but the hostess said you had left. I drove to your apartment, but you weren't there. I waited a while but you never came back."

"I stayed the night at Beth's. We'd been drinking and she didn't want me to go home." I paused to collect myself. "She drove me here this morning so I could get my car, I didn't want to disturb you."

"You didn't want to disturb me or you didn't want to see me?"

"I didn't know if you wanted to see me," I admitted.

"I sat in front of your apartment building for three hours last night, Avery. I came home, paced for a while, drove back into town, and waited a while longer but you never came home." He blew out a long breath. "I was so worried about you. I figured you were with Beth, so I thought I would give you a little time. I'd hoped I would see you today."

"You never called."

"I was pretty sure you'd ignore my calls, and what I had to say to you I didn't want to say on the phone. I did call later, when I couldn't find you or stop worrying, but it went straight to voicemail."

"My phone died and my charger was in my bag here."

"Yeah, I saw it in the side pocket. I assumed, if you were with Beth, you'd eventually show up here to get your car. I've been waiting for you all night."

"So you thought you'd block me in to stop me from leaving?"

Without a word, he reached forward, shut off the engine, then dragged me across the seat and out of the truck. He lifted me off my feet, and pressed me against the side of the vehicle, pinning me to the cold metal of the truck with his body.

"I couldn't risk you leaving. Not before I had a chance to talk to you."

"Talk to me then."

"I want to apologize for last night. I realize what I said was hurtful, and though I didn't mean it that way, it's how it came out. I was stressed and tired, but that's no excuse." He sighed. "It was thoughtless and I'm sorry. More than I can say."

"I'm sorry, too."

"What are you sorry for, Sprite?"

I shrugged, feeling self-conscious. "I am a nervous driver. I always have been."

"Still, it didn't give me the right to tease you, or behave the way I did."

"I overreacted."

"We both did for different reasons. I was overtired, not thinking, and being an idiot." He hesitated and touched my cheek with the tip of his finger. "And I think something I said brought up a bad memory for you, am I right?"

"Yes."

"Tell me."

"My last boyfriend didn't think very highly of me and liked to point out all the things I did wrong, which by the end of our relationship seemed to be almost everything. The day he broke up with me he said a lot of nasty things, including the fact I was a boring stick-in-the-mud, nothing but trouble, and he was glad to be rid of me."

"And I said the same thing."

I bit my lip, unsure if I trusted myself to speak. My throat was tight with emotion.

"I don't want rid of you. I want you with me—always." He inched forward, his voice softening. "I thought I would go crazy not being able to find you. All I could think about was I had blown the best thing I'd ever found in my life."

"All I could think about was I couldn't stand to not be perfect in your eyes," I admitted, my eyes filling up with tears.

"You are perfect," he insisted. "You're perfect for me."

"Bad driving and all?"

"You aren't a bad driver—a little overcautious, but not bad. I'm sorry I said that." He tightened his hands on my hips. "Can you forgive me?"

"Yes. Am I forgiven?"

"Always. It was an argument. One we're going to move forward from—it's not the end. Did you really think it was?"

As I nodded, admitting my fear, relief flooded through me and tears ran down my cheeks. He wiped them away tenderly.

"It's not. Far from it. Don't, Sprite. Don't cry."

I sniffed. "Sorry. I guess I'm being a girl."

"My girl," he stated firmly. Daniel stared at me, his gaze turning from serious and sad to a warmer, gentler expression. "I guess we just had our first fight."

"I guess so."

His hands slid to my waist as he dropped his head to my neck. "Do you know what that means?" His hot breath drifted across my skin, making me shiver.

"What?"

"It means we need to make up now." He lifted his head, his expression mischievous.

"Is that a fact?"

"It is." He shifted, lifting me higher, so my legs wrapped around his waist. "In fact, I need to make up with you really, *really* hard."

I gasped as he surged into me, showing me just how hard he intended to make up. Our eyes held: anxious green meeting intense blue. His warm, toned body trapped me against unforgiving, cold steel, the contrasts so great; and yet so right. He tightened his hands on my hips, flexed his fingers, rubbing small circles on the bones, then traveling upward. He delved under my shirt to the bare flesh, skimming the length of my torso, causing my breathing to increase.

"I didn't know if I'd get the chance to touch you again." He traced the shell of my ear with his tongue. "Feel how soft your skin is. How you respond to me," he continued, cupping my breasts in his large hands, caressing the nipples.

I tightened my legs around him, arching into his touch, breathing his name.

"Are you still mine?"

"Yes," I pleaded.

His lips hovered over mine. "What if I want you right here— against my truck, in the open? What if I want to hear your forgiveness shouted into the dawn?"

I grabbed the back of his neck. "Yes."

His lips crashed to mine—they were hard, hungry, and desperate. Our tongues tangled, pressed, and stroked, the urgency mounting. His mouth claimed mine, stealing my breath, leaving me longing for more. It was the same every time he kissed me. Only this time, there was an edge to his caresses—a desperation we were feeling.

Daniel's hands roamed over my skin, touching, teasing, his

fingers restless, grasping at the fabric of my shirt, sliding up to fondle my breasts, then traveling back to grasp my ass as he ground against me.

"You taste so damn good." His tongue dragged along my bottom lip. "How many mints did you eat this morning?"

"Seven, maybe. I don't know—I lost count. I have none left." I confessed in a whisper. I had continually crunched them all morning.

"Damn it, I wanted to steal one."

"I'll let you later."

He kissed me again, even deeper this time.

"Tell me," he commanded in a low voice. "Tell me to take you inside and make love to you."

"No," I gasped, clutching his shoulders, "I want you here. *Now*."

His mouth grazed along my neck, his teeth nipping as he bunched up the material of my skirt, tearing away my thong. He trailed his knuckles along my folds, groaning at the slickness he found. "I love you wear skirts all the time. It's so convenient for me." His fingers slipped deeper, teasing me. "Is this for me? You want me, Sprite? *Tell me*. Tell me how much."

"I want you, Daniel," I begged, my head falling back to the hard metal as he slid two fingers inside, pumping slow and deliberate. "I *need* you."

"What do you need?"

"You. I need you to *fuck me*."

He bit down on my neck. "With pleasure."

An impatient tug, he tore down his sweats. One powerful thrust and he was buried deep inside me, his body slamming me into the inflexible steel behind my back. Bracing one hand behind my head, and the other on my hip, he started to move, his body pinning me in place. His eyes locked on mine; dark, piercing, and swirling in desire and need as he took me, hard and rough.

I clutched at his broad shoulders, my blunt nails sliding across his damp skin. Needing as near as possible, I wound my arms around his neck. I held myself close, licking and kissing his neck, moaning his name, letting him move me whichever way he wanted.

He answered with grunts and groans, breathing my name. He tangled his hand into my hair, tugging my face back and capturing my mouth. He enfolded me in his arms, holding me tight, his hips driving fast, his tongue mimicking his rapid actions.

My body began to tighten as my orgasm approached.

Daniel's motions picked up, his cock slamming into me ferociously as I screamed my release into his mouth. He shuddered as he spilled inside me, his body stilling as he climaxed, my pussy clamping down around him.

A long tremor moved down his spine, his body relaxing into mine. He dragged his mouth up my neck, and spoke low in my ear. "I feel forgiven."

"You are."

He smiled against my skin.

I ran my fingers through his hair, as I made my quiet confession. "I hate driving. I know I'm bad at it, which is why I walk most places. I'm probably worse than an old lady behind the wheel."

He leaned back, keeping his face near mine. "No, I just said that wrong. I know you dislike driving. But I can help you. We can work on making you more relaxed behind the wheel." He ran a finger down my cheek. "Or maybe it means I need to drive you places and keep you safe. Once I convince you to move in with me, we'll have to discuss that."

"You still want me to move in?"

"More than ever. And one day soon, I'll convince you."

He stepped back, his cock slipping from me, leaving me feeling empty without him inside me. "In the meantime, I'm taking you into the house, getting you cleaned up, and we're getting some sleep."

"I was going to go home. I'm sure you have lots to do today . . ."

I stopped talking at the intense look on his face.

"Everything I want to do today, involves you. We're spending the weekend together, just as we planned. We're gonna talk, and I'm going to have sex with you all over my house." His lips curled into his mischievous grin, one corner higher than the other, causing his eyes to crinkle. "Think you can keep up with that, *old lady?*"

"I can certainly try."

He hitched me higher, pulling me away from the truck. His hands curved around my ass, holding me tight as he strode toward the house. "Then let's go, happy bum."

"Happy bum?"

He laughed, the sound loud in the open air. "Glad ass—happy bum, what's the difference?"

I tried to fight my grin at his lame joke, but I couldn't. I was in his arms, with the weekend still ahead of us, and we were together.

I laid my head on his shoulder and joined his laughter.

Twelve

Daniel

AVERY SLEPT SOUNDLY, her head burrowed in the pillow and the blanket clutched around her. I had slept for a while, waking up to her gentle breath drifting over my skin as she slumbered.

After the disaster of the previous night, I was ecstatic the way the morning had turned out, and she was now beside me. All was right again in my world.

Caitlin always chided me on the fact when I was tired I didn't realize the tone I spoke with at times, and last night proved her correct. What I'd meant as teasing came out condescending. It destroyed our plans, and led us to our first disagreement. For a moment this morning, I was worried we were about to fall right into a continuation of the same argument, but we managed to stop it before it restarted.

I hated how tired she looked, and I knew she could see the same exhaustion reflected in my eyes. When I had reached for her it was to simply hold her and reassure us both we were okay. I hadn't planned to fuck her against my truck. However, it seemed every time I had Avery close and there was an immobile surface behind her, all my common sense evaporated and the caveman in me took over. As soon as I had her trapped between the metal and me, I had to have her.

And I did have her—thoroughly.

I ran my knuckle down her cheek. Her nose wrinkled and her lips pursed, then she burrowed a little deeper, making me chuckle. She loved to sleep.

The sound of her phone drifted up from the floor, and with a frown, I rolled over, reaching down to find her skirt. She had plugged it in to charge while we had coffee, then slipped it back into her pocket before we came to bed. It had been buzzing almost constantly, and I thought, perhaps it might be important. I had to stop the laughter as I reached into the pocket of her skirt and my hand came back with not only her phone, but also the numerous empty wrappers from all the mints she had eaten. She had severely misjudged the number she had consumed. There were a dozen wrappers in my hand—maybe more. I let them flutter to the floor, and peered at the screen, seeing her friend, Beth, was the person contacting Avery. There were several texts and two missed calls. I realized Avery hadn't let her know she was okay, and Beth was worried. I typed a quick text to her, letting her know it was me and Avery was safe, asleep, and we were okay. Her reply was prompt.

You messed up. Don't do it again.

I replied. *Don't plan on it.*

Her response was fast.

You better not. You'll have me to deal with.

I liked her protectiveness. Avery needed friends like Beth. After a moment, I sent another text to Beth, asking if I could make up for the previous night by taking her and Ryan to lunch. After she agreed and we set a time and place, I rolled back to Avery, nuzzling her cheek.

"Hey, Sprite, wake up."

She opened her sleepy eyes and peered up at me. "Hi."

I kissed her fast, unable to resist, yet knowing if I lingered we'd never make it out of this bed. "We need to get up. We have a date."

"A date?"

"We're meeting Beth and Ryan for lunch."

"Uh, o–okay?" she replied, obviously confused.

"She kept texting. I replied for you and thought I would offer to make up for last night. We're meeting them in an hour." I rolled out of bed and bent down to pick up the wrappers. "And we need to talk about your addiction to these mints, Avery. You must have eaten a dozen or more."

"Is that both pockets?"

My eyebrows shot up and I grabbed her skirt to check, fishing out yet more empty wrappers, adding them to the pile on the bed. "Your dentist must love you."

She sat up, dragging her finger through the pile. "I'm not usually that bad—only when I'm nervous."

"Or upset."

She nodded. "Or upset."

I hovered over her, dropping another kiss to her mouth. "We'll pick you up more on the way to meet them. I'll do my best to make sure you don't need to OD on them again. Deal?"

"Deal."

I started to walk to the shower, then turned around. "Avery—"

"Yeah?"

"You still owe me a mint. I plan on collecting."

She smiled wide. "Okay."

"Okay."

Avery

MY HEAD FELL back in laughter as Beth finished off another one of her entertaining stories of the escapades we had shared. Daniel had been roaring with laughter most of the lunch with Beth's lack of filter. Ryan was used to her forwardness, never once reacting to her bold statements with anything except a grin. When she had begun the conversation, asking with a sardonic grin who drove into town, I felt Daniel tense up, and I narrowed my eyes in warning.

"*Daniel* drove his truck in."

She winked at me subtly. "You were later than I expected. I thought maybe you had driven."

I knew she was trying to test the air and to tease me. I tossed my hair. "We were delayed leaving."

"Oh?"

This time I winked. "The shower was particularly enjoyable."

Daniel began to chuckle.

Ryan looked shocked, and Beth held up her hand. "High five to that."

Daniel draped his arm over my shoulder, drawing me close. "I'll second that."

I turned to him with a wink. "You already did."

We all laughed.

"GOOD LORD, I may explode," Beth grumbled, leaning back in her chair. "I ate way too much."

"You drank a lot, too."

She pointed in front of me. "Pot, meet kettle."

I giggled, realizing she was right. The mimosas tasted exceptional today, and I'd had quite a few. The whole room seemed a bit fuzzy.

"I think I need to take you home for another nap," Daniel mused, glancing up from perusing the dessert menu.

I looked at him, and my breath caught.

Was he always this good-looking?

His messy hair gleamed under the lights. He hadn't shaved today and his chin looked sexy covered in stubble. I wanted to lick it. The dark frames of his glasses set off his eyes that were staring at me with an intensity that made my thighs clench. He was entirely fuckable at that moment.

I needed to get him home, and fast.

He bent close, his smile so wide his eyes almost disappeared. He brushed his lips across my ear, his voice low. "Filter, Sprite. I'm not sure the woman at the table behind us needs to know how fuckable I am."

I slapped my hand over my mouth, and he laughed, pulling it away and kissing the palm. "I'll take you home."

Beth laughed. "I have no idea what you've done to her, Daniel, but keep it up. I like seeing this *wild* side of her."

Daniel's gaze never left mine. "I plan on it."

WE SAID OUR goodbyes in the parking lot. Beth and Ryan left with promises of another get-together soon. I leaned against the side of the truck, staring at Daniel. He stepped closer, drawing his finger down my cheek. "I need to take you home."

Turning my head, I caught his finger between my lips, running my tongue over it. "Yes, you do."

His eyes darkened. He started to lower his head when a voice ran out.

"Daniel?"

He pivoted, shocked. "Karen?"

His firm body was suddenly gone, and I watched as the gorgeous, perfect ex-girlfriend flung herself into his arms. He laughed as he spun her, then dragged her to him and hugged her hard.

I thought I growled. I knew my eyes narrowed, my back tensed, and an emotion I had never experienced flooded my body.

Jealousy.

He was hugging her enthusiastically. She was touching what was mine with the same zeal. I dug into my pocket, fished out a mint, and chewed on it furiously.

She stood in front of him, talking, laughing, touching his chest, arm, shoulder as she spoke, her golden hair fluttering in the breeze as she beamed at *my* boyfriend. She was tall with long legs, and as beautiful as I knew she would be. I had to hold myself back from stomping over and removing her hand from his torso. I tilted my head to the side. She had particularly long fingers—like talons—and the way her hand rested on his chest it resembled a claw. I felt another wave of anger build when I realized Daniel hadn't even glanced my way—he was too busy listening to Ms. Perfect's long, rambling story.

I popped another mint.

"She doesn't mean anything by her actions, you know," an amused voice spoke from beside me.

I turned my head to meet the dark gaze of a man, grinning at me.

"Excuse me?"

"My wife. She's harmless. Karen is simply being Karen. She has no idea about personal space."

"Um. I wasn't worried."

He chuckled, the sound low in his throat. "If you hold onto the door handle any harder, you may rip it off. I don't know Daniel very well, although from what Karen has told me, he would probably prefer it stayed in place."

I glanced to the side, realizing how tight I was holding onto the metal. My knuckles were white.

He stuck out his hand. "I'm Buck."

I uncurled my fist and shook his hand.

"I am going to assume you are Avery."

"How did you know?"

"Karen and Daniel keep in touch. He raves to her about you."

I was dumbfounded. I had no idea.

"He didn't do you justice."

I looked down, shy from his words.

Buck laughed at my reaction. "I see why Daniel is so taken with you."

He leaned casually against the truck, crossing his arms, completely relaxed. He was tall and broad, with brown hair graying around the temples, hanging to his collar. He carried himself with a confidence that was at once easy, yet projecting.

I glanced at him, meeting his amused eyes.

"It's always the same when they see each other. They practically talk over the other one."

My gaze cut over to Daniel and Karen. Daniel was talking, Karen nodding, her smile wide. She was *still* touching him. I dug out another mint.

"It doesn't bother you?"

"One of things I love the most about my wife is her openness. She grabs life and she lives it. Every day she reminds me of how to embrace the joy that is all around us. She is very fond of Daniel—as a friend." He emphasized the last few words. "She's thrilled he has found someone; the same way he was glad when we met."

He pushed off the truck and held out his hand in invitation. "They could be a while. Want to go inside and grab a drink?"

I looked toward Daniel. The way Karen chatted, they *were* going to be there for a while. I moved away from the truck. Another drink in the cool air of the restaurant seemed a better idea than standing by the truck watching my boyfriend chat with his ex.

As I moved forward, Daniel suddenly stepped back, with his gaze focused on Buck's outstretched hand. He came toward us, covering the distance in long strides. She followed him, a grin on her face.

He came beside me, his arm going around my waist, tugging me to his side. He extended his free hand. "Buck. Good to see you again."

Buck shook his hand, his expression one of amusement. "Daniel."

Karen joined us, stepped in front of me, and flung her arms around me, hugging me hard. "It is so good to meet you, Avery! I've heard so much about you!"

"Nice to meet you," I mumbled, unsure how to react to her enthusiasm.

She released me, standing back. "The two of you are perfect together!" She beamed at Daniel. "You look so happy. So in love!"

He dropped a kiss to my head. "I am."

My heart sped up. *He was in love?*

With me?

Buck spoke up. "We were going to go grab a drink and let you two catch up."

Daniel's arm tightened. "Thanks for the offer, but we have to get going."

Karen frowned and sounded disappointed. "Really?"

He nodded. "Avery and I have to be somewhere. We're already late. But it was great to see you."

"We're only here for another couple days. Lunch, maybe?"

"Sure. I'll call you Monday. I'll come meet you and Buck."

"What about you, Avery? Can you join us? I'd love to get to know you more."

I studied her briefly. Her expression was open and friendly. She stood beside Buck, her arm wrapped around his waist, her head resting against his shoulder. She appeared to be everything Daniel and Buck said: affectionate, real, and simply Karen.

"Sure, if I can arrange it at work."

"We'll work around your schedule," she assured me.

"Okay."

She stepped forward, kissing Daniel's cheek, dragging him in for another hug. I found the last mint in my pocket.

"Don't forget to call," she teased. "You know I'll chase you down."

He chuckled. "I'm aware. Enjoy your lunch."

They walked away, already lost to each other, talking.

Daniel steered me toward the truck, opened my door, lifting me into the cab before I could scramble in. He leaned forward, his chest pressing me into the leather upholstery. He crashed his lips to mine, kissing me, hard and deep.

"What was that for?" I gasped, trying to catch my breath.

"Reminding you who you belong to."

I arched my eyebrow. "There was a question of that?"

"You were going to go have a drink with Buck."

"May I remind you that you were so engrossed talking to your *ex-girlfriend* you didn't even notice I was standing there anymore?"

He laughed low and husky in his chest, his breath floating over my skin. "I knew exactly where you were every second, Avery. I was chatting with Karen but most of the time my eyes were on you. I saw you gripping the door handle. I watched you eat your way through four"—he kissed me, stealing the last mint from my mouth with a wide smile—"make that three mints. What do you think she was teasing me about? She said she'd never seen me look so happy— or so protective. She had to remind me Buck was just being Buck."

"He said the same of Karen."

"They're inseparable. I was thrilled to see her, but I was as aware of you as I always am."

"Oh."

"Jealous, Sprite?"

"Yes."

His face morphed into a grin. "I felt the same way watching you talking to Buck. I guess we're quite the pair, aren't we?"

"You were jealous?"

"When he held out his hand, I thought I was going to come over and punch him if you took it."

I ruffled his hair. "He was trying to give you some time together."

"I'll see *them*"—he emphasized the word—"at lunch. The only person I need time with right now is you."

"Yeah?"

"Yeah."

I paused and glanced away.

"What?"

"Karen . . . what she said—about you being in love . . ."

His face changed expression, his gaze becoming tender and filled with emotion. "I wondered if you noticed that."

I could only nod, not sure how to ask the question.

"I am in love."

"With me?"

"Yes, of course with you." He cradled my face, his thumbs

running small circles on my skin. "I didn't mean for you to find out in a parking lot with my ex-girlfriend in the mix. I wanted to tell you in a romantic setting."

I shook my head, wrapping my hand around his wrist. "I don't need romance, Daniel. I only need you. Because I feel the same way."

"Say it, Avery. I want your words."

"I love you, Daniel Spencer."

"I love you, Avery Connor." He covered my mouth with his, kissing me hard, the passion simmering right on the surface of his caress.

"Even though I'm a terrible driver? And I was so jealous watching her touch you, I wanted to rip her hand off?"

"I love you more for both of those. It gives me something to do for you—drive you places so you're comfortable, and as for the jealousy part, I feel the exact same way concerning you."

I gazed at him, a feeling of belonging washing through me. He loved me. This wonderful, incredible man loved me. I had never been loved by anyone, and I knew being loved by Daniel Spencer was going to be life-changing. He made me feel differently about the world, and myself. With him, I felt right. Accepted. Adored. It was a powerful emotion.

"I need three, Avery."

I smiled, knowing the three he needed were about him. *Us.*

"I love how it feels when you say my name."

"*Sprite,*" he breathed out.

"I love how you treat me—as though I matter more than anything or anyone."

"You do."

"I love how it feels when you're inside me, when we're connected in every possible way."

With a hooded gaze, he lowered his mouth to my ear. "I fucked you against this truck this morning. Right now, I feel like fucking you in it, just so you remember you're mine. How would you feel about that?" His lips trailed down my neck, grazing across my cheek, teasing the edge of my mouth.

"It's a parking lot," I squeaked out.

"The windows are tinted. My place is too far away right now."

"My apartment is ten minutes away."

He pulled back with a nod and traced his finger over my lips. "Only you, Avery. I've only ever felt all of these emotions, these reactions with you. You bring out something in me I don't understand. I didn't like the idea of Buck, or anyone else for that matter, touching you."

"I didn't like the way she was touching you, either."

"Then let's get somewhere alone, so you can fix that, yeah?"

In a move he didn't expect, I grabbed his shirt, yanked him to me, kissing him long and hard. "Yes."

His eyes crinkled as I released him. He pulled the seat belt over me, securing it with a click. "Hold tight, happy bum. Mario is about to take over."

I laughed as he slammed the door. I was okay with fast right now.

Daniel

WE BARELY MADE it into her apartment before I had her tight to the wall, trapped with my body. Hearing her tell me she loved me made me wild. I had been holding back in order not to scare her by moving too quickly, but she was right there with me.

I made short work of her skirt, pushing it past her hips along with her lacy underwear, and lifting her to wrap her legs around my hips.

My pants hit the floor, the belt buckle making a loud thunk, and I was inside her. I surged deep and hard, needing the feel of her around me.

Her fingers clutched at my hair, her body shaking as I slammed into her. Her moans and whimpers were a low echo of the roar in my head that built along with the orgasm building in my body.

"Come with me, baby. I can't hold on," I pleaded, my mouth pressed on the soft skin of her shoulder.

She tightened her legs, arching her body, letting me deeper inside. My arm shot out, a loud crash exploding in the room as the lamp fell over. I hit the table with my hip and the dish she kept her beloved mints in scuttled over the edge, hitting the floor, candies scattering everywhere. Papers and mail followed, the sounds small echoes in the room. It did nothing to stop me.

"I'm fucking destroying your apartment."

"Destroy *me*, Daniel. *Fuck* me," she begged, in a husky voice.

Her words did me in. Hearing her curse and plead threw me over the edge, and with a low growl, I came so deep inside her, I knew she'd feel me for days. I wanted her to feel me—to know she was mine. Every part of her.

Avery hid her face in my neck, crying out. Her fingers tugged on my hair as her tongue swirled on my skin, her lips drawing into a pucker.

I pushed her face in harder as I felt the sting of her teeth sinking in. "Yeah, baby, mark me."

She shuddered, and her body became loose and heavy in my arms. She eased the sting of her bite with teasing caresses of her tongue, and I turned my head to drop a kiss to her hair. She lifted her face to mine, and minutes passed as we kissed, the intense passion draining into something softer—sweeter.

Gathering her to me, I stumbled back to the sofa, sitting down heavily, holding her. I snagged the blanket behind me, wrapped it around us, and relaxed back with a sigh. She rested her head on my chest, nestled tight. We were quiet, letting the emotion pass and calm to settle.

"Okay, Sprite?"

She peeked up at me, her sleepy eyes shining. "I'm good."

"You bit me."

"You fucked me."

"Touché."

"What is it with you and walls? I feel like an Avery filling in a Daniel and wall sandwich these days."

"Best damn filling ever." I ran my finger down her cheek, laughing. "And it's not just walls. Any hard surface will do."

She rolled her eyes at my words.

"I don't know," I confessed. "You bring out a passion in me I've never felt for anyone. I want you all the time. Besides," I added, lowering my head to hers, "you feel so damn good pressed between me and the wall."

"Or the truck," she quipped.

"Or the truck. The shower. The barn is pretty awesome, too."

I was granted another bout of her giggles. I loved making her laugh. I tucked a stray curl behind her ear. "I can control myself if you want me to."

"No," she admitted. "I like that you are so passionate with me. I've never had that until now."

"Get used to it, because I'm not going anywhere." I tucked an errant curl behind her ear. "I love you."

Her smile was like sunshine. "I love you."

I held her to my chest, dropping a kiss to her head.

She shifted a little and grimaced. "All this filling makes me a little messy, though."

I stood, taking her with me. "I think I hear another wall calling my name, Avery. I seem to remember a good non-slip mat in your shower."

"Yep," she happily agreed, kissing my shoulder. "An extra-good one."

"Perfect."

I WOKE UP, warm and entwined with Avery. We had spent the rest of the afternoon making love, fucking, napping, and talking. Mostly the first two. Her bed was a mess—blankets strewn around the floor, items knocked over on her dresser. I had also proven to her that kitchen counters were a great place for showing her how tasty of a filling she was, making her come with my mouth and fingers multiple times, until she was a shaking mass of nerves in front of me.

I carried her to the bathroom for yet another shower. As I adjusted the temperature, she shocked me by pushing me against the wall, grinning wickedly. "My turn for a Daniel filling."

I groaned as she sank to her knees, taking me into her mouth, her hands pressing my back into the cold tile. It was unexpected and highly sexy. She stared up at me, her mouth filled with my cock, and began a tortuous circuit with her hands, cupping my balls, rubbing my thighs, and teasing me with her lips and tongue. The erotic sight of her doing that to me, the warm water raining down over us, and the intense pleasure of her mouth was too much. I came down her throat, throwing my arm out to steady myself as I roared her name. I brought the entire shower curtain and rod down around us, as the steam billowed and my orgasm raged.

With mumbled promises of cleaning up all the damage, I tugged her back to her bed, found a blanket to cover us, then we fell asleep.

I blinked in the early evening dusk and glanced down at Avery. She was watching me with a small smile curling the edge of her lips.

"I don't think I have ever spent this much time in bed on the weekend," I rasped through my dry throat.

She leaned over and offered me a bottle of water. I accepted gratefully, drinking down in long swallows.

"We've been very lazy."

"We've been very destructive."

She laughed, the sound low in the dim light. "Nothing major. We'll clean it up fast." She frowned. "I am starving, though."

I finished the water. "Me, too. I'll take you out?"

"Don't really want to."

"Pizza? I can order in."

"Yeah, that sounds good."

"You have a number?"

She slipped out of bed and padded down the hall, returning a few minutes later with a menu. She laid my pants and shirt over the chair and handed me the menu. "I picked up the lamp, or at least what was left of it."

"What else broke?"

"Nothing. I picked up the bowl and the papers." She shrugged. "I sort of kicked all the mints under the table. I'll deal with those and the messy papers later."

"I'll fix the shower curtain."

"Okay."

"And replace the lamp."

She shook her head. "I was never overly fond of it. Luckily, it sort of broke in pieces."

I ordered the pizza, making sure to get plenty of olives on her half, and held out my arms. "Come here. I miss you."

She curled into my chest. "You're crazy."

"I am about you."

She burrowed closer. We lay enjoying the quiet, both of us drifting off. The knock at the door roused us, and I stood, grabbing for my pants, pulling them on, not bothering to do them up. I didn't plan to keep them on for long. "I'll get the pizza."

She sat up. "Okay. I'll get dressed."

I handed her my shirt. "This is all you need."

She laughed, accepting it. I bent low and kissed her, just as another knock, heavier this time, sounded.

"Impatient pizza guy." I huffed.

"He always is."

"Stay here. We can eat in bed and watch a movie." I plucked the shirt from her hand. "Actually, you won't need this after all."

She beamed at me. "Okay."

I made my way to the door, digging out my wallet. Another knock sounded. I flung open the door, not looking up as I took out some money. "Sorry, man. Got here as fast as I could."

All I heard was a muffled gasp, followed by a low curse.

Startled, I looked up and froze.

Thirteen

Avery

I CURLED UP, holding my pillow. It smelled like Daniel. Fresh grass, citrus, something musky, and all him. I pushed the book teetering on the edge of the nightstand back into place. We had certainly left a trail of our lovemaking behind us. I knew the term fucking was more accurate, but every time Daniel touched me, every time he was inside me, no matter how frantic it was, it still felt as if he were making love to me.

And he did love me. The way he said it in the truck, the emotion in his eyes, I could feel it everywhere. I could feel him everywhere. He filled up every corner of my mind—and my heart.

I rolled over to study the few movies I had piled up by the TV, wondering if he would want to watch any of them, when I heard hurried footsteps.

I sat up as Daniel came in, shutting the door behind him. I tried not to drool as I looked at him. His hair was disheveled, sticking up everywhere from my fingers. His torso was bare. His pants hung low on his hips, the button open. There were two marks on his neck and another on his chest from my passion earlier. He looked like sex. Walking sex. Then I met his gaze. His wide, panicked gaze.

"Daniel, what's wrong? Where's the pizza?"

He stepped forward, crouching down, holding my arms. When

he spoke, his voice was low and intense. "That wasn't the pizza, Avery."

"Oh Lord, was it Beth?" A chuckle escaped my lips. "She got an eyeful, didn't she?"

He shook his head wildly, and something in his expression made me realize he was being serious.

"What is it? Who was at the door?"

"Avery," he began in a nervous tone, "your parents are in the living room."

I SCRAMBLED OFF the bed, staring at Daniel in shock.

"What?" I prayed I hadn't heard him correctly.

"Your parents are here. In the living room."

I blinked, swallowed, then reached past him, grabbed a mint from the bowl and started chewing. Watching me fidget, he handed me another one.

"Say something."

I indicated him with a wave of my hand. "They saw you—like that."

"Yes."

"My father." I snagged another mint. "He saw you half-undressed and looking so . . ."

"Recently fucked, yes."

I shut my eyes, drawing oxygen into my lungs slowly to remain calm. When I opened them, Daniel was still watching me, apprehension in his gaze.

"You have to run."

His lips twitched. "Where would you like me to go, Sprite? Out the window?"

"It's only two stories. The worst that can happen is a broken leg."

"Ah, no. I don't think so. That would leave you here to face them alone."

"He won't kill *me*."

Leaning down, he picked up his shirt. "He won't kill me either."

"What did they say?"

"Your mother kinda gasped and your dad cursed and sputtered a lot. He thought he had the wrong apartment."

"Oh, God."

"I let them in and told them I would come get you."

"I don't know what to do."

He smiled in reassurance. "You go and say hello to your parents, and properly introduce me." He held up his hand. "After you get dressed that is."

I grabbed some yoga pants, and yanked them on, then I searched in the closet for a long-sleeved shirt, pulling it over my head.

Daniel handed me a brush, and I impatiently tugged it through my hair. I added a spritz of perfume, hoping it covered the smell of sex I had all over me.

Daniel was all over me.

I looked up at Daniel in trepidation. "I take back that statement. He might kill us both."

Daniel wrapped his arms around me. "He won't kill anyone. He—they both—are a little shocked, but they're your parents and they love you. They came to surprise you."

I couldn't help the hysterical giggle. "I think they got the surprise."

His chest rumbled with suppressed laughter. "They did." He dropped a kiss on my head. "Go see your parents, baby. I'll tidy up and be out in a minute."

"Do I look okay?"

"You look too good for me to be alone with you much longer. I don't think your parents would survive the shock." He pushed me gently to the door. "Go see them."

I grabbed a final mint. "Okay."

I ROUNDED THE corner. My parents were sitting with their

heads close together speaking quietly. I tried not to think about the fact Daniel and I had sex on the sofa only a few hours ago. I stole a glance around the room, grateful I had picked up the lamp and bowl earlier. I only hoped my mother wouldn't notice the mints.

I sucked in a long breath. "Hi."

They looked up. My mom stood, opening her arms. "Avery!"

She enveloped me in her embrace and I inhaled her scent. It was the same perfume I had known all my life—Elizabeth Arden's Blue Grass. She never changed. She smelled like Mom and home. I hugged her hard. Drawing back, she cupped my face. "You look so good!"

"I am," I assured her. "I am."

My father cleared his throat, and I smiled tentatively at him. "Hi, Dad."

He tilted his head. "Cupcake."

I relaxed a little. If he was still calling me Cupcake, he wasn't going to kill me.

"I'm sorry we came unannounced, and ah, interrupted your weekend." My mom patted my arm. "Your father wanted to surprise you."

"Actually, I wanted to find out why you never seem to be home when I call, and what was going on in your life," my father interrupted. "I guess I got my answer."

Before I could say anything, Daniel's voice broke in.

"That would be my fault, Mr. Connor. I work such long hours in the week, I tend to kidnap Avery on the weekends to my place outside the city."

My father regarded him. "Is that so?"

Daniel moved closer. His shirt was on, the collar hiding his neck. His hair was combed, his pants buttoned and when I looked down, even his socks were in place. He held out his hand to my father. "We haven't been properly introduced. I'm Daniel Spencer." He added after a slight pause. "Avery's boyfriend."

My father glowered at him. "I've never heard your name until now."

Daniel didn't waver, his hand never moving. "I've heard a lot of great things about you and your wife, sir."

My father finally shook his hand.

My mother smiled at him. "She mentioned you to me. A few times."

My father's eyebrows rose in surprise.

"It is nice to meet you, Daniel. Please, call me Janett." Mom paused eyeing my father, who didn't say anything. With a small shake of her head, she added, "And this is my husband, Doug."

"Pleased to meet you both."

An awkward silence ensued.

I shuffled my feet; feeling as if I were ten years old again and got caught doing something naughty. A small, nervous giggle escaped my mouth when I thought of just how naughty I had been all day. Three sets of eyes looked at me. My amusement stopped, and I felt as if I was going to throw up. A heavy knock at the door startled us all.

"The pizza this time, I presume," Daniel stated dryly. "I'll get it."

"I'll get some drinks. Excuse me." Then, like a coward, I escaped to the kitchen. I made some coffee then opened the cupboard and retrieved some mugs. I was reaching in the freezer for some cupcakes I knew I had in there, when Daniel walked in, carrying the pizza. He slid it in the oven and turned to me.

"Are you okay?"

I nodded. "You can go, Daniel. I'll visit with them and come see you later."

He took my hand, kissing the palm, holding it over his heart. "Nope."

"I have to talk to them."

"We'll talk to them together."

"You don't have to do that."

"Yes, I do."

"Why?"

"So one day when we tell our kids the funny story of the first time I met their grandma and grandpa, I can tell them how I stood beside you, then charmed the pants off both of them. Add in the story of how we met, and we have entertaining things to talk about at parties for years."

"Well, I'm not sure how fast my husband will give up his pants, but keep talking about a future with my daughter, and you have a good chance of getting mine, young man." Mom chuckled as she stepped in behind Daniel and winked at him. "I would like to hear about how you met, and why we haven't heard more about you until a few minutes ago." She reached for the tray. "I'll take the tray, Avery. Try to keep her away from the mints, Daniel. Hugs can usually help her calm down, too."

I gaped at her and Daniel smiled. His best, jaw-dropping, sexy smile that got me every time. He leaned down and dropped a kiss on my mom's cheek. "On it."

She picked up the sugar, adding it to the tray, trying not to grin. "From what I saw earlier, that much is obvious. Try to rein it in while Doug is around. His eye is twitching."

"I can do that."

"Good. Bring the coffee when it's ready. Oh! Cupcakes. Your father's favorite. That will help."

I stared after her as Daniel wrapped me in his arms. "Your mother's orders." He pressed a kiss to my head.

The coffee maker beeped and he picked up the pot. "Let's go face the music."

I poured some cream into the jug. "Okay."

Daniel

I FINALLY UNDERSTOOD the expression "cut the tension with a knife." No matter what I did, how polite I tried to be, I couldn't get Avery's father to talk. All I got were a few humphs, and a grunt to my queries of their trip. Doug Connor was going to be a hard nut to crack.

Not that I could blame him. I knew what it looked like when I answered the door. Well, it looked like exactly what it was. I had spent the afternoon fucking his daughter. I saw the way his gaze swept around the apartment, lingering on the broken lamp pieces, the dented shade, and the mess of papers haphazardly piled up on the table by the door—and the scattered mints. I swallowed thinking of the bathroom. If he got there ahead of me and saw the shower curtain on the floor and the towels strewn around, soaking up the puddles of water, I was undoubtedly, as Avery feared, a dead man.

Avery sat beside me, her fingers worrying the long hem of her shirt. I knew she was eyeing up the mints across the room, but didn't want to get up and get them.

I slid my hand into my pocket, fishing one out and slipping it into her palm.

With a small sigh, she popped it in her mouth, crunching away. It was the biggest tell for her. If she sucked on it, it was for enjoyment. If she ate it, she was tense. Judging from the sound of the candy being crushed, I would say she was beyond tense. Not caring if her father was watching us, I wrapped my hand around hers and lifted it to my mouth, kissing the knuckles, leaving our entwined fingers on my thigh.

He glared at my leg, but I refused to let Avery's fingers go. I knew what he was trying to do, except I wasn't going to let him intimidate me.

Finally, he set down his mug, with a loud thunk.

"What is it you do that is *out of town*, Daniel? Besides, of course, spending the weekends with my daughter."

I didn't react. Instead, I drained my mug, squeezed Avery's hand, and dropped a kiss to her head. "Great coffee."

I turned to her father. "I'm a vet. I run a practice with my brother-in-law and sister."

"How wonderful," Janett gushed.

"You live with them, too? Is that why you *escape* on the weekends?" Doug asked sardonically.

Avery began to speak up, but I held up my hand.

"No, sir. I own my own home. I own the practice as an equal partner. My truck is paid for in full, I have a good investment portfolio, and no huge debts. I'm close to my family, and for the record, I don't usually come here on the weekends. I have Avery stay with me since she enjoys getting away from the city."

"You have women stay at your place a lot?"

"Dad," Avery hissed. "Knock it off."

I waved away her objections. "Avery is the first woman I have had stay at my home. I don't do casual relationships, Mr. Connor. In fact, I'm rather insulted you think Avery would be involved in one. I think you know your daughter better than that."

"Is that a fact?"

"It is. Another fact is, although I'm sorry we met under such, ah, *uncomfortable* circumstances, I am pleased to meet you. Avery means a great deal to me, and I hope, at some point, we can be friends."

"Friends?" He snorted.

"The person I spend the rest of my life with will be my family; therefore, her family will become part of mine. Friends would be the least of what I hope we will become."

Avery's eyes widened at my declaration. Her mother gasped and clutched her hands together. Her father's shoulders sagged a little.

"Well, let's not get ahead of ourselves," he muttered. "I was just asking. It's my job, you know."

I eased back, not releasing my grip on Avery's hand. "Understood. However, I'm not Tommy Forsyth," I stated, reminding him of Avery's teenage first date he terrified all those years ago. "You can't scare me that easily." Letting go of her hand, I wrapped my arm around her shoulder, drawing her close. "I love your daughter, and she is too old for your curfews anymore."

"You think so, young man?"

I met his gaze. "I know so."

"We're not finished yet."

"I hardly expected to be. Just stating my case."

Avery leaned forward. "You *are* finished, Dad. I love him. He's the best thing that has ever happened to me. And he treats me like a queen."

"A little warning might have been nice."

"Right back at you."

He pursed his lips, studying his daughter. "Not quite the same, young lady."

She smiled; one that curled her lip to the side so it was crooked and sweet. "I wasn't ready to share him yet. I knew you'd get all overprotective and *fatherish* on me. I was worried you'd show up and embarrass me."

He winked, reaching for a cupcake. "Good thing that didn't happen."

It was as if the air grew ten times lighter. Everyone relaxed and I turned to Avery, thrilled at her declaration. That was twice today her words undid me. Hearing her declare she loved me did something to my body, infusing it with heat and the need to be connected to her. Slowly, I slipped my hand up her neck, enjoying the feel of her soft skin. I knew I was being watched, but at that moment, I didn't care. I tugged her to my side, pressing a kiss to her full lips. "Thanks, Sprite. I needed that."

"Anytime," she promised.

I chuckled against her mouth. "Let's hope this is a one-time occurrence."

Her father cleared his throat.

I took my time drawing back, refusing to let him dictate when I could show Avery affection. I enjoyed touching her too much. I dug into my pocket, snagging the last mint, and slipped it between her lips. She hummed, this time savoring the treat. I watched, fascinated as she rolled it on her tongue, humming in enjoyment. It reminded me of the shower earlier, and the way she had used her tongue on my cock. I blinked and breathed to control my body's response to the memory in my head. I stood, excused myself, and hurried down the hall to the bathroom—both to distance myself from being so close to Avery and to set the room to rights before her parents saw it.

I might have won over Janett, but Doug wasn't a sure thing yet.

I'd made my point already, but there was no need to poke the lion with a stick. I'd save that for another time.

Fourteen

Daniel

AFTER RETURNING FROM righting the bathroom, I sat with Avery and her parents for a short while. Then I made a few excuses to leave. I knew she needed time with them to discuss what they had discovered was happening with her life. As much as I hated leaving her, it was best to give them privacy.

Prior to leaving, I invited them to brunch at my parents' the next day. My thoughts were twofold. I could see Avery again, they could meet my family, and they would know I wasn't some sort of degenerate who lived with his sister and sponged off his family. I could talk all I wanted, but to see my life would convince Doug and Janett how serious I was about Avery.

Avery walked me to the door and stepped out in the hall with me.

"I'm sorry," she whispered, winding her arms around my neck.

Chuckling, I lifted her up. "Nothing to be sorry for, Sprite. It was certainly a unique way to meet your parents, but I survived."

"You don't have to leave."

"Yeah, I do. Spend some alone time with them. Call me when they leave. I'll be here in the morning to pick you all up."

"Can you come early?"

With a groan, I slid my hands down to grip her firm ass. "Give me five minutes, I could come right now."

Her laughter was muffled, but it made me smile.

"Can I have three from you?" she asked quietly.

I turned my face, my lips by her ear. I could give her a hundred, but three was easy.

"I love your light and goodness."

She held me tighter.

"I love your beautiful eyes."

She hummed.

"I love the way you take care of me."

"We take care of each other."

I set her down, cupping her cheeks, holding her gaze. "That's why we're perfect for each other."

She smiled up at me, eyes glowing.

"I don't want to leave, but I have to. I'll be here by ten. It's probably best if your parents don't show up and find me looking the way I did earlier today. Not sure your father would survive a second incident."

She wrapped her hands around my wrists, her thumbs caressing my skin. "Okay. I love you."

I yanked her back, kissing her hard. My tongue sought hers, tasting the sweetness of her and the sharpness of her mints. Burying my fist in her hair, I held her close, unable to find the strength to break apart from her.

Until I heard her father's voice, too close to the door for my liking. He asked if they were going to eat the pizza soon, or let it dry out in the oven. Regretfully, I released her, stepping back with a heavy sigh.

"I love you, Sprite. I'll talk to you later."

She ran her finger over her swollen lips. I liked the way she always did that—as if she was sealing in my touch.

I hated walking away from her, and even though I would see her in the morning, the rest of the evening felt endless.

THE NEXT MORNING, I drove in, picked them up, and took them

to my parents. Janett and Doug were welcomed by all, and as I expected, they warmed greatly to me due to the interactions they saw with the people I loved. Just to stack the odds in my favor, I had invited Beth and Ryan to brunch, as well. It turned out Ryan loved to cook, and he made the best French toast I had ever tasted. The way my family attacked it, I had a feeling they would be included in our brunches from now on. With the addition of Avery's best friend, it was a lively bunch at the table, with lots of laughter and teasing.

Janett watched me carefully while I played with Chloe. When my niece crawled into Avery's lap and snuggled close, falling asleep with her head on Avery's shoulder, her eyes misted up and her smile grew wide.

I met Janett's gaze, knowing she saw what I did. Avery fit in there, with us, *with me*, seamlessly. Even Doug was relaxed, talking football with my dad, and discussing past players they were both familiar with. His loud laugh reminded me of Avery's.

She was built like her mother, short and curvy, but her coloring and eyes, uniquely Avery. Janett's eyes were a vivid green and Doug's an unusual gray, which resulted in the silvery-jade I loved so much in Avery's gaze. Of the two, she was fairer, her skin pale and snow-white hair, while Doug's complexion was ruddier and his hair a dark gray. I had seen pictures of Janett's mother, and Avery did resemble her grandmother in many ways. Although, I thought Avery was more beautiful. Janett and Doug made a striking couple, and I could see bits of each of them in Avery—the shape of her mother's eyes and nose, the freckles, and wide smile from her father. The most amusing part was the fact Janett had the same habit of mumbling her thoughts aloud. More than once her musings made me chuckle. Apparently, she liked my tattoo—and my broad shoulders. I had to hide my smile.

I glanced around the table, sipping my coffee, relaxed. Caitlin smirked at me and pushed a football schedule my way. "The Argos defense sounds promising this year."

With a grin, I picked up the paper. "I hear Edmonton's offense is going to be unbeatable."

"Oh yeah? Care for a little bet again?"

I rubbed my hands together. That was one of our standing bets. I won more often than I lost. "Yep. Wager?"

She rifled through the paper and tapped her finger on an ad. "You have to take this pole dancing class. All six weeks."

I studied the ad. Pole dancing. It didn't sound fun, except I didn't plan to lose. My intel was solid. One of Dad's friends was a coach with the team.

I smirked at her, catching Avery's eye. She didn't look too upset at the thought of pole dancing. Maybe she'd enjoy the benefits if I lost this one. I might even be able to convince her to go with me. That would be a bonus.

"Pole dancing it is. You lose, and you have to wear a fake Justin Bieber tattoo for two weeks."

I held up my hand before she could agree. "I choose the tattoo and placement." I winked. "It will be visible."

Avery and my mother groaned.

Mom shook her head. "Will the two of you ever outgrow this?"

Sitting back, I laughed. "Nope." I ran my finger down Avery's cheek. "Besides, the last bet got me Avery. I doubt Caitlin is gonna get so lucky while she's sporting her Bieb's tattoo."

Caitlin snorted. "I hope you enjoy humiliation, Daniel."

"Bring it on."

Janett laughed. "I love how you two get along. Now tell me how you and Avery met, and what a bet has to do with it."

Beth held up her hand. "Oh, me! Pick me! I want to tell this story!"

Everyone laughed over her enthusiasm.

Avery narrowed her eyes at her friend. "My parents," she warned.

Beth waved her off. "Don't worry, Avery. I won't mention how the two of you tongue dueled five minutes after meeting each other." Dramatically, she covered her mouth. "Oops."

In that moment, I saw the distinct resemblance between Avery and Doug. Both of them looked scandalized, their eyebrows so high up on their forehead it was comical.

Janett only laughed and picked up her coffee mug. "Well now, this I want to hear."

Doug crossed his arms. "Yes, do tell us, Beth."

I saw the twinkle in her eye, and I leaned back in my chair, draping my arm around Avery's shoulders. Beth was so going to hang us out to dry on this.

I caught Avery's hand and snagged the mint from it before she could reach her mouth. Her mint eating habit was addictive. I knew she had plenty, and there was no way I could take it the way I preferred. Even with my parents there, her father would erupt if I stole it from her mouth. This would have to do. She frowned at me, then fished another from her pocket.

We sat, crunching away, as Beth regaled Avery's parents with the story of how we met, and I wondered if I would ever get off Doug Connor's shit list.

Avery

I WAVED GOODBYE to my parents as their car pulled away from the curb. I stood there long after the car had turned the corner, feeling the same sadness I always did when they left. A week was never long enough, and the time had gone by too fast. An arm wrapped around my waist, and Daniel's full lips pressed a kiss to my forehead.

"You okay?"

I peered up at him, offering a sad smile. "Yeah."

"They'll be back in a few months. They agreed to come for Christmas."

"I know."

"I know, you'll miss them." He tucked me a little closer. "I'm here, Avery."

I nuzzled his shoulder. "Yes, you are. Alive and kicking."

He chuckled, the sound rumbling in his chest.

After Beth had told her story, making sure to highlight and overdramatize every detail, I was certain Daniel and I needed to run. Except my mother had laughed so hard over the squashing of my fingers, the halitosis worry, and my fear of Daniel being a closet clown that even my dad relaxed and chuckled at her amusement. Luckily, Beth did tone down the kissing part and amped up the romantic angle. She talked about the ice pack and how he insisted on taking care of me, then invited me to dinner. Her story seemed to satisfy my dad, and he let it go. He adored Beth, and the way she told the story was hilarious.

More stories were shared of the over-the-top wagers between Daniel and Caitlin, much to Daniel's chagrin. Some of their antics were downright inane, but I still enjoyed hearing them.

When we left brunch, Daniel drove us to his house. He showed my dad around the clinic, and they disappeared to see the horses, leaving my mom and me to talk. I showed her the house and we walked the grounds. At one point, I saw Daniel and my dad in deep conversation by the barn. I started to walk toward them, but my mom insisted I leave them to "work it out on their own."

"If Daniel is going to be part of your life, you need to let them hash things out. Your dad will have his say, and Daniel can have his."

"Can he? Will Dad let him?"

She smiled, linking our arms, tugging me away. "I'll let you in on a little secret. Your dad isn't so bad. He's just being a dad. And he likes Daniel. He liked the way he stood up to him yesterday." She waggled her eyebrows. "That was quite a sight that greeted us when he opened the door. Your father didn't know where to look."

I sighed, thinking about how hot he had looked prior to the panic.

"Your man is rather sexy, Avery."

We both giggled.

"I know, Mom. I know. But he is even more amazing inside. He makes me feel so loved."

"He's the whole package."

I tried not to laugh at the fact my mother said package—or to think *about Daniel's package. I failed at both. Luckily, she laughed with me.*

She shook her head. "I think, however, next visit, we'll call ahead."

"Good idea. I thought Dad's head was going to explode."

My mom fanned herself. "I thought I might." She winked in an exaggerated fashion. "I swear, daughter of mine, if I was forty years younger and not so in love with your father . . ."

I didn't tell Daniel. I was sure his head would have been the one to explode that time.

I smiled up at Daniel. "They liked you—once they got over the shock."

"Good, because I'm not going anywhere."

"Good."

A wide, mischievous grin lit up his face.

I gasped in surprise as he swung me up into his arms, striding toward my apartment.

"What are you doing?"

"Your parents are gone."

"And?"

"Alone. We're alone for the first time in a week."

"Oh. *Oh!*"

His voice was a low growl in my ear. "I think it's time to find a wall and celebrate, Sprite."

A long shiver raced down my spine. "Walk faster, Daniel."

RAIN HIT MY window, the sound steadily beating against the glass. I glanced at my watch with a frown. Daniel was late.

He had called to say the roads were bad, but insisted on coming in to see me, even though I wanted to cancel.

We had been busy since my parents left, and it had been three days since I saw him. Tonight, we were going to dinner and a movie, then I would go back to his place for the weekend.

I sighed as I looked around my apartment. It no longer felt like home, but rather a place I lived. Daniel's place felt like home, because he was there. I planned to surprise him this weekend when he asked me to move in, as he always did, by saying yes. He certainly wanted it, and it didn't matter in the end what anyone thought, or said. It was right for us and I wanted it. I wanted to be with him more.

I already knew what would happen when I told him. His warm, blue eyes would light up, and my favorite smile would appear. The one that made his eyes crinkle and the dimple in his chin stand out. It changed his face from one of handsome to devastatingly irresistible. I loved making him look like that. Then he would find the closest wall and thank me the way only Daniel had ever thanked me.

My phone rang, and I grabbed it, not surprised to see Caitlin's number. She had been busy organizing that week's brunch and her calls had been frequent to check details.

But when I answered, it was the anxiety in her voice that instantly made me nervous.

"Avery?"

"Caitlin? What is it? What happened?"

Her words made my blood run cold.

"There's been an accident."

My heart raced in my chest, and my breath came out in heavy pants as I gripped the phone. "Daniel?"

"You need to meet us at the hospital. Don't drive—the roads are too bad. I already called a cab for you."

"Is he all right?"

"His truck was totaled. I don't know much about his injuries. Just get here, Avery. Town General."

Tears made my voice thick. "I'm on my way."

THE CAB WAS waiting when I exited my building, and despite the weather, I begged him to go as quick as he could. The fear in Caitlin's voice had shaken me. The thought of Daniel hurt, or worse, made me panic. The entire ride I prayed and pleaded, begging God to let him survive. As long as he was alive, it was fine. We could handle it together. But a world without Daniel seemed too much to face. He had to be okay.

I raced through the doors of the emergency room, immediately finding Daniel's family. His parents were standing together, his father holding tight to his mother. Caitlin was sitting, legs bouncing. Steven paced, holding Chloe, keeping her occupied. Caitlin saw me and stood, hurrying over, hugging me hard. I felt the tremors running through her body.

"How bad is he?"

"He's unconscious. We don't know the extent of his injuries. He's still being assessed."

"Where?"

She knew exactly what I was asking.

"His shortcut."

I shut my eyes, trying to hold it together. He promised me he would be careful. He told me he wouldn't speed on that road anymore.

"He was coming to me," I breathed out.

She stood close, shaking my arms. "Don't do that. You aren't to blame for this accident. He's used that road for years."

I opened my eyes and met her gaze. Eyes so similar to Daniel's stared back at me. There was no blame or anger in them. Only fear and anxiety.

"He's going to be okay," she assured me.

Inside, I was screaming. He had to be okay. I *needed* him to be okay. All I could do was nod. "He's tough."

"He is. He's Daniel." A tear slid down her cheek as she gave me a small smile. "I'm winning the bet right now. I plan on collecting."

"They only won the preseason, Caitlin."

She shook her head, speaking with conviction. "I'm still ahead. He *is* going to get better, and he *is* going to pole dance."

I hooked my arm through hers. "Okay then."

WE WAITED, ALL of us anxious and silent as we shared hugs and spoke quiet words to each other. I held Chloe so Steven could comfort Caitlin. Sean kept his arm around Julie, a pillar of strength for everyone, despite the worry I saw on his face. They had each other, but the person I needed to comfort me was somewhere in this building, injured and alone. I tried to stay calm, offering brave smiles and words of encouragement. Daniel would want that.

Finally, a doctor came out and spoke to the family. Daniel's arm was broken, three ribs were cracked, he was covered in contusions and bruises, and he was still drifting in and out of consciousness, but the tests showed no brain trauma. The air bags had saved his life, but his truck was a complete write-off.

Julie sank into Sean's chest, tears of relief flowing down her cheeks. Caitlin pressed her face into Steven's neck with a long, shaky exhale of air. I fought back tears, placing a kiss to Chloe's head, breathing out my thanks.

"Can we see him?" Sean queried.

"Family only and just a short visit. He will be in and out, probably more out than anything for a while. We'll monitor him closely."

Julie stepped over to me, her voice firm. "Avery is family. She's his fiancée."

I hid my surprise at her announcement. If it meant I could go in to see him, I was fine with her small fib.

The doctor nodded. "I'll make sure she is on the list." He paused and regarded us all. "He looks bad. There's lots of swelling and bruising, but I assure you he is stable. Keep that in mind when you see him. He might be fuzzy when he's awake, and that's normal. He has suffered a major trauma. He'll need a while to recover. However, I think he's going to be fine."

I tried to hide my tears, except it didn't work. A huge sob of relief escaped and instantly I found myself in Julie's tight embrace.

"He's going to be fine, honey."

I nodded against her shoulder. "You need to go see him."

"We all do."

"You go first with Caitlin and Steven. Chloe and I will wait here." I hugged her small body closer.

They seemed to realize I wanted to see him alone, and without arguing, they went down the hall. Once they disappeared, I sat down heavily, the relief in my body making my legs shaky. I sucked in some deep breaths, all while patting Chloe's sleeping form.

He was going to be fine. He would need time to recover, but he *would* recover. I said a small prayer of thanks, and waited.

WHEN IT WAS my turn to see Daniel, Julie came with me. Caitlin, Steven and Chloe left, Sean walking them out to their car.

He was so still when I walked in. I had to grab the bed rail for a moment as I stared at him, reminding myself he was going to be okay. His handsome face was bruised and cut from the broken glass of his windshield. His arm was encased in heavy plaster, and I knew under his hospital gown his ribs were taped. More cuts and bruises were on his arms and neck. He was hooked up to various machines, and although I knew they were for precaution more than anything, it was still a shock to see them.

As I discovered early on in our relationship, Daniel was a restless sleeper, his feet moved and his hands twitched. He often muttered in his sleep, lips pursing or frowning as he dreamed. But in the hospital bed, he was still, arms and legs unmoving. His eyes were shut, his chest rose slowly, and his face was impassive. I swallowed, trying not to cry again. Julie slipped an arm around me.

"He woke up a couple times earlier. He asked for you."

I could only nod, trying to fight down the emotional response I was feeling.

"Go to him. He needs you."

Hesitantly, I approached him, my hands hovering, needing to touch, to feel him, unsure where I could place them so they didn't cause him any pain. Finally, I traced my finger over his cheek, stroking the skin on the right side, which wasn't as bad as the left appeared to be.

Daniel rolled his head, leaning into my touch. His eyes flickered open, his gaze unfocused. He blinked, his eyes drifting shut again.

One corner of his mouth curled slightly, then he became still once more.

I ghosted my lips on his cheek. "Sleep, Daniel. I'll be here when you wake up."

He made a noise—somewhere between a groan and a grunt, and his fingers twitched by his side. I sat down in the chair beside his bed and slid my hand into his. There was the slightest of pressure before his body relaxed.

Julie laid her hand on my shoulder. "He's glad you're here."

"There isn't anywhere else I'd be." I cleared my throat. "And I'm not leaving until he does."

She chuckled softly and dropped a kiss to my head. "I'd expect nothing less."

IT KEPT RAINING. The sound was a constant dull beat against the window as I continued to sit beside Daniel's bed. The ward was quiet aside from the busy tasks of the nurses and doctors as they came and went. Daniel drifted in and out, mostly out. His eyes would open, his weary gaze finding mine, occasionally looking around the room, then closing again. He muttered incoherent words at times, and other than the random groan or mutter, was silent.

The chair I sat in was uncomfortable, but I refused to move. I held his hand, stroked his arm and head at times. He seemed to like it, his breath leaving his body in a long sigh as my fingers combed through his hair in gentle passes. I would get up and stretch, sip at some water, then return to his side. They assured us he would be fine. His body needed the rest. He would wake up in short order, and be more coherent.

It took me a long time to convince them, but finally Julie and Sean left after I assured them I would be staying. The ICU ward wasn't full, and although it was against the rules, I had managed to convince the staff to allow me to stay, since Daniel was in a private room, and I was very quiet.

It was now the middle of the night. I had been at the hospital for eight hours, waiting and watching, needing Daniel to wake up and say my name. I had kept myself together, for the most part, shedding some tears of worry in the bathroom. I had cried when I called my parents, who had immediately offered to return, but I assured them if I needed them I would let them know. Their offer, however, meant one thing to me. They liked Daniel and wanted to be there as much for him as for me. They had gotten along very well after the first disastrous meeting, seeing him for everything he was—kind, caring, and as in love with me as I was with him.

"Don't cry, Sprite." Daniel's low, raspy voice, broke the silence.

I sat up, startled, gripping his hand tighter as I stood.

I hovered over him, and caressed his face. "You're awake."

"Sort of."

I bent down to brush my lips over his cheek. "I'll take it."

He cleared his throat, and I reached for the ice chips, sliding one between his dry lips. He hummed in appreciation, opening his mouth for another one.

"I'm sorry I upset you."

"Stop it."

He tugged at my arm, asking me silently to come closer. I leaned in, lifting his hand to my mouth, kissing the bruised knuckles.

"What do you need? Are you in pain? Can I get the nurse?"

"No. I need you to know . . ." He cleared his throat again, the sound rough. I gave him more ice chips, letting the cold soothe his pain. When he spoke, his voice was quiet.

"I wasn't speeding. A deer ran out in front of me and I swerved to avoid it. I lost control."

"I know. The doctor said you couldn't have been going too fast or the damage would have been much worse." I hesitated, gathering myself, because "much worse" had deadly implications. "Your truck is totaled, though."

"Damn. I liked that truck."

"It doesn't matter. The truck can be replaced, you can't. You're here and that's all that matters."

"Yeah." He exhaled. "I remember the deer and the rest is a blur.

I sort of recall being airborne and the world spinning." He licked his lips. "I woke up here."

"Don't think about it. You need to concentrate on healing and feeling better."

He looked down at his body with a grimace. "Do I want to know?"

I listed his injuries with a steel resolve to stay calm. "You'll be off work a while. You won't be able to drive, either."

He frowned. "How will I come get you?"

I rolled my eyes. *That* was what he was worried about?

I cradled his face in my palms, and met his gaze. "You don't have to come get me, Daniel. Not anymore."

"Why?"

"Because I will be right there with you."

"I don't understand."

"I'm moving in with you."

All the pain and worry disappeared as his smile broke out. It was exactly the way I pictured it—aside from the cuts and bruises marring his handsome face. "Yeah?" he breathed out.

"Yes."

"Soon?"

"I'll bring my stuff gradually. But I'll be there to look after you."

He tugged my arm, and I lowered my face closer to let him kiss me. I knew what an effort that was, so I stood back. "But for now, you're going to rest."

"Already bossing me around."

"Get used to it."

He squeezed my fingers. "Happily."

I sat down, stroking his arm.

We were quiet for a few minutes.

"Avery . . ."

"Hmm?"

"Can I have three?"

I held his hand to my face. "I love you so much, Daniel Spencer, and I can't remember what my life was like before I met you."

"Hmmm."

"I'm going to nurse you back to health."

His lips curled up. "Does that include sponge baths?"

I chuckled, then stood and pressed my lips to his.

"I am never letting you go. Ever."

"Perfect."

I kissed him again, smiling when his lips moved against mine. "Here's a bonus. I can hardly wait to live with you. I want to be with you every day."

He sighed, eyes drifting shut. Our short exchange had exhausted him. But a smile played on his lips.

"I like the bonus."

Fifteen

Daniel

"**IS THIS THE** last of it?" I asked.

Avery nodded her head as she looked around her apartment.

"Are you sure you don't want any of this furniture, Sprite? We have lots of room."

"No. These are all just pieces I picked up second hand, and a few were already here when I came. The girl moving in is thrilled to have them. My bed can go in the guest room, and we already took the few pieces I wanted to your house."

I dropped a kiss on her cheek. "Our house," I reminded her in a gentle tone.

"Our house," she agreed. "Our home."

I kissed her again. It was a home only when she was there, and now she'd be there every day. I was spoiled always having her around.

I had spent a couple days in the hospital, relieved when I was released and able to return home. I ached all over, my arm uncomfortable, and my ribs felt as if they were on fire every time I moved. It had felt awesome to walk in my front door though, even if I moved at a snail's pace.

Over the next few weeks, I learned how short my patience was with my physical limitations. I needed help to do everything, and I had to rely on my family and Avery for it all. She took some time off and was with me for the first couple weeks. She handled my recuperation better than I was able to, rarely losing patience with me. I hated that I needed help to shower, dress, sit, and even shave.

I discovered quickly I was shit when it came to using my left hand; the nicks on my face and neck were proof, after I insisted on shaving myself the first day. Avery had teased me as she blotted the blood on my skin. *"Really, Daniel. You survive a roll over, then take yourself out with a razor because you're so stubborn?"* I laughed because she was right.

She refused to allow me to feel sorry for myself or to do too much. I had to admit I enjoyed the naps she insisted on taking. They started out as a necessity for the first few days, then became an excuse to lie down with her nestled beside me. We watched movies, talked, and she read to me, her voice soothing and relaxing me.

As my energy returned, we walked around the grounds, exploring and enjoying the time together.

However, she had to return to work, and after a few days alone, I was going stir crazy and started wandering to the clinic on a regular basis. At first, Caitlin and Avery objected, but Steven was on my side and we came to an agreement. I couldn't lift or examine animals, but I could help consult and offer suggestions. I was careful not to overdo, and it helped pass the hours of the day.

Avery brought a few things with her every night when she returned. Beth and Ryan were amazing and helped her on the weekends, bringing more of her possessions to the house. She put the boxes in the guest room, unpacking them gradually, and today was the final lot. I drove in with her; not once did I make fun of her driving. The few lessons I had with her had helped her relax behind the wheel, but I knew she would always be an overcautious driver. I didn't suggest we take the shortcut. I knew she would never drive that road again, even on the sunniest, driest of days.

I had my dad drive me there one day to see where the accident occurred. Evidence still remained of the damage my truck had done when it flipped over.

My stomach lurched when I saw the massive upheaval of earth and roots the truck had driven in the ground.

Dad stood beside me, his hand firmly on my shoulder as we surveyed the area.

"Avery hates it when I use this road."

His voice was low when he spoke. "Your mother hates this road, too, Daniel."

I glanced at him. "She never said anything."

"You're a grown man capable of making your own decisions. So she kept her opinion to herself. But I think now you have two very important women in your life who hate it. You may want to make a change." He paused for a moment. "Caitlin isn't big on it, either."

"Oh."

"Neither am I."

I nodded, surprised at the thickness of his voice. There was no choice to be made in the matter. "Well then, I guess the majority rules."

We were both glad to leave the scene. The fact I wasn't the only vehicle on the road that fateful day was a miracle. The person following me had been the one to call 911, and because of them, I was rescued promptly. The EMT who arrived on the scene knew me and called my father as soon as we were en route to the hospital. I still had only vague recollections of what transpired, and I was okay with not remembering. I knew how upset Avery got when someone broached the subject.

"Will you miss your own space?"

She shook her head. "No. I look forward to our life together, Daniel."

"You may change your mind when I start physio next week and am grumpy all the time."

She laughed, bending over to pick up a box. I had to resist taking it from her. I knew my limitations, even if I tried to push the boundaries at times, a full box was impossible.

"You're already grumpy, so I think I can handle it. We'll figure out a goal for you to work toward, and perhaps that will help."

"I have three goals in mind."

"Ah, the three. Go ahead."

"Yep. My dad and I are going to start looking for a new truck in a couple weeks when the cast comes off."

"Okay."

"I'm going to start more hours at the clinic."

She pursed her lips at my announcement, but didn't argue. "And the third?"

I wrapped my good arm around her, tugging her close. I buried my face into the crook of her shoulder and dropped a kiss onto her neck, smiling at the shiver that ran through her. "That one is a two-part goal."

"Oh?"

"Sex with you as soon as possible."

"I like that goal."

I pressed my mouth to the sensitive spot behind her ear, flicking my tongue on her skin. "And as soon as possible, we're going to test every wall in our house, Sprite. Every. Single. One. We'll revisit a few, too."

She whimpered. I knew physically, she missed being with me as much as I missed being with her, but it had been impossible, and the few things we could manage hadn't been enough for either of us. Once the cast was off, and my ribs healed more, all bets were off.

I eased back, grinning at her flushed cheeks. "But for now, let's get you home where you belong. Maybe we can celebrate a bit later, yeah?"

She lifted up on her toes. "Yeah."

Three months later

THE SUN WAS bright, the warmth soaking into my skin as I bent down, and snapped another small flower off the stalk, placing it into the small bouquet I was creating. Below, the wind stirred up the water, the waves hitting the sand rhythmically.

We had sat by the water when we first arrived, then spent the hours enjoying the late fall sun and the lushness of the hilltop. Avery loved to go there and enjoy the peacefulness of the secluded area. I enjoyed having her all to myself.

Inspecting the arrangement, I had a feeling it wouldn't pass Caitlin's scrutiny, but I knew Avery would love it. At that point, there weren't many flowers left to pick, but it did the job. Kneeling, I pulled the ribbon I'd taken from her drawer of hair things out of my pocket, clumsily tied it around the stalks, then made one last addition.

I looked over toward the thick grasses. Zen grazed a few feet from Avery who sat cross-legged on the blanket, book open, an apple clutched in her free hand, no doubt forgotten as she lost herself among the words in front of her. I loved how she could go hours without moving when she read. Often, I would wake up and find her nose-deep in a book, or with the light of her Kindle shining as she read in the dark. I could watch her without her knowing, delighting in her facial expressions as she discovered some new world or fell in love with some strapping hero in a sweeping saga.

I glanced down at the bouquet. It was time to start a sweeping saga of my own. Taking in a calming breath, I walked over, stopped in front of Avery, and kneeled. I waited patiently until she finished the page, closed the book, and shifted her attention to me.

"Nice walk?"

My muscles were still stiff, and my arm ached at night, but I was almost as good as new. Therapy was complete, and I worked diligently on my own, making sure my muscles stayed strong. I had used the excuse of needing to move around in order to prepare my surprise for Avery.

I nodded, bringing out the small nosegay from behind my back, swallowing my nerves. "I picked these for you."

Her eyes filled with delight, and she took the flowers, with a happy hum. "So pretty! Thank you, Daniel," she sighed as she ran her fingers gently over the blooms.

Her response pleased me. She adored simple, heartfelt gestures, and I knew she loved the funny-looking bouquet I picked for her as much as if it had been a huge arrangement delivered by a florist, because I had done it myself.

However, my ragged offering was special. I waited, nervous, as she sniffed and gazed at her flowers. I knew the instant she spotted the addition.

Her eyes grew large, shoulders tensed, and a small gasp flew from her mouth. When her eyes found mine, love and tears were overflowing.

I picked up her small hand, clasping it over my heart. "This is yours, Avery. It has been since the very second I stepped on these fingers and held them in my hand." I lifted her hand and kissed it, holding it against my mouth. "These lips became yours the instant they touched your sweet mouth. My life became yours. You became my entire world." I took the ring from its bed of green leaves, slipping it onto her finger. "Wear this and show the world you belong to me." I paused to gather my nerves. "Marry me. Please."

"Daniel," she breathed out my name as tears ran down her face.

"Happy tears?"

Her book flew to the side as she launched herself at me, dropping tiny, wet kisses all over my face. "Yes!" She sobbed. "Yes!"

"Yes, happy tears, or yes, you'll marry me?"

"Both!"

I held her tight to my chest, blinking at the surge of emotion that welled up.

She said yes. She was mine.

AVERY WAS WRAPPED around me, her head resting on my chest. Every so often, I felt her hand unfurl as she stared at her ring.

"How did you know?" she murmured.

I cupped her chin, lifting her face up. "Beth," I admitted. "I know you don't wear much jewelry, but I noticed you seemed to wear older-looking pieces when you do."

"I love jewelry that has a history," she confessed, twisting her hand so the stones caught the light.

"Beth gave me the name of the little shop you like to go to and I went in and spoke to the owner. She had recently acquired this ring from an estate auction."

"It's perfect."

"The story is it was purchased in England and brought here for his betrothed—hence the rose gold. The couple was madly in love and married for over sixty years. The ring was passed down to their son, who never got married. It was part of his estate." I picked up her hand and kissed it. "It was part of a great love story then—and now."

"It's perfect. If I could pick any ring in the world, this is exactly what I would pick. I love it." She pressed her lips to mine. "I love you."

"Good thing." I traced my finger down her skin. "You agreed to marry me."

"I did."

"Soon?"

"If you want."

"I want. Why wait? Unless, you want a big, fancy wedding?"

"No."

I huffed a sigh of relief. I didn't want a big one, either. "When?" I implored.

"A couple months?"

"Next week."

She laughed. "And you called me impatient the first day we met. One month."

I smirked. That was easier than I thought. "Done." I held her tight. "One month today. Where?"

"The house?"

"Perfect. Guests?"

"Family. Friends. Small."

"Perfect. My mom is gonna freak."

Avery snickered. "My parents have barely recovered from me moving in with you. Now I have to tell them we're getting married."

"Not an issue. I already spoke with your dad."

"You did?"

"I told him the first weekend, when we were walking around the grounds, that you were it for me, and I planned on marrying you. He gave me his blessing before they left."

Her eyes shone verdant green in the sunshine.

"So we can tell my family tomorrow." I smirked. "No doubt, they'll drag you off and commence wedding plans."

"Probably. With their help, it will be easy. I don't want anything over the top and fancy."

"What about me? What do you want me to do?"

Avery pressed her lips to my ear, making me shiver. "Honeymoon," she murmured, a husky note to her voice.

I dropped my face to her neck. "Hmmm. I can handle that."

"You have to tell me what to pack."

"Your toothbrush." I swirled my tongue on her silky skin.

"Nothing else?"

"No." I moved my mouth to her ear, nibbling on the lobe. "You, me, and a sunny, private beach. No clothes needed."

"Daniel—"

"Okay, a couple of dresses. Little ones. And a few pairs of shorts for me in case we run out of milk." She giggled as I rocked, sending us tumbling to the blanket, then I hovered over her. "Otherwise, you're naked. I'm in charge of this honeymoon thing, so what I say goes. Got it?"

She gazed at me tenderly, her eyes warm and bright. They were filled with love—love that was mine and mine alone. She would belong to me for the rest of my life. And beyond. Her arms wound around my neck, pulling me down to her mouth. "Got it."

I was going to like this marriage thing.

Eighteen months later

I ENTERED THE house, and my heart dropped in my chest at the silence. I knew what time of the month it was. I knew how hopeful Avery tried to be. She remained doggedly cheerful every month, and then when we failed to conceive again, her pain was tangible. The sobs she thought I didn't hear when she shut the door leading to the bathroom tore my heart out. More than once, I had found her weeping into a towel, trying to hide her anguish, and I would gather her up into my arms and hold her until the storm passed. Every month it got harder, though—on each of us.

My feet dragged as I walked down the hall. I pushed open the door, expecting to see a small ball of misery in the center of our bed. Instead, Avery was sitting against the headboard, reading a thick file, Dex curled up by her feet. She looked up startled, as I walked in.

"Oh! Daniel, I lost track of time. I don't even have dinner going."

I sat down beside her, relieved, stroking Dex's head. He was a constant companion to her most days. She still looked sad but not as devastated as usual.

"How about some noodles and Kung Pao?" I offered. "I'll go pick it up?"

She nodded, but that was her only response.

"Are you, um, okay?"

She was resigned. "I'm not pregnant."

I leaned forward, nuzzling her cheek, trying to offer what comfort I could. "I'm sorry, Sprite."

"I made a decision."

I rubbed my hands up and down her thighs in comforting strokes. "Tell me."

"I went and saw the doctor today. She gave me a referral to the fertility specialist."

"Okay, this is good." We had talked about the possibility of taking that course of action. We'd been tested and tried other solutions. That was the next logical step.

"I see him in two days." She held up the file. "She gave me a bunch of stuff to read."

"Okay. I'll read it when you're done."

"Can you come with me?" She sounded unsure.

I kissed her. "Try to keep me away."

Six months later

I PATTED LUCY'S head. "She's doing great, Mrs. Thomas." I made a note on the chart. "Hopefully I won't see her again for another year." Escorting her to the front, I smiled. "Caitlin will send you the reminder. If you need anything before then, we're here."

"Thanks, Dr. Spencer." She beamed in gratitude. "Oh, hello, Mrs. Spencer!"

I looked up, surprised to see Avery. It was only two o'clock. Moving forward, I wrapped my arm around her, bending to kiss her cheek.

She surprised me by turning her head, pressing her mouth to mine. Hard.

Her eyes were dancing when she drew back, smiling. "Hi," she whispered.

"Hi, your own sweet self. This is a nice surprise." I nuzzled her lips. "You okay?"

She had been fighting the flu the past week or so, sleeping a lot, and her appetite had been off.

"Yep. I'm good. Caitlin says Steven can handle the rest of the afternoon after your next patient. Can you come home?"

I tightened my arm. "You sure you're okay?"

She nodded. "Come home as soon as you can."

I watched her leave. She didn't seem upset. She didn't seem anxious or worried. She was calm, and her eyes were clear. Maybe she simply wanted my company—or even better, perhaps she wanted something else.

During the past months, we tried so hard not to let the romance leave our lovemaking. While it was never a chore to make love to my wife, there were times it was frustrating for both of us to have to schedule it. We preferred spontaneity. Maybe Avery was feeling . . . frisky, which meant she *was* feeling better. Maybe we needed to saddle up Zen and take a short ride to our beach. However, a glance out the window changed my mind. It looked as if it would start to rain soon.

Oh, well. A warm soak in the tub or a hot steamy shower would work, as well. We'd gotten good in each of those places.

Whistling, I walked to my office. "Let me know as soon as Mr. Warren's here, Caitlin. My wife is waiting."

I heard her chuckle as I sat at my desk and transcribed the last patient file, grateful the next animal was for a vaccination. I'd be home soon.

IT STARTED TO rain while I walked the short distance to the house. I found Avery sitting at the kitchen table, sipping a cup of tea, a plate of her cupcakes in front of her. I poured myself a cup and grabbed one of the treats, leaning over to kiss her as I sat down. "Tea? That's unusual for you."

She spoke over the edge of her cup. "Easier on the stomach."

"Um, I think you should go see the doctor, Avery. It's been a week, maybe even more."

"Good idea. You can come with me."

I blinked, and was sure my mouth dropped open. She rarely agreed when I worried about her.

Still smiling, she dropped a couple sugar cubes in my tea and handed me a spoon. "We'll go next week. Tuesday, in fact."

"Avery—"

"Stir your tea, Daniel."

Frowning, I mixed in the sugar, wondering why it was so freaking important right now. I tapped the edge of the spoon on the cup with a little more pressure than needed, glancing down at the spoon as it slipped from my fingers, the light glinting off the silver. It wasn't one of our regular spoons—it had writing on it. I tilted my head and picked up the spoon to study it closer. My eyes widened as I read the small inscription.

YOU'RE GOING TO BE A DADDY

My head snapped up to meet Avery's glowing countenance. "Sprite?"

"Congratulations."

I was on my knees in front of her in a split second, one hand stretched across her stomach while the other hand buried itself into her thick hair. Luminous green met awestruck blue. Tears shimmered in her gaze, but the pure joy that was radiating from her, left me breathless. My mouth covered hers in a deep, soul-shattering kiss that left us panting. I leaned my forehead against hers. "Say it."

"I'm pregnant."

I drew back, cupping her face. "They said it would take time, maybe more than one round . . ."

She ran her fingers through my hair. "I know. I wasn't even thinking when I saw Dr. Hastings this morning. She did a pregnancy test, then told me the news." Her mouth curled into a small smile. "I was so shocked when she asked about my period, and I realized it was late."

"You waited all day to tell me?"

Avery rolled her eyes. "I saw her three hours ago. I was so dazed I sat in my car for a while. Then I had to go and find your spoon."

"Are you okay?"

"I'm good. I have to go see Dr. Pritchard next week."

"Tuesday."

"Yes."

"That's why you've been so tired."

"Yes, it is."

"I want to take care of you. Both of you."

"Oh, Daniel, you already do," she crooned. "We're so lucky to have you."

"Do you need anything? Is there something I should be doing?"

"No. Let's just enjoy this and celebrate." She covered my hand with hers. "Our baby."

"Our baby," I repeated in awe.

Her lip quivered. "Yes."

"My parents, my sister—Beth . . . *God,* they're going to be so excited. When can we tell them?"

"Let's wait 'til after next week." She decided. "I picked up some other spoons, too! They'll love it!"

"I love *you.*"

She cradled my face between her palms, her expression one of joy. "I love you."

I WAS ANXIOUS as I paced the small room.

Avery laughed at me. "Relax, Daniel."

I stared at her, incredulous. How could she be so calm?

The ultra sound technician and the doctor would arrive any minute, and I knew—I was *certain*—they were going to tell us Avery was having twins. They had told us it was a possibility with the fertility treatments, and although we'd been fine with the idea, the thought it might be a reality, was making me nervous.

When I had brought the idea up, Avery remained composed, only shrugging and stating we would know soon enough. But she was already huge. Not that I would ever tell her that—again. I had discovered only a few weeks into her pregnancy she was freakishly strong. The word "huge" would never pass my lips again, and I wasn't sure my right nipple would ever be the same.

At only eight weeks, she looked bigger to me than I would've expected; even given her tiny stature. I was so confident last night, I got up and measured the room Avery wanted as a nursery; to make sure we could fit two cribs and dressers, and a change table in it.

The door opened, and Dr. Pritchard came in smiling as he looked at us. Tall and older, he radiated a calm Avery and I liked. "How are you?" he inquired as he shook my hand.

"I think it's twins," I blurted out.

His eyebrows shot up as he snickered. "Well, I guess we'll see in a few minutes. Should I ask why?"

I arched my eyebrow at him and side-eyed Avery. I didn't want to say it out loud. She might hurt me again.

"He thinks I'm already showing too much for it to be one baby. *Huge*, I think, was the word he used. Right, Daniel?" Avery smirked at me from the examination table.

I found the smirk rather sexy.

Dr. Pritchard started to laugh. "Oh, Daniel." He clapped his hand on my shoulder. "I'm surprised you're walking upright." He pulled up the stool, still laughing. "You'll learn, son. You'll learn."

"I already did," I murmured, absently rubbing my nipple.

He chatted with Avery and took some notes while the technician got everything ready. I sat down beside Avery, held her hand, grinning as she gasped over the cold gel, and watched eagerly as the wand began to move. Dr. Pritchard was quiet as he checked and measured, his eyebrows rising as he peered at the screen and then threw me a smirk. "So you think it's twins, Daniel?"

"Yes, I do."

"Looks as though you're correct."

I felt a little smug. I knew she was too big to be carrying only one baby. I smiled down at her, trying not to chuckle over her panicked expression.

"It's okay, Sprite. We'll figure this out. We'll have plenty of help," I assured her, pressing a kiss to her palm.

Dr. Pritchard suddenly barked out a laugh. "Well, it looks like you're going to need it."

I looked at him puzzled. "Oh?"

"You were wrong. I was wrong. It's not twins."

"Oh, well, one is fine." I squeezed Avery's hand, wondering if she was upset, but she wasn't looking at me. Instead, she was staring at the monitor.

He turned and faced us fully, his finger tapping the screen. "I hope you have a big house. It's triplets."

Now, she looked at me, her eyes as big as saucers.

The word echoed in my head.

Triplets.

The last thing I heard was my voice, loud and ringing in my ears. "The cribs won't fit!"

MY EYES FLUTTERED, and I frowned. Why did my head hurt so much? I looked around. Why the hell was I lying on the floor? My puzzled gaze met Avery's startled eyes, and it all hit me.

Avery was having triplets.

Triplets.

Three babies. We'd made not one, not two—as I'd suspected—but three babies.

I was gonna be a daddy to three babies. All at once.

How the hell did I get on the floor?

Dr. Pritchard chuckled as his hands slipped under my arms, pulling me off the floor. "Up you go, my boy. Sit beside your wife." Still laughing, he handed me an icepack and my glasses. "You might need that. Nice goose egg."

I looked at Avery sheepishly. "Oops."

"Are you okay?" She stroked my head, concerned. "I guess that was a bit of a shock?"

"Three babies, Avery!" My hand flew to her stomach.

That changed *everything.*

She smiled, her eyes wide, beaming with happiness. "I know."

"The nursery will have to be down the hall. Three cribs won't fit in the room."

She laughed. "So you yelled just before you passed out." She cupped my cheek, brushing her lips over my skin. "It's okay, Daniel. We'll figure it out."

I pulled her close, burying my face in her neck. "Avery, we're gonna have three babies. Three!"

"Your favorite number."

I kissed her and ran my hand in small circles over her stomach where my children were growing. "These are the best three of them all. Thank *you*, my beautiful wife."

Panicked, I looked at Dr. Pritchard. "Did I miss the heartbeats?"

Both he and the technician laughed. "No, Daniel. You, ah, interrupted the ultrasound."

"Sorry."

"You up to finishing the scan?"

I nodded eagerly, wincing a little.

"Okay. Let's finish this up, then we'll go to my office and talk. I've no doubt you have many questions. I'll give you some Tylenol, as well." He threw me a grin as he lifted Avery's T-shirt. "Try to stay upright, Daniel."

I chuckled. "Just don't change your mind and tell me you missed another one."

"Don't even say that!" Avery gasped, her fingers pinching my side.

I groaned as I rubbed the sore spot and kissed her head in apology.

Freakishly strong.

I needed to remember that if I was going to survive this pregnancy.

And then . . .

The rapid sounds of multiple heartbeats filled the room and nothing else mattered.

Only Avery and my three children.

My family.

Sixteen

Daniel

I SLIPPED IN the side door, to greet my mom, and Janett. She had arrived a few days prior to help Avery during the last part of her pregnancy.

"How is she?"

Janett shrugged. "Cheerful. Tired. Crying. Anxious. And all in the space of about ten minutes."

"Uh, yeah." That was about normal these days. "Is she asleep?"

"I think so."

"I'll go check."

"Don't wake her if she is, Daniel."

I held up my fingers. "Scout's honor."

My mother snorted, looking up from peeling potatoes. Avery had a constant craving for them now. "You were never a scout, Daniel."

I chuckled. "I won't wake her up."

I peeked in the door, my lips curling into a smile at the sight of my wife asleep on her side. There were various pillows surrounding her, to support her now undeniably huge stomach, but I was sure she was still uncomfortable. We only had a short while to go, then Dr. Pritchard was confident the babies would be fine if Avery went into labor. She was confined to bed, and if needed, he was prepared to put her in the hospital. She didn't want that, so she was following his orders to the letter.

Some days were harder than others were, though.

Most of the time, Avery was strong. Happy. So thrilled to be carrying our children, the difficult days were easier to handle. She was usually more tired and worried on those days, and the thing that seemed to make it easier on her was if I was beside her. I would talk and tell her stories, stroke her hair if she cried, and I'd kiss her until she fell asleep.

I'd kiss her a lot.

It was, my Sprite informed me, still her favorite thing.

It was mine, as well.

I started to step back when her wide eyes met mine and I realized she'd probably been awake the whole time. Slipping inside, I lay beside her, my hand rubbing her stomach in large, soothing circles.

"You're supposed to be asleep. One of our moms will kick my ass." The two of them were a force to be reckoned with, and I didn't want to test it.

"I rest better when you're here." Her hand covered the top of mine. "Can you stay?"

I kissed her forehead. "For a while. I want you to shut your eyes and rest."

"I'm tired of resting."

"You only have to make it another couple days, Mommy."

I knew she wanted to last longer and give the babies more time inside her. None of us expected her to make it this far, but she proved to be right. My wife was stubborn to the core. The problem was that they were getting bigger, and she was so small.

"You've done so well, Sprite."

A small tear rolled down her cheek and I kissed her smooth skin. "Don't cry, Avery. Please."

"Can I have three?" Her voice was soft and pleading.

I leaned my forehead to hers. She needed lots of threes these days.

"Everything is fine. You and the babies are doing well. We'll get to hold them soon." I pressed another kiss to the side of her lips. "And here's the bonus. I love you."

A small shuddering sigh rippled through her. "I love you, too."

"Then everything is good. Right?"

"Another kiss would make it perfect."

I nuzzled her mouth until she was asleep.

I STOOD, LOOKING down in amazement at what Avery and I had done.

Our children.

All three of them—at once.

Two boys and one girl.

I thought I was ready for today. I had read up on the subject of multiple births, I knew everything that could occur, and I was ready for all emergencies.

Nothing I read prepared me for the emotion of seeing my children as they were born.

Nothing prepared me for the incredible joy I felt when I knew they had all arrived safely, and Avery was fine.

I took more pictures and a short video, then left them sleeping to go back and check on my wife.

I walked into her room, meeting her exhausted, but happy eyes.

"They're perfect, Avery."

I showed her the pictures and video, reassuring her that they were all doing well, and she would be able to see herself the next day. "And for the first time since they were born, all three of them are asleep at the same time."

That made her laugh. They had been active and fussy, but finally exhausted themselves and slept.

I leaned down and kissed her. "And Mommy should be sleeping, too. You must be exhausted. You were amazing today, Avery. Just amazing."

"You'll stay close to them?"

I wrapped my hands around hers, squeezing them in comfort.

Our children had to stay in NICU for a while since they had been born early. Avery's biggest concern was the fact she wasn't able to be beside them every moment.

"As soon as you're asleep, I'll go back."

Nothing was going to keep me away from my children.

"They're so small." She looked back at the pictures. Her lip started to tremble as she gazed at our children.

"Small but healthy," I insisted. "Dr. Pritchard is in awe of how long you carried them. He was sure you wouldn't make it to thirty-four weeks. You gave them the best chance we could have hoped for, and in a few weeks, we can take them home." He was filled with praise for Avery, and he had been a constant support to us during the delivery.

"Things will certainly feel real then."

I ran my fingers through her hair. "It's all worked out. Between our moms, Caitlin, Beth, and the nanny we hired, we're covered. You can recover, our children will be cared for, and we will find our way. Together—the way we have from the start."

She nodded, eyes heavy, fighting the weariness I knew she was feeling.

"Sleep, Sprite."

"We have to choose their names."

"After you sleep, before the crowd arrives."

I knew my dad was holding them back; otherwise, the room would already be full. The last I heard, he had made a list and assigned times to everyone, so we weren't overwhelmed. My mom laughed at him, but he insisted a schedule was the best way to go.

"I'm sure there will be lots of people, more flowers, and presents arriving." The room was already full of packages and bouquets from friends and patients. The one set of flowers that arrived with clown balloons attached was carefully removed before Avery saw the scary faces on them. I could only imagine the reaction they would have caused.

My gift to her was still in my pocket. When we were alone later, I would give it to her. Three slender white gold rings to represent each of our three children. Two were delicate woven vines and the middle one was a simple band, and they all fit together perfectly. Scattered with diamonds, they caught the light beautifully and I knew she would love the rings.

She fell asleep fast, exhausted from everything she'd been through. I sat beside her, wanting to make sure she stayed asleep before I left and went back to our children. I heard the door open behind me, and my mom entered in the room. She walked over and wrapped an arm around my waist. "How is she?"

I smiled. "Magnificent."

She smiled in agreement. "I popped in and saw the babies. The nurses said they're all doing well."

"They are. I was going back as soon as I knew she was asleep."

"You go be with your children," Mom urged. "I'll stay with my girl here. Janett will be here shortly, too. When she wakes up, we'll let you know."

I watched my mom stroke Avery's hair, her eyes filled with love for my wife. She had become a second daughter to her and my dad, and the sister Caitlin never had. I had become Doug's "favorite son-in-law,"—a term he enjoyed throwing around when teasing me. He and Janett had become part of the family and visited regularly during the pregnancy. I had a feeling we'd see even more of them now the babies had arrived.

I dropped a kiss on my mom's head, a gentle one to Avery's smooth cheek and left to go back to my children.

THE UNIT WAS quiet when I returned the next day with Avery. We watched our little miracles together, our hands held tight. Her poignant reaction to seeing them made my throat ache with emotion.

"Dr. Pritchard says he is sure they'll only have to stay a few weeks," I told her, keeping my voice low.

"I can't wait to hold them."

I knew how she felt. We were allowed to touch them gently,

skin to skin, but as a precaution, we hadn't held them yet.

"Soon, I promise. Only a couple more days." I kissed her hand. "You ready to choose their names?"

"Maggie Rose," she replied with no hesitation.

I laughed at her decisive tone. She'd been firm on that name for a while. I liked it; it was pretty, so I nodded in agreement.

"And?"

"You choose the next one."

"I still like Carter as a name. And we can use your dad's as the middle one."

"Suck up. You're already the favorite."

I laughed at her teasing. "Just cementing it in for life."

"Carter Douglas Spencer?"

"Yes. It's a good strong name for our oldest."

Avery grinned. "Oldest by one minute. Carter Spencer. I like that."

Both boys had been born before Maggie—a fact I knew they would hold over her the rest of their lives.

"Okay." I reached into the tent, placing my hand on my son's back. "Our middle child."

"Our troublemaker."

Avery insisted he was the one who caused her the most grief in her pregnancy—pushing on her bladder and shoving the other two for room. One of them had been in constant motion, often a tiny hand or foot clearly visible through her skin, pushing and shifting. My other two children came out quiet and laidback, but he arrived, screaming and red-faced, arms flailing and legs kicking, letting us know he wasn't pleased to be outside his warm nest. It only made sense he'd been the active one inside, as well.

"Dylan?" I offered. It had been on both our lists. "It sounds like a good name for a troublemaker."

"Dylan," Avery repeated. "Dylan Spencer. What about a middle name? Sean after your dad?"

"Dylan Sean Spencer," I mused. "It does sound good." I transferred my hand to each of the other babies, keeping my touch light as I gazed down on them. I sat back down beside Avery. "Carter, Dylan, and Maggie. Yes?"

"Yes."

"I have a feeling those three names will be shouted out in succession many times over the next twenty years. Although, if he holds true to your prediction, Dylan's name will be the first one I shout."

Avery cupped my cheek. "You're going to be a great daddy."

I covered her hand with mine as my eyes filled with tears of tremendous emotion. The last couple days, the stress, and excitement crashed over me, and I felt vulnerable. It was something I knew only Avery would understand. "I love them so much," I whispered. "I love you."

She moved closer, and I met her partway so there wasn't more pressure on her incision. Her lips met mine. "We love you. All of us."

I kissed her with utter abandon. Everything I felt for her was in my kiss. Love, happiness, lust, gratitude, and complete adoration.

All for my Avery. My Sprite.

For what she meant to me.

For the blessing of my children.

For the rich, full life she'd created with me.

I pressed another light kiss on her lips, both of us smiling and breathless when we broke apart. Without a word, I slipped her rings on her right hand and bent down to kiss her finger where they rested. I held them against my mouth unable to form the proper words to express how profound my feelings were for her. I lowered my head to her shoulder, needing the comfort of her touch. Her hand slipped into my hair, caressing my scalp in light, loving touches, conveying her own silent feelings.

As the crest of emotion passed, I lifted my head and entwined our hands, her new rings glinting in the light.

Together, we watched our children sleep.

I HUFFED A sigh. *"Really*, Beth. You had to put bows around my children?"

She laughed. "It's just for the pictures, Daniel. You can add in their names and use them as announcement cards, too. Avery thought they were cute."

I looked back and had to grin. They were adorable, and if Avery liked them, then it was fine. All three of them were asleep, their little bums sticking up in the air and a huge silky bow—blue for the boys and pink for Maggie, who was always between them—resting on top of their diapers. It would make a cute photograph; although, I could imagine the horror the boys would experience when they saw the picture as teenagers. I could already see Avery cooing in delight as she showed it to their girlfriends and went on about how precious they were as babies.

Maggie, of course, would not have to suffer that indignation, since she wouldn't be allowed to date until she was thirty—at the earliest.

We'd only been home for about a week with the babies. They had done surprisingly well. After two weeks in NICU, they were ready to go home, and I loved having my family all together.

Avery was discharged after five days, but we'd spent most of our time at the hospital to feed and be involved hands-on with the babies. If Avery had her way, she'd have been there 24/7, but she did listen to Dr. Pritchard and came home in the evenings to rest and look after herself. I loved being able to care for her during those short hours, and I catered to her every whim, wishing there was more of them. She was an easy patient.

Now she was home for good, the house buzzed all the time. There were constant feedings, diaper changes, and people milling around. My favorite time of day was late in the evening, when it was only Avery, our little ones, and me. I'd carry them in, and we'd sit on our big bed, cuddling and talking to them, delighting in every noise and facial expression they made.

The first time I held them in the hospital was one of the most profound moments in my life. Feeling their tiny, warm bodies snuggle into mine had brought forth the most intense, protective feeling I had ever experienced, only rivaling the one I felt for Avery. I knew there was nothing I wouldn't do for my children; I would protect and love them at any cost. Seeing Avery hold them brought tears to my eyes at the utter joy in her expression. I felt complete.

Together, we had become a family.

Avery came in, smiling at our babies, ghosting her hands over their backs. Her rings glinted in the light, small sparkles reflecting on the walls around us as her hands stroked and soothed the tender skin. Bending down, she kissed all three, then finished with a lingering kiss to my mouth. Not one to miss an opportunity, I dragged her face close to mine and kissed her again. And again. Each one deeper, longer, and more passionate.

She whimpered against my lips. "Is six weeks up yet?"

I rested my forehead to hers. We were having trouble waiting, but knew we had to follow the doctor's orders. "Soon," I promised.

She dropped another lingering kiss on my face. "Good." She chuckled. "If we can find any time."

I laughed into her hair. "I'll hire a night nanny, as well. I have a feeling we're going to need one, anyway."

Right on cue, she yawned. "I might let you do that without much fuss," she admitted.

Neither of us were getting much sleep, and we knew things wouldn't change for a while. My mom knew someone who was happy to work nights, helping new parents. I'd get her number.

I hugged her close. "I'll call Phyllis tomorrow."

Beth came in holding her camera. "Okay. People are arriving. Let's take these pictures, then we can get the munchkins dressed."

I stood up grumbling. I knew I'd agreed to the small get-together so our friends and other family could meet the triplets, but I still hated sharing. I wanted every moment when I wasn't at work with them. "I won't even get to hold them this afternoon. Everybody will want a turn."

Avery laughed as she handed me Maggie. "It's only for a couple hours, Daddy. Then you can have your baby girl back."

Maggie snuggled into me, and I held her close, breathing her in. She had me wrapped around her tiny finger so tight I would never be free again.

"Okay, fine." I pouted, knowing Avery would kiss me if I did.

I was right.

HOURS LATER, MY favorite time of day arrived. It was just my family and me. I stood over the cribs, looking at my children—who were all asleep at the same time, for a change. It had been a big day for us. They were passed around, cuddled, kissed, and cooed over all afternoon. I'd never been hugged that much in my life. Avery was pampered non-stop, and given more advice than she could possibly remember.

We had all been thoroughly loved.

New presents were piled on the dressers. Stuffed animals, dozens of pieces of clothing, toys, and books were all there. Caitlin had tracked a careful list of the gift and giver, so thank you cards could be sent later. Tomorrow, I'd have the picture of the triplets done into the right format, and Avery would start the process. Of course, I would do everything I could to avoid helping with that task, aside from signing my name at the bottom of the note.

I stepped into our room, my eyes falling on the gift that now hung over our bed. The moment Avery opened it and stopped crying, she begged Ryan and me to hang it. It was a collage done by Beth with the inscription "It Started with a Kiss" across the top. It was our life in a combination of special photos. The center was a screenshot she had taken from our first gentle kiss at the studio. Around it were pictures of our wedding, Avery round and glowing with our children, and finally, one of us she had taken recently. It was of Avery and me together with her on my lap and all three babies held by us. My entire family encased in my arms.

It was, as Avery stated, the most perfect gift—ever.

Arms slipped around my waist, and I grinned as Avery appeared at my side, snuggled under my arm. I nuzzled her hair as we both stared at the picture.

"Who knew?" she breathed out. "Who knew the day I walked into the studio, scared and worried, we'd end up here?"

I tugged her tighter to my side.

"I still owe Caitlin for that one. I'll never be able to repay her. Best bet I ever lost."

"You changed my life, Daniel. You kissed me and changed everything."

"You made mine complete."

She turned in my arms, and her eyes met mine. They looked up at me with the same sweet expression they did the first day I met her. A swell of tenderness filled my heart as memories of that day flooded my head.

Smiling, I reached over and slid off her glasses, as I pushed mine up into my hair.

"Avery, can I try something?"

Her smile—that special smile she had only for me—curled up the corners of her inviting mouth.

"Anything, Dr. Spencer."

We were smiling as our lips met.

Epilogue

Dates with Maggie

Age Three

I YANKED ON my tie. I couldn't get it straight—the damn thing was crooked again. Groaning, I shook my head.

Why the hell was I so nervous?

Caitlin appeared behind me, having overheard my mutterings—a habit I picked up from my wife. "Because the last date you went on, brother of mine, was with Avery, and that was yeeeeeeeaaaars ago."

I smirked. "Thanks."

She laughed and grabbed my shoulders, turning me around. She fiddled with my tie then stepped back. "There, perfect."

"Okay."

"You made the reservation?"

"Yep."

"Flowers?"

"In my office."

"Music?"

"Loaded."

"Then all you need is the girl."

"You're right."

The girl.

My baby girl.

C⟍

I ROLLED MY shoulders and knocked on the door. I could hear muted voices, picking out Avery's easily. Then behind the wood, I heard my Maggie, calling to her mother. "Da handle's too high, Mommy."

I kneeled down and turned the knob, pushing the door a little to help her. Maggie's sweet face and wide smile greeted me as the door swung open. "Daddy!" she crowed, clapping her hands. "You's hewe!"

I handed her the small bouquet of baby pink roses.

Pink roses for my Maggie Rose.

Her little mouth formed an 'O' as she stared at them. She always loved it when I gave Avery flowers, dipping her little head into the blossoms and sniffing. This was the first time she'd been given flowers of her own.

I was starting a tradition.

"So bootiful!" she lisped, gazing up at me.

"So are you, Princess. Is that a new dress?"

She nodded, excited, twirling around. I bent over to stop her from hitting the door after her second twirl. She was just like her mother and too familiar with the floor and edges of furniture. I lifted her into my arms, delighting in her little butterfly kisses she dropped all over my face. It was her favorite game: grabbing my face and kissing it until I laughed. It was my favorite, as well.

"Yook!" she squealed, pointing to her feet. "Mommy gots me new shoes, too!"

I lifted one tiny foot, admiring the pink and white shoe.

"It's got bows, Daddy! Yike my hair! Dey match!"

"Did Mommy do that for you?"

"Yes. I kisseded her for it."

"Good. Mommy deserves lots of kisses."

Avery appeared from the kitchen, smiling and shaking her head. "I see your date has arrived, Miss Maggie, and he's already talking about kissing. Tsk, tsk."

Maggie giggled—a sweet, high-pitched, little girl giggle that always made me smile. "He's funny, Mommy."

Avery's loving eyes met mine. The silvery-green, and deep emotion held within them, still made me breathless when she looked at me.

"He is funny." She laid her hand on my arm, her lips skimming my cheek. "And wonderful," she breathed into my ear.

I shifted Maggie into one arm so I could wrap the other around my wife. "Everything set for tonight?"

"Yes." She winked at me and kissed Maggie. "Are you taking your flowers with you, young lady?"

Maggie nodded. "To the restwant."

Avery smiled and repeated the big word slowly. "Rest-au-rant."

Maggie frowned. "I saided dat."

Chuckling, I dropped a kiss on Avery's head. "Yeah, Mommy. She did." Looking at Maggie, I grinned. "Ready to go, Princess?"

She clapped her hands eagerly. "To da date, Daddy!"

We were walking down the steps when Avery called out. "Remember what I said to tell your date, Maggie!"

"Oh, yeah." Maggie looked up at me, serious, as I lifted her into her car seat. "I haf to be home by seben. Dats my bedtime."

I glanced at my watch. Three hours.

I only had three hours?

I looked back to Avery. "Eight!"

She laughed as she went back in the house. My wife knew me well enough to know three hours wouldn't be enough time with my girl.

A lifetime wasn't enough.

MAGGIE'S FAVORITE SONGS from *Frozen* were on repeat in the car. Luckily, we arrived at the restaurant before my voice gave out. We did great duets together. It was another tradition when we were in the car.

I carried her inside, since she didn't want her new shoes to get scuffed up. I settled her into a booster seat, and once she was satisfied her flowers were okay in the glass of water our waitress kindly provided, I ordered her favorite dinner: cheese pizza for two. Since it was our first date, as a treat, I also ordered her all-time favorite beverage: chocolate milk.

Once she'd had a couple sips, I grinned, running my fingers through her curls that spilled over her shoulders. Carter and Dylan both had my brownish-red colored hair, but Maggie's was even brighter than her mother's was. Her hair was a mass of blonde curls, the color so light it was white when it glinted in the sunlight. Her eyes were hazel, often more green than blue, while her brothers had my blue irises. They towered over her, always having been in the top percentile of their range, while she had remained in the bottom, small and perfect, just like her mother. "You ready?" I asked, knowing what she wanted me to say.

She nodded.

"Go!"

What came next was our daily ritual. One I had with all my children. It was their time to tell me everything that happened while I was away from them. I sought out each of them, one by one, to listen. Although, usually, what happened, was I'd end up on the floor with all three of them piled on top of me, talking at once. I loved hearing their excited voices and laughter.

Maggie more than made up for her brothers not being with us as she babbled away. She'd had such an exciting day of shopping, exploring, discovering a new kind of jam for her toast Mommy had let her try, and even found her lost button we'd hunted for the other night. She filled me in on how Dylan had been bad—not a big surprise—Carter had scolded him, Mommy had made cookies after lunch, and Grandma had stopped by for a visit. Her eyes were serious as she assured me she'd scrubbed "extra hard" behind her ears for our date.

"See?" she demanded, leaning over and turning her head.

I inspected the smooth skin and bent down, blowing a raspberry behind her ear. Her loud giggles made me laugh, and we were still smiling when the pizza arrived.

A non-stop monologue continued over dinner. I kept interrupting by slipping bites of pizza in her mouth, knowing Avery wouldn't be happy if she found out Maggie hadn't eaten. Shamelessly, I bribed her with dessert if she finished her dinner, and finally, she tucked in and polished off her slice. Dessert disappeared significantly quicker. I barely got my spoon into the gelato.

Again, just like her mother—and I wouldn't have it any other way. My girls owned me. Totally.

Back in the car, I changed Maggie's shoes and we went to the park. The slide was out, because of her "pwetty dwess," she informed me, but the swings and teeter-totter were her go-tos, anyway. I pushed her higher and faster, loving her laughter. On the teeter-totter, I was rewarded with her giggles when I would "bump" her hard enough she'd "pop" off the seat.

We ended up with more ice cream, sitting under a tree. I gathered her onto my lap, occasionally licking the cone when it melted, saving her new dress from complete destruction.

"Daddy?"

"Hmmm?"

"Is we gonna haf anofer date?"

"Yep. Every second month. You and me."

"What 'bout the ofer months?"

"Those are fun nights for me with the boys, so you and Mommy can have girl time." I had tried taking them one at a time, but the boys preferred to go together. Avery and I decided to try it, and it worked well. Everyone was happy, so that was all that mattered, and I got more date time with Maggie.

"Can we go to putt putt?"

I chuckled, tucking a stray curl behind her ear. "Mini golf?" They all loved playing games.

She nodded; her mouth full of ice cream.

"Sure, my girl. Whatever you want."

All of a sudden, though, she yawned. Her eyes scrunched up,

mouth wide, the remains of her ice cream still lingering in the corners. I glanced at my watch, surprised to find it past seven. Time had flown by. It always did when I was with my kids.

I wiped her mouth and popped the last of the cone into my mouth. She snuggled tight to my chest, happy to be still and held close. I knew she had to be tired, since she was never quiet.

She grew heavier and I stood, carrying her to the car. She slept the entire way home.

Avery met us at the door, a tender smile on her face. "Hey."

I bent down, to kiss her full lips. "Hi, Sprite."

"Good date?"

"The best."

"You tired her out."

"Yeah, but we had a great time. Why don't I go tuck her into bed, then we'll see if I can tire you out?"

Avery laughed. "Good plan, Daddy."

I smiled all the way down the hall.

I liked this tradition.

Age Fourteen

"DAD!"

"What?" I smirked, nuzzling her head.

Maggie pushed away from me. "You can't hug me in front of the kids at school!" she scolded, looking around, then scampered into the car.

I chuckled as I went to the driver's side and slipped in. "Is this a new rule?"

There were always new rules in Maggie's world.

She rolled her eyes, tossing her hair over her shoulder. "Mom gets it."

I pulled away from the curb. "Mom gets everything—she's cool. You gotta cut your old man a break, Mags."

Maggie's voice changed. It softened and she smiled at me.

"You're pretty cool too, Daddy."

I squeezed her hand. "Thanks, Princess."

"Are we going for pizza?"

"Your turn to choose—whatever you want." She was old enough now I let her choose our date locations. We had our favorites, but we tried to vary them.

"How about Chinese? I feel like some noodles."

"Sounds good. After?"

"Mini golf. I've got a score to settle with you."

I laughed. "Bring it on, little girl."

I LOOKED AT her wide-eyed across the table. "Dylan did *what?*"

She giggled—the sound that still made me smile. "He did, Daddy. Three Cokes, one after the other, then he walked past Mr. Victor's table and burped. It was so loud everyone in the cafeteria heard it. It was epic."

I groaned. Dylan was in constant trouble with his history teacher. No doubt, Avery would be telling me the whole story when I got home.

Only then, I couldn't laugh about it.

We had a strict policy about date night. What we talked about remained between us. It was the same as girls' night and when I was with the boys. Unless Avery and I thought it was something important we had to share, we kept our children's confidences. Luckily, nothing major had ever come up, until now.

"What happened?"

"Dylan stopped and looked horrified. He gave the best apology you ever heard. He even sat down and told him about how the phrase 'excuse me' started." She giggled again. "He spent all night last night looking it up. Not even Vicky could be upset after his little speech."

"Mr. Victor," I corrected.

She waved her hand. "He's such a jerk, Daddy." She scowled. "I don't like how he treats Dylan."

I smiled at my girl. All three of my children were close and protected each other fiercely. Dylan and Carter might drive her crazy, but if someone so much as looked at either of them funny, she'd go all momma bear on them. The boys were even more protective of their only sister. Nobody was allowed to mess with their Mags.

"Dylan likes to wind him up."

She snorted—another trait she had picked up from her mother. "He needs to be wound up. He's the most boring teacher we have." Leaning over, she grabbed another egg roll. "Seriously, I learn more from Uncle Steven and Auntie Caitlin during our family dinners than from old Vicky. He's useless."

"I know, kiddo, but he's your teacher and he deserves your respect."

She opened her mouth to argue, but I gave her my patent don't-argue-with-me look and she dropped it.

She finished her egg roll, wiping her fingers on the napkin. "Daddy?"

"Yeah, my girl?"

"I love my flowers."

I still bought her a bouquet for every date. Avery told me she pressed one flower from each bunch I had ever given Maggie, and they kept them in a special book. I tried to change it up, but after ten years, I knew I'd repeated a few.

"Good."

"Can I ask you something?"

"Anything."

"If there was something I wanted, would you let me have it?"

I shifted in my seat. That was dangerous ground and I'd fallen for it before. "It depends."

"It's nothing dangerous or illegal."

I felt slightly better, but still suspicious.

"What is it?"

"Josh asked me to his prom. I want to go."

I gaped at her. "His *prom*? You're . . . you're fourteen!"

"He's ahead of me in school."

"You're too young to date."

"We'd be going with a group of friends, Dad."

Oh—now I was Dad, not Daddy.

I preferred Daddy.

I decided to buy myself some time.

"I'll talk to your mother."

"I already did. She said I had to talk to you."

Damn it.

"Have I met Josh?"

She rolled her eyes. "Yes, Daddy. Many times. You like him."

So many kids hung around my house day in and day out; especially after we installed the in-ground pool and the kids began swimming. I wasn't sure which one was Josh. "Which one is he?"

"Tall, dreamy eyes, and dark hair. His dog is Rufus. You look after him."

I snorted. "Well, I don't recall the dreamy eyes, but I do remember how tall he is. Rufus is a great dog. He treats him well."

Her hand covered mine. "Please, Daddy. I–I like him. I want to go."

The kid was friendly and polite—I remembered that much. His dad, Jeff, was a good guy, too. There was only him and Josh; his mom passed when he was little. Jeff had done a great job raising Josh.

"I'll talk to your mom."

"Okay." She squeezed my hand. "You could even be a chaperone, if you want."

Hmmm.

I shook my head as I laughed. "You're good, my girl."

"It was Mom's idea."

I knew I was going to lose if I objected. I could at least keep an eye on them if I was there. I drew in a calming breath, unexpectedly feeling old. "I think we can work something out. But there'll be rules. My rules."

She rolled her eyes. "There always are." Then she smiled; that beautiful Maggie smile I could never resist. "Thanks, Daddy."

I signaled for the check. "Okay. Let's go play some golf."

"Daddy?"

"What?"

"I'm glad you didn't freak out or anything. But you're still going down."

I laughed.

There was my Maggie.

cN

Age Seventeen

"MAGGIE, PRINCESS, TELL me what's wrong."

She looked up from her uneaten pizza, eyes bleary and sad. I should have known something was drastically wrong when she asked to go for pizza, then ordered a plain cheese pie and chocolate milk. She hadn't ordered that combination since she was ten. Not even my flowers had gotten much of a reaction. She kissed my cheek. That was all.

The only conversation I'd gotten out of her was short, monosyllabic answers. Tugging on my hair in frustration, I tried again.

"Sweetheart, you can tell me anything."

"Why are boys such jerks, Daddy?"

I inhaled sharply. That wasn't what I expected.

"Um, is this a general question, Maggie, or do I need to go find Josh and have a talk with him?"

"I don't understand him!"

I bit back my amusement. "We generally don't understand you either, my girl." I wrapped my hand around hers. "What happened?"

"I asked Josh today if these jeans made my butt look big."

Oh, God. He hadn't.

Any male over twelve knew the right answer to that question.

"What did he say?" I was prepared to tell her how her butt was not big and Josh was an idiot.

"He said no. Then he walked away." Maggie's lip trembled, then suddenly she started to cry—big, wet tears rolled down her face. I pulled her into my arms, attempting to soothe her, as I tried to figure out how to get Avery to join us.

If he said no, I didn't understand the problem; so obviously I was missing some huge key in the girl world. Avery would know what to say and do to make Maggie feel better.

After a couple minutes, she drew back and wiped her face.

"Do you want to go home and talk to Mom?" I asked.

"No. I want a guy's perspective."

Shit.

Things were so much easier when I could buy her a new My Little Pony.

"Did you want to go to the mall and buy a new pair of shoes . . . or something?"

She glared at me, picked up her chocolate milk and downed it, then stood. "I'd like another glass of milk. I'm going to go wash my face."

As soon as she was gone, I called Avery, and told her what just happened. "What's going on with her?"

She chuckled. "I think it's PMS, Daniel."

Shut up.

"My Maggie? *PMS?*" I whispered-yelled.

"She was a little emotional this morning, as well. She'll be better tomorrow. I'll give her some Midol when she gets home. In the meantime, get her some more chocolate milk."

Oh, Lord, I was in way over my head.

"Never mind tomorrow, what about now? She wants to talk boys," I hissed.

She chuckled. "Then talk boys. Give her your expert opinion."

"My opinion is I think they're all after one thing and she should be locked up 'til she's thirty, but you won't let me."

"Go ahead and share that with her today," she retorted dryly. "She'll punch you."

"I need you here."

"Nope. She wants her daddy. I gotta go. See you later. Love you!" She hung up.

Maggie returned, looking calmer. I slid her fresh glass closer, hoping the chocolate would help. It always helped Avery.

I exhaled and straightened my shoulders. "Okay, Maggie. I don't understand. Josh didn't tell you that your, ah, butt looked big, so tell me why you're so upset."

She regarded me as if I had sprouted an extra head. "He didn't tell me it looked good either."

I blinked.

Then I glanced around the restaurant, wondering if I was being set-up. Was I being *Punk'd*? Was Avery standing somewhere with Beth, taping our conversation, laughing as I tried to figure out what to say?

I looked back at Maggie, then took a drink of water, wishing it was alcohol—very strong alcohol.

"Did, you, um, ask him?"

"What?"

I cleared my throat. "Did you ask how your butt looked in your jeans? Directly."

"No."

I warmed to the subject a little. "We men are fairly simple creatures, Maggie. If you had asked him how your butt looked instead of asking *if* it looked big, I think you would have liked the answer better."

"Really?"

I nodded. "Our brains don't work the same as yours do."

She frowned, grabbed her phone, and sent off a text. Picking up her milk, she sipped, watching the screen. "Is that because teenage guys are always thinking about sex?"

The water I was swallowing caught in my throat, and I coughed loudly. "Where did you hear that?" I sputtered.

"Everyone knows that, and I asked Dylan—he said it was true. Plus, I've heard you say it often enough."

Oh.

"I'll talk to Dylan, and sometimes I say things I shouldn't. Ask your mom. She'll tell you I'm whacked." I lowered my voice. "Is Josh, ah . . . ?" I left the question hanging.

Her mouth dropped open, cheeks flaming. "No! Daddy—no! He knows I'm not ready. We're both waiting."

The fondness I had for Josh increased tenfold. "Oh. Well, good to know."

Her phone buzzed and she picked it up, reading the screen. A huge smile spread across her face and she typed back a reply. She picked up her pizza, took a large bite, and chewed happily. "Are we going to play mini golf after dinner?"

Her sudden change in mood surprised me. "You, ah, want to?"

"Yeah, that'd be great."

I looked around once more. I'd missed something. "You feel better now?"

"Yep. I asked Josh. Just like you said."

"Oh."

She beamed. "He said my ass looked fantastic. The best ass in the whole school."

Oh, God.

If that was how things were going to go down from now on, Avery was coming with us on our next date.

Age Twenty-Six

MAGGIE DROPPED A kiss on my cheek before sliding into the booth. "Hey, Dad."

"Hi, my girl." I was only Daddy on the rare occasion now.

She picked up her bouquet I had waiting, and inhaled the pink and white roses, sighing with pleasure.

"You look beautiful today."

She smiled at me, fingers tracing over the blooms. "Gran says I look just like Mom did when you married her."

"You do."

She was Avery all over again. My sons were both tall—taller than I was—but Maggie took after Avery, in every aspect: her light-colored, curly hair; her small stature; and her gentle, caring spirit. She carried peppermints everywhere she went, and she even hated clowns. They were so similar it made my chest ache.

Her eyes were the only difference. Swirls of blue and green made up the hazel irises. Their color caught the light and reflected her moods. Today they were calm, the green more predominant, and she did look like Avery. Her hair was caught up in clips and it hung down her back in masses of curls. She claimed to hate it, but I loved it. So did the other man in her life.

I poured her a glass of wine, remembering our earlier dates of pizza and chocolate milk. Now they consisted of wine and some interesting entrée she would choose for us. As a food critic, Maggie loved trying new food, and we'd been to many different restaurants over the past few years.

"How's your mom?"

Her eyes crinkled in amusement. "I exhausted her today, I think. The boys were taking dinner to her."

"Good. Everything set?"

"Yes." She grinned, looking more like a teenager than a young woman. "Two days from now I'll be married! Can you believe it!"

I shook my head, still unsure where the time went.

Our children were all grown and on their own.

Carter was married already, with our first grandchild on the way. Avery and I adored his wife, Suzanne, a soft-spoken, kind woman. He worked in the clinic with me; his path as a vet set early on in life, and he never wavered.

For the longest time, we thought Dylan was destined to be a wild bachelor, forever coming home for meals and to have his laundry done—until the day he met Laura. The transformation had been mind boggling. Dylan settled down, his priorities and lifestyle changed drastically. Avery considered Laura an angel. He still traveled a lot as a freelance journalist, but his life had developed into something resembling normalcy.

Maggie lived not far from us, and as of Friday, would marry her high school sweetheart, Josh. He'd been part of our lives for many years; he was already like another son. The day he came to Avery and me, to ask for permission to marry Maggie, there'd been no hesitation from either of us. We were thrilled to have him as a permanent part of the family. He'd called Avery his adopted mother for years, and she was pleased to know he would officially be her son now.

"I guess our dates are done."

"What? No, Daddy! I don't want them over!"

My chest warmed at her endearment. "Really?"

She covered my hand with hers. "I love our time. I'd miss it too much."

I squeezed her fingers. "So would I."

The entrées came, and I smirked. "Maybe we could stick to dinner. I'm getting a little old for mini golf."

She giggled, the sound making me feel nostalgic. "You're not old, Dad. Mom still says you're the sexiest man alive."

Avery did still think that way. I thought she was pretty hot too, and I showed her as often as possible, but I didn't tell my daughter. She'd probably cover her ears and leave the table, gagging.

"Regardless of how sexy your mother thinks I am, I'm tired of losing to you young people."

"But maybe every so often? For old time's sake?"

I relented. I could never say no to her. "Every so often."

She talked during dinner about some wedding details. Over coffee, I sighed. "Next time we do this, you'll be a married woman."

"I'll still be your little girl, Daddy. I always will be."

"My Princess." I reached into my jacket and took out a small box, sliding it across the table. "For you."

"Daddy?" Her voice was thick with emotion.

"It's from your mother and me. She told me to give it to you tonight. Open it."

Tears filled her eyes as she looked down at the necklace. A single teardrop sapphire glinted and caught the light, hanging on a white gold chain. A set of earrings went with it. Simple. Elegant. Just like the beautiful woman who would wear them. My daughter.

"Mom thought they could be your something blue," I offered, fighting the emotion welling in my chest.

"And new. Oh, Daddy, they're perfect." More tears formed in her eyes. "Just perfect." She looked up at me. "Thank you." Leaning over, she clasped my hand. "I love you."

All I could do was nod.

AVERY WAS SITTING on the front steps, waiting for me, when I climbed out of the car, feeling every year of my age hitting me. She handed me a glass of wine as I sat next to her, resting my head on her shoulder.

"Did she like her gift?"

"She cried." I sighed and rubbed a hand over my face. "I did, too."

"Hard night then, Daddy?"

"Where'd the time go, Sprite? How can our baby girl be getting married? We're going to be grandparents." I shook my head. "My God, Avery, I'm over fifty. How the hell did that happen?"

She laughed. "Time flies." She ran her fingers through my hair, pressing a kiss to my temple. "It's been a great life. You're as sexy now as you were the day I met you . . . and kissed you for the first time."

"My hair has more gray—and there's less of it."

"Not really."

"I have to wear glasses all the time now."

"Your glasses only make you sexier, Daniel."

I chuckled at her words. She only ever saw the good in things. Including me.

I looked at her beautiful face. "You haven't changed a bit. Except, you've gotten lovelier over the years, which I didn't think was possible."

"Look closer, my darling husband. You're missing the wrinkles and bifocals. You see me with love."

"Back at you."

She bumped my shoulder. "Then we're still okay."

Lifting her hand, I pressed it to my lips. "Yes, we are." I was quiet for a minute, sipping my wine, when I noticed the thick book sitting beside Avery.

I looked at it, and my throat closed with emotion. I knew exactly what it was: Avery had saved one flower from every bouquet I had given Maggie, one flower for every date I'd had with my girl over the past twenty-three years.

Twenty-three years of flowers and memories.

"Maggie's book," I murmured.

"Yeah, I was looking through it tonight; thinking how many years had flown by, and remembering how Mags chose one flower from every bouquet, and I helped her dry and save it. She loves this book."

I picked up the book and set it on my lap. Flipping through it, I paused, read the dates, and looked at each dried, pressed flower. Under every flower was a short note, written first by Avery, then by Maggie, as she got old enough to do it herself, of what our date consisted of that night. There were lots of mini golf nights, many more spent at the park, and as she matured—movies, ice-skating, shopping, and coffee shop talks. She'd kept movie stubs, concert tickets, and programs to plays we'd gone to, carefully adding them into her memory book. As I turned the pages, she grew up, and her writing changed from a childish scrawl in crayon to a cursive, elegant script—her words longer and more descriptive.

"She'll have to add in tonight's flower."

I nodded. There were still empty pages—all of which I planned to fill. Years more of memories to create with my Princess.

I took a deep breath, smiling, and after closing it, brought the book to my chest and closed my eyes, savoring all the memories flowing through my mind.

Avery leaned her head on my shoulder, slipping her hand into mine and squeezing. "Need three?"

I rested my head on hers. "Yeah."

"We raised three great kids together."

"We did."

"We've had an amazing life so far."

"Yep."

"We have lots more years together."

"I'm looking forward to them."

"And here's your bonus. I love you as much today, if not more, than I did all those years ago."

"I love your bonuses." I pressed a kiss to Avery's head. "I'm the luckiest man in the world."

She hummed, and we were silent for a moment.

"How about a vacation, Sprite?"

"Yeah?"

We'd had plenty of family vacations over the years, and we tried to get away on our own from time to time, but it hadn't always worked out. I wanted to take her away, spend time with only her, and create more memories of *us*.

"Yeah. Some time for us. You, me, a beautiful beach, and very little clothing. Just like our honeymoon." I ran my finger over her smooth cheek. "I want to spend a day kissing you. Endlessly kissing you."

"I'd love that. But why now?"

I shrugged. "Because we can? After the wedding, before the baby comes. The practice is doing great. I can take some time away." I wrapped my arm around her waist, drawing her close. "We've raised our family, Avery, and we have the rest of our life to enjoy them. Let's enjoy *us*."

"That sounds fabulous."

"What if I told you I was going to semi-retire? Ask you to find someone to take over the books?"

After becoming pregnant with the triplets, Avery left the accounting firm. She worked on the books for the clinic and stable, allowing Caitlin more time to help expand the practice. It proved to be successful for all of us. She still did them because she enjoyed it and it kept her busy.

"Suzanne can step in. She does a lot now."

"Perfect. It's settled. As soon as the wedding is over, we're paying a visit to the travel agent. You pick the first destination."

"Hawaii," she replied with no hesitation. It was one of our favorite places. Then she grinned. "England, next. You get your beach; I get my history."

"Done."

Standing in one swift movement, I surprised her by scooping her up into my arms and carrying her inside; pausing only once to set down the precious book on the hall table.

Her little gasp made me smile. "I thought you felt old, Dr. Spencer?"

I turned and pressed her into the wall, smirking at her playfully, as she yanked off my tie. "Suddenly, Mrs. Spencer, I feel remarkably frisky."

A brilliant smile graced her lips. Reaching up, she pulled her hair from its holder, the long blonde waves falling around her shoulders. Her eyes glowed in the muted light.

In that instant, she looked like the Avery from the first day I saw her, crouched in the doorway, and fell in love with her.

I carried her to our bed, tossing her on the mattress, listening to her carefree laughter.

My sweet, little Sprite. I wanted her as intensely now as I did back then.

I always would—until my last breath.

Her arms opened.

I went willingly.

Acknowledgments

THEY SAY IT takes a village to raise a child—the same can be said of writing a book.

Caroline, thank you for your help. Your keen eyes and support mean so much.

To Karen, Beth, Shelly, Janett, Darlene, Lisa, Kristi, Carrie, Jeanne, Claudia, Pamela, Suzanne—I cannot even begin to thank you. All your encouragement and the love you have shown to me and my work the past months is priceless. The friendships I have found with you all are a treasured gift.

Deb—another book done, my friend. You constantly push me, helping me continue to grow as a writer. Your efforts make my words better. Thank you for everything.

To all the bloggers, thank you for everything you do. Sharing your love of books, posting, reviewing—your recommendations keep my TBR list full, and the support you have shown me is greatly appreciated.

To my fellow authors who have shown me such kindness, thank you. I will follow your example and pay it forward.

To Christine—thank you for making my words look pretty!

And, of course, much love to the ladies at Enchanted and my group Melanie's Minions. You rock!

Finally—Matthew. My world. I love you. Always.

About the Author

NEW YORK TIMES/USA Today bestselling author Melanie Moreland, lives a happy and content life in a quiet area of Ontario with her beloved husband of twenty-seven-plus years and their rescue cat Amber. Nothing means more to her than her friends and family, and she cherishes every moment spent with them.

While seriously addicted to coffee, and highly challenged with all things computer-related and technical, she relishes baking, cooking, and trying new recipes for people to sample. She loves to throw dinner parties, and enjoys travelling, here and abroad, but finds coming home is always the best part of any trip.

Melanie delights in a good romance story with some bumps along the way, but is a true believer in happily ever after. When her head isn't buried in a book, it is bent over a keyboard, furiously typing away as her characters dictate their creative storylines to her, often with a large glass of wine keeping her company.

Books by
MELANIE MORELAND

Into the Storm

Beneath the Scars

Over the Fence

The Contract

It Started with a Kiss

60072460R00132

Made in the USA
Lexington, KY
25 January 2017